Tilly's Tearoom Mysteries
Open for business

Written by
AW Harrison

Copyright 2022 and 2024
All Rights Reserved

Preface

The idea for *Tilly's Tearoom Mysteries* came to me in April 2020 during the first coronavirus pandemic lockdown. My wife and I were house-sitting for friends in the village of Kelsall in Cheshire for a few months and some of the scenes in the story are based on the Kelsall and Willington area.

The lockdown has led people everywhere to assess what life is about and everyone has been forced to examine their own navel, repeatedly! It has brought out the best and the worst in us, but at the same time provided the time to prepare for the future in a more meaningful, informed way. This is one good thing that has come out of the tragedy that has hit the world. However, you may have found you have unresolved issues in your life, things still simmering in the present, or things from the past, things you have done to others or things others have done to you. Resolutions are often not simple as we are complex beings, but if Tilly should arrive on the scene of your life, she would discover all the ins and outs, and would suck out the poison, which is quite painful at times.

This story deals with normal people, sometimes people who have done abominable things. Tilly's Tearoom addresses the elephant in the room like a creeping angel of judgement; sometimes it is an act of vengeance, and sometimes it is a case of redressing the balance. It may even be an emotional healing or simply a chance to resolve those complex issues or make amends.

Even though this book has a unique story in each chapter, it also describes a logical sequence of events, as a sub-storyline runs parallel throughout, connecting the dots along the way. This connecting thread comes in the form of a small group of investigators who are keen to solve the mysteries surrounding Tilly's Tearoom. But will they succeed in solving the puzzle of Tilly and her tearoom mysteries?

Be warned! If you have an unresolved issue in your life, especially if you have a dark secret, think twice before you enter Tilly's Tearoom, as I can guarantee you will not come out the same you went in!

Andrew Harrison

Contents

Chapter 1
Blow the Man Down   5

Chapter 2
Grind My Bones   16

Chapter 3
The Meaning of Ug   28

Chapter 4
Venus   40

Chapter 5
Alison   51

Chapter 6
The Keeper   62

Chapter 7
The Pattering of Eight Little Legs   79

Chapter 8
The Criminalist   91

Chapter 9
Let's have some Happy!   102

Chapter 10
Firestone Village   119

Chapter 11
Tilly Goes AWOL   129

Chapter 12
A Saw Point   140

Chapter 13 It's All a Matter of Perception	151
Chapter 14 Rosie Warm-Cheeks	165
Chapter 15 Not a Penny, Nor a Kiss	172
Chapter 16 The Tank	185
Chapter 17 I Scream	199
Chapter 18 Finding Santa (Don't Tell the Children!)	209
Chapter 19 Tilly Goes to Ground	220
Epilogue Six Months Later	226

Chapter 1
Blow the Man Down

"Ooooh, it's blowing a gale out there!" said Tilly shuddering behind the tearoom serving counter while she fluttered around its immaculate, gleaming surfaces with a cloth. Everyone in the tearoom heard her voice but they did not see any point in responding as they were all very much part of the furniture. "We can't allow the dust to stir up again yet, can we?" she said fussily, and everyone ignored her again.

The tearoom was square, small and quaint with an old-fashioned yet pleasant décor. It was however not full of dark woodwork as you might expect, as it was painted white, giving it a clean, clinical look. Its overall effect was kitchenesque with its dash of light turquoise tiles here and there throughout the room. The tables and chairs were sturdy and each dainty table cloth supported a central box of cutlery and condiments. "Let's hope nobody calls it a café or a tea shop today," Tilly added as she floated up to the door to turn the sign to 'Open for business.'

You may be wondering why there were already customers in the tearoom even before Tilly had turned the sign on the door, but that was characteristic of that particular tearoom in that particular place at that particular time, as you will no doubt discover later.

Meanwhile, Jim and Trudy Tailor were travelling home in their Peugeot after having spent two relaxing weeks with friends at their holiday home in Redruth in Cornwall. And it was with some reluctance and trepidation that they were returning to their normal work-life. It was true, they were very successful, and their careers very lucrative, but it was hard work nonetheless. Trudy was the owner of a dental practice on Clifton Road in York, and Jim was a senior manager for 'Selby and Samson,' a successful construction company in Yorkshire.

"How on earth can you see where you're going, Jim!" said Trudy.

"It's okay, I've been in worse storms than this," responded Jim.

"We're going to have to stop soon anyway because I'm in desperate need of the loo; where are we anyway?"

"To be frank, I have absolutely no idea where we are," replied Jim.

"That's a first!"

"It is," he agreed.

"Oh look, there's a tea shop or something over there, they should have a loo we can use," suggested Trudy.

"It'll be closed by now, it's teatime."

"Well the lights are on, we might catch them just before they close," urged Trudy.

"If they're open we can get a bite to eat as well," suggested Jim hopefully.

Jim pulled up the Peugeot alongside Tilly's Tearoom and through the heavy rain he could just make out the sign 'Open for business' on the door. They both got out of the car and rushed into the tearoom under their jackets. There was a tinkling sound when they walked through the door into the tearoom and Tilly gave them a welcoming smile from behind the serving counter. "Welcome to Tilly's Tearoom," she said, "Please take a seat; would you like a towel to dry your hair?"

Trudy did not know whether to be happy about the welcome or cringe at the over familiar suggestion that their hair was unkempt, especially as their hair was not wet - they had only just stepped out of the car! "Oh, no thank you, but if you could point me in the direction of the Ladies …?"

"Certainly, but I am sorry to say our lavatories are out of service today; please use the public conveniences just outside the tearoom and to the right … you can't miss them."

"Okay, thank you," Trudy said, and her face winced at the prospect of going outside into the raging storm again. She decided to choose a decent table before she went out. Some of the tables alongside the walls were taken, so they just sat at the one in the middle of the room.

Whispering to her husband, "Disgusting, they should have toilets in the café, not send customers out into the pouring rain!"

"Shhhh!" responded Jim, "At least there IS a loo AND food. Come on, choose something from the menu."

Shuffling on her bottom, Trudy quickly glanced through the tearoom menu, and Jim squinted around the room at the customers. The hostess was a bit of a stereotypical country bumpkin, not quite obese, but heading in that general direction. However, her accent surprised him as it was quite dignified and betrayed no particular localised dialect. Against the wall facing Jim was a middle-aged man in a grey suit, perhaps a business man, tapping furiously on his lap top while gulping gallons of filtered coffee. Behind Jim was an elderly woman in tweeds, knitting contentedly. Beside her, on the table, sat two woollen dolls that she had no doubt proudly knitted on a previous occasion. She gave Jim a sinister, toothless smile as he turned his head.

"IT'S A TEAROOM!" shouted a voice from a table at the back of the room. Trudy jumped up in surprise and nearly went to the toilet there and then. They both looked to see where the voice came from; it seemed to have come from a scruffy looking man who was sat at a table with his back to them. He was wearing a black coat over his broad shoulders down which crawled wavy, dark, greasy hair.

Jim whispered to his wife, "This is a weird place."

"It certainly is, anyway, we need to eat. Order a cheese toastie with a side salad for me would you please? I'm going to find that loo."

"Okay, don't be long!" Jim said as Trudy went out into the hurricane. Jim looked up with a fake yet polite smile towards Tilly behind the counter to find her scowling at him with her arms folded. He quickly averted his gaze towards the menu and thought he would go with the steak and kidney pie. He turned back to the service counter with, "May we have …?" and was shocked to see Tilly, the hostess, standing right beside him.

"I'm terribly sorry about your wife, sir," she said.

"Er, what do you mean?"

"That she had to go out into that awful weather."

"Oh that's okay."

"It's not something I'm accustomed to doing," she said.

"Sorry?"

"Sending people out into stormy weather, that is."

"Oh, I see, it's all right, it really is," said Jim.

"Well if it's all right with you, then everything will be okay, won't it? Now, what can I get you?"

"Er, may we order a cheese toastie with side salad and a steak and kidney pie for me, please?"

"Of course, and I guess you would like some gravy with your steak and kidney pie …?"

"Er, yes please."

"I will bring out the boat then," Tilly said.

"Excuse me?"

"The gravy boat, I'll bring out the gravy boat for you, is that all right for you?" asked Tilly, sounding a little annoyed.

"Oh, okay, yes, that would be wonderful, thank you," said Jim, politely.

"In the drink?"

"Sorry?"

"And a drink? Would you like a drink?" Tilly asked.

"Two Americanos please."

"There are no Americanos here," said the hostess.

"Well, what do you …?"

"We be 'avin' filter coffee, we beee," she said, changing her accent for some unknown reason.

"SHIVER ME TIMBERS!" shouted the scruffy man on the table at the back of the tearoom.

"Look, is there something going on here?" asked Jim.

"Somethin' goin' orn? Nay, there be nothin' goin' on'ere!"

"Okay, two filter coffees will do, that's my order, thank you," said Jim, hoping his wife would return quickly so they could do a runner.

Tilly had not left him long before he heard a SMASH! A teacup had fallen onto the floor off the service counter, and Tilly exclaimed, "Man overboard!"

"HA HA HA!" laughed the scruffy man.

"Exactly where are these toilets?" Jim asked Tilly.

"Just round the corner, your wife would be havin' just about finished a-relieving of 'erself by now, don't yer think?"

"Yes, of course."

Jim did not realise at first, but the tearoom was uncannily beginning to sway. Swaying was not such an unfamiliar experience for Jim as he was a keen sailor and had been on his yacht in Cornwall just a week before. But with all this talk of 'man overboard' and 'shiver me timbers' came a raw and recent memory. He thought back to being on his yacht with his wife Trudy and a couple of their friends, Heather and Mark:

"I'm sorry to bring you out into such a dreadful storm, it has rather taken us by surprise," said Jim, struggling to control the yacht, his voice sounding strained and faint with the tempestuous noise in the background.
"It's okay," said Heather, "We could have said 'no' if we'd wanted to."
"We'd all had such a skinful, so none of us checked the forecast properly," said Mark chipping in.
"Still, it's my boat and I'm responsible," said Jim.
"Or not very responsible!" added Trudy, his wife.
"Look, just concentrate everybody, otherwise we're not going to get back to land!"
"Keep your shirt on Jim!" exclaimed Mark, "Everything's going to be all right."
The four of them were reasonably fit and strong, quite capable of lasting out the storm, but tensions began to mount as they tossed up and down.

Like a damp dog, Jim shook himself in an attempt to remove the raw memory, but the images clung to him like a wet towel as he shuffled in his chair in the tearoom (I dare not call it a café or a tea shop! Don't want to incur Tilly's wrath!).

"Are ye al'right there me darlin'?" Tilly asked Jim.

"Yes, quite all right, thank you," said Jim, sweating. "I'll just go and check how my wife is getting on…"

BOOM went the fist of the scruffy, six and a half foot, stubbled, wavy haired man on Jim's table. "MARK!" he bellowed.

"What?" said Jim, trembling.

"Mark my words, Jim lad!"

"How do you know my name's Jim?"

"Name? You don't deserve a name. Just you mark my words, you'll never get away with it!"

"Get away with what?"

"You're gonna walk the plank for it!"

"That's enerf Captain, be a-sitting if you will, leave the poor man to 'is sorrows!" interrupted Tilly. The scruffy man returned to his seat.

"What makes you think I've got sorrows? I'm perfectly fine thank you very much; now please serve the food and we'll be on our way."

"Right you are, sir, right you are … it be plain sailin' it be," said Tilly.

"Stop with the seafaring terminology!" exclaimed Jim, as it was all feeling too personal.

"Just trying to make somethin' nice to tide y'over."

Jim could not stop shaking in his confused struggle to fathom what was going on around him, especially as the tea room still seemed to be swaying. He looked up to try and find some scrap of normality, and unconsciously glanced at the business man on the table in front of him who was typing even more furiously now, as though in a panic. The scruffy man to his side had his back to him again, so he was safe from him for a while, and in his continuing subconscious desperation to establish everything around him was reasonably sane and stable, he turned his head to see what the elderly woman was up to. With relief, he saw that she was still knitting, and the two knitted dolls were still on the table beside her. But he had to squint as the faces on the dolls reminded him of people he knew. He told himself not to be stupid, but could not resist trying to make out the names that were written at the bottom of each one. They were called 'Flotsam' and 'Jetsam.' Jim's mind was again assaulted with the painful memory of being on his yacht in the storm.

Jim, Trudy and Heather were frantically trying to rescue Mark from the raging seas after he had been knocked overboard by the boom of the main sail.

"MARK!" shouted Heather, his girlfriend.

"It's too late! We can't find him, he's gone!" said Trudy.

"Why don't you have a lifeboat or at least flares! By law ..." added Heather.

"I've called for help," Jim said, "I don't know what else I can do."

"He'll drown before they get here!" shouted Heather.

"We have done everything we can possibly do; he should have grabbed the life rings, but he didn't," said Jim.

"DO SOMETHING!" Heather shouted.

"Shut up!" screamed Trudy, slapping her round the face. "He's called for help, there's nothing else we can do."

Heather returned the favour by slapping Trudy back round her face and then she started laying into Jim, screaming, "You've killed him! You stupid fools!" Trudy grabbed hold of Heather, threw her down onto the deck, and turned to Jim.

"How long did they say they'd be, Jim?"

"The radio's broken."

"You've got to be kidding! Don't tell her."

"She's going to find out when and if we ever get back to shore."

"What are we going to do?"

Heather pulled herself up by the grab rail and set on Jim and Trudy again. Trudy thumped her fist down hard onto Heather's head and she crashed to the deck again, unconscious.

In the tearoom, Jim came back to his senses when he heard another SMASH. It was another teacup falling from the serving counter and Tilly exclaimed, "There goes another one!"

Again the tearoom was swaying and Jim slowly stood up, intending to leave. "I don't feel so good," he said.

"Feelin' seasick are ye?" asked Tilly.

"He's just about ready to keel over," said the elderly woman behind him with a croaky voice. Jim turned to see her knitting a Skull and Crossbones. He ran to the door and opened it, but the wind and water blew him inside again, right onto his back, dazed. All he could think of was that raw memory swimming around in his head.

Heather was on her back out cold on the tossing yacht.

"Actually, nobody knows about this boating trip," said Trudy.

"What are you suggesting?"

"We can throw her overboard, we don't want the media to splash all over the place that we didn't have emergency equipment and that we're responsible for Mark's death. It's OUR yacht! We are screwed!"

Trying to think of all the reasons why he could safely avoid doing what Trudy was suggesting, Jim said, "People will understand."

"We'll be ruined!"

"Mark's probably still alive anyway, and he'll get back to shore, and ...."

"Jim, listen! You know that's stupid! He's gone!"

Just then, Heather began to stir again.

"It's now or never," said Trudy.

They both picked up Heather's body just as she was becoming fully conscious. She just managed to utter, "What are you doing! You murderers!"

"Sorry, Heather, we have no choice," said Trudy.

They threw her over the stern, but she managed to quickly grab the pushpit. "No you don't!" Heather screamed, but Trudy frantically punched at her hands. This did not work, so she finally prised Heather's fingers away, causing her to fall into the deep. As she fell, Heather screamed again, "YOU MURDERERS!"

Jim stood up in the tearoom and shouted, "GET ME OUT OF HERE!"

The scruffy, stubbly-faced giant man stood up again and shouted, "GUILTY!"

The elderly woman croaked, "GUILTY!" as she continued knitting, and Flotsam and Jetsam tumbled off the table. The business man also cried out "GUILTY!" but then continued typing more frantically than ever.

Suddenly, everything went dark as the strong, tall, scruffy man threw a sack over Jim's head.

"Let me out!" screamed Jim, but it was useless because Tilly helped to restrain Jim as he wriggled about. The three of them tumbled around on the tearoom floor as Jim cried out, "Trudy! Trudy! Ring the police!"

At that moment, a short man emerged from a back room and asked Tilly in a very nasal voice, "Shall I call the Sweepers?"

While wrestling Jim with the scruffy man, Tilly replied, "Yes, better call the Sweepers."

Soon after this, the sack was removed from Jim's head, and he found himself in a dull, damp, dreary room in complete contrast to the bright, clinical tearoom he had been in earlier. He was being held by two hooded, strong men, facing a huge vat of boiling water. Above the vat, he could see a series of thick, metal chains within which was fastened a metal chair. In the chair was his wife, Trudy, alive but muzzled. She was wriggling and trying to scream through the muzzle.

"WHAT ARE YOU DOING?" screamed Jim, "LET HER DOWN!"

Another hooded figure nearby then began to turn a wheel and Trudy was lowered towards the boiling water.

"NO! I DON'T MEAN LIKE THAT! STOP, PLEASE, I'M SORRY, I'LL CONFESS!!"

The hooded figure nearby stopped turning the wheel for one moment, but then carried on turning the wheel.

"NO, STOP! TELL ME WHAT I MUST DO, ANYTHING!!"

The hooded figure turned the wheel faster.

"I AM GUILTY, I KNOW I AM, I PROMISE YOU, WE WILL BOTH CONFESS!"

The hooded figure stopped again.

"THANK YOU, thank you, please let us go, we know we're guilty, SO guilty!" confessed Jim.

But then the hooded figure turned the wheel a few more times and Trudy dropped into the vat of boiling water trying to scream and escape as she went. She splashed around in the boiling water for a few moments and then stopped. Jim sobbed uncontrollably at the sight.

"Is there no justice? It's not fair, it was an accident!"

At that, the two men restraining him pulled Jim closer towards the boiling vat of water where his wife was cooking.

"What are you doing? Do you realise what you're doing? You can't do this ... you're not allowed to do this!! It's against the law!!!" Jim kicked against the vat to push himself back from it as the men were clearly attempting to lift him into the vat to join his wife. But the men were too strong for him and lifting him up by his legs, they threw him in too. Jim screamed in agony as he grabbed at the edges of the vat while burning in the boiling water. The two hooded agents of vengeance punched at Jim's hands and prised his fingers off, and it was not long before he went quiet.

The following morning, Tilly was fussing around in the tearoom with her duster while her regulars were doing ... well ... whatever it is they do, when the short, nasally man came into the room with a couple of bags. "Here's some more steak and kidney for you, Tilly."

"Thank you kindly," she replied as she gratefully took the bags from him. "Now you'd better leave me in peace while I finish my cleaning; got to get it all shipshape and Bristol fashion!"

It was not long after this that four people were reported missing in the UK Daily:

DAILY TITBITS
by
Justin Caadfar Esquire

Jim Tailor and his wife Trudy Tailor, a married couple from Yorkshire, and their friends Heather Tilbury and Mark Pickering from Cornwall have been reported missing today. All four are known to be good friends, but police are not sure whether their disappearances are connected. Mr Tailor is a senior manager for 'Selby and Samson' in Yorkshire, and Mrs Tailor owns her own dental practice called 'York Dental.' Mr and Mrs Tailor are said to be a very happy and friendly couple, well respected in their community. They have known Mr Pickering and Miss Tilbury since Secondary School in Hampshire, and have often met up in Cornwall for holidays.

Mr Pickering, who works for 'Clear View Opticians,' and Miss Tilbury, a pub manager in Redruth, were last seen on the 12th of February this year by someone who noticed them talking to a couple, who are believed to have been Mr and Mrs Tailor, on Fowey Harbour. However, Mr and Mrs Tailor were last seen a week later at a service station on the M5 in Somerset.

If anyone knows the location of these missing persons, please contact the UK Daily. Police are not treating their disappearances as suspicious at this time, but any information would be appreciated.

On a more positive note, the Easter Holiday is round the corner and it is forecast that it will be a real scorcher, so get out your bottles of sunscreen early and protect your skin from those ultra-violet rays! You may be boiling in the heat, but don't waste the chance as experts predict that Summer is going to be pretty damp this year.

Bon Voyage!

Chapter 2
Grind My Bones

The Sweepers were tidying the back room of bodies and body parts. This was a regular practice but there was sometimes a bit of a backlog. The incinerator was working to capacity even before they hauled a forty-stoner onto the conveyor. It was a bumpy ride towards the flames, which shot out to scorch the hoods and sleeves of the Sweepers as they had to open the larger door to the furnace. Even so, the humongous body got stuck in the opening, so they had to poke at the mass of flesh with metal rods until it relinquished its right to a raw existence. The body of a teenage boy was next in line, but he had a bit of a long wait ahead. There was still some life in him, but the Sweepers did not worry about that as he was strapped down.

A while later, the ashes were collected from the incinerated monster of a man, and the bones were set aside for grinding. This was the job of the female Sweeper; she enjoyed this process as the sound of the grinding made her feel alive and significant somehow. The bones were ground again and again into a fine powder and added to bags of flour for Tilly. The short, nasal man was stood there waiting to collect the bags, but there was no conversation between them. The only voice that could be heard was that of the teen being transported on the conveyor into the incinerator. But his echoing screams for help did not make the nasally imp-like man flinch as he collected four big bags of bones and flour.

"Here's your flour, Tilly," he said in his characteristic creepy voice on entering the tearoom.

"Thank you, just leave them on the counter for me," Tilly replied.

"You can use it in your tiffin!"

"I will, it gives it a proper crunch, doesn't it?"

"It certainly does!"

"That'll be all then," Tilly said, dismissing the imp back to his lair while she got on with the cleaning and preparations. After the imp left, she fussed around, muttering to herself. "It's such a responsibility ...

such a responsibility ... all this poking about in people's monkey business ... problems sprouting up everywhere. Seems to be no end of loose ends to tie up. So many strange people, no morals ... no morals ... not a scrap of common decency! It's none stop, really is ... I need a holiday, that's what I need. Why can't someone else deal with them all? My poor little tearoom! Why does it have to put up with all this clamour? It makes such a mess!"

Three young men and a young woman were hovering over the satnav in Mike's Volvo through the Devon countryside on the way back from a beach party after excessive drinking and drug-taking.

"Ha! There it goes again!" spurted Jock, "How did you get the satnav to fart, Mike?"

"Easy when you know how," replied Mike, barely able to speak due to the chemicals in his system.

"So, you programmed it to fart every time you come to a speed camera?" asked Melany from the back.

"Yes! It just brings a bit of humour into the world," slurred Mike.

The satnav farted again and they all rolled about laughing hysterically as the car swayed around on the dark country road.

"Come on, concentrate on your driving Jock, I need to get back home, I've got work in the morning!" exclaimed Paul who was sat in the back with Melany.

"Call in sick! I would, especially if I was as stoned as you are!" suggested Melany.

"If I lose this job, I'll never forgive you, Jock, come on!"

"All right, all right, keep your hair on!"

"And don't crash my car!" warned Mike.

"I won't!" Jock tried to assure them all of his excellent driving ability as he strained to see in the dark.

In the tearoom, Tilly's late-night patrons were dressed unusually. The elderly lady had donned a blonde wig and was wearing a shiny, golden dress, humming a melancholy tune to herself while strumming her fingers through her hair. The six and a half foot tall man was sat dressed as a beach bum – in nothing but a pair of trunks and playing around with a snorkel. As for the middle-aged man, he was dressed in white like a pharmacist, frantically swopping pills from one bottle to another at his table, and sticking labels on them.

On the back seat of the car, Melany started to kiss Paul just at the moment the car bumped the side of a curb. Melany and Paul's teeth clinked against each other. "Hey, careful, you're gonna break our teeth!"

"Sorry!" said Jock swerving back into the middle of the road.

Mike hoped to get an honest answer from Jock over something everyone was wondering about. "Where did you get all that money from Jock?"

"None of your business!"

"Come on, otherwise we'll think you stole it," urged Mike.

"It's just my secret stash, nothing to worry about," insisted Jock.

"You must have, like, a hundred thousand!"

"Three hundred thousand to be precise," said Jock.

Paul and Melany were still kissing as Mike continued to pry. "You can tell us, we're your friends, we won't tell anyone. How did you get it?"

"Yeh, tell us Jock," said Melany coming up for air.

"Nope."

"Suit yourself, keep your dirty secret!" said Melany before she sank into another snog.

"Your satnav's useless, Mike!" said Jock, changing the subject.

"Why, what's wrong with it?"

"Well, according to your satnav, we're in Paris!"

"Don't be stupid!" said Mike, squinting at the satnav. "What makes you think it says Paris?"

"Look, there! It says we're near the Eiffel Tower," said Jock, pointing furiously at the screen.

Just then, the car mounted a bank and Melany screamed at Jock again.

"I can't control it!" shouted Jock, "The steering wheel's got a mind of its own!" The car continued coasting over grass until it crashed into a tree and the satnav let out a final fart.

"You fool! Look what you've done!" shouted Mike, "You've crashed my car!"

"It wasn't my fault, it's your stupid satnav!"

"How can you blame my satnav?"

"It doesn't work properly 'cos you've been messing about with it too much."

"The satnav wasn't driving the car, you were!"

"No, actually, I wasn't, it's like something else was controlling it," argued Jock.

"That's just because you're stoned like the rest of us!"

"Look, stop arguing you two, we need to call breakdown thingamajiggy!" said Melany.

Mike got out of the car and tried to phone his breakdown service, but his phone didn't work. Nobody else's phone worked either.

In the distance, through the darkness, Paul saw a light on in a building farther along the road. They all set off on foot to see if they could borrow a phone.

"You do know it's two in the morning, don't you?" said Melany. "They're not going to take too kindly to you knocking on their door at this hour!"

"I don't care, it's an emergency," said Paul.

"Hey, what if they call the police? We have all been drinking and doing drugs, you know," said Melany.

"They won't, we just want to call roadside service, they're not going to care," added Paul.

When they got closer, Jock read the sign over the entrance, "It's a café! It says 'Tilly's Tearoom.'"

"Looks like a family business or something, there's a house attached to the back of it," said Melany.

On arriving, they looked through the window and saw people inside, and the sign on the door read, 'Open for business,' so with some relief, they entered to ask if they could use their phone. There was a tinkling sound as they opened the door.

"Hi, our car's broken down, has anyone got a phone we can borrow?" Paul announced.

Everyone in the tearoom just stared at them.

"Hiya! A phone? Has anyone got a phone?" repeated Melany, sounding annoyed.

"We only have one phone in here," said Tilly who was polishing a dainty light turquoise and white teacup. There was a pause.

"Okay ... can we use it?" asked Mike, "I need to call my breakdown service and our mobiles don't work."

"There are no mobiles in here!" exclaimed Tilly, looking put out.

"Look, we don't care!" said Jock, "We just need to use whatever phone you have, so my friend Mike can phone breakdown cover, so they can come and fix the car."

"You're not allowed to take it away with you!" said Tilly, concerned.

Frustrated, Jock said, "We're not going to take the phone anywhere, we just want to borrow it!"

"But how do we know you won't steal it?" asked Tilly, and the other three patrons of the tearoom stared directly at Jock, giving suspicious nods.

The elderly lady in the blonde wig joined in the conversation, croaking out the words, "You've got your head in the clouds if you think you can get away with stealing anythin' from 'ere!"

Melany sniggered at her and turned to Paul, "Look at her in that wig, soooo weird!"

Paul asked Tilly, "Is it a land-line?"

"Wha'ever!" Tilly replied. "I'll bring it out and you can look at it. Please sit there on the middle table where we can keep an eye on you all, and if you want anything else, you'll have to pay up front."

"Of course," said Mike obligingly, "and we'll pay for the phone call as well."

All four of them sat down. Melany kept whispering to Paul about the strange patrons surrounding them, not being able to take her eyes off the tall man sat with his back to them wearing nothing but swimming trunks and practising breathing through his snorkel. "Look at the hairs all up his back!"

"He is a bit of a gorilla," said Paul chuckling.

"You're a right handful, you young'uns," said the golden lady.

"And I expect you were a bit of a handful yourself when you were young," responded Jock, trying not to sound TOO impolite.

"How dare you, I'm not old!" she said. Then she looked over at the pharmacist, "Did you 'ere that?"

"Yes I did," he replied.

"This young boy just said I was old; he needs punishment!"

"He does indeed," said the pharmacist.

"Yes he does!" added Melany, sniggering.

The elderly woman started to stroke her hair and hum to herself, and all four of the young people burst out laughing.

"I know you're laughin' at my beau'iful singing," the elderly woman in the golden dress said.

"Very beautiful singing, we're just jealous, that's all," said Melany, tongue in cheek.

"That's the truth, because HE wants to kidnap me so he can make money out of me, don't ya!" said the elderly woman, pointing at Jock.

All four of the young customers burst out laughing again.

Tilly arrived with the phone. It was shaped like a cow jumping over the moon. "Here you are," she said, giving it to Jock. "Don't steal it!"

"I won't steal it! Just because we're younger than you doesn't mean we're criminals!" exclaimed Jock.

"Well I'm staying here while you use it, I'm not taking any chances," said Tilly with her face right up to Jock's. "Am I big enough for you?"

"Yes, too big," said Jock as he handed the phone to Mike. Mike tried several times to phone the breakdown service, but each time he got a voice saying, 'Welcome to Paris!'

"There's something wrong with your phone, it keeps saying, 'Welcome to Paris,'" said Mike.

"Welcome to Paris?" said Tilly.

"Welcome to Paris?" said the pharmacist.

"Welcome to Paris!" exclaimed the giant beach bum.

At that moment, a troupe of five Can-Can dancers in traditional French dress, wearing long skirts and thick petticoats, entered from the back of the tearoom in a line doing high kicks while music blurted out of the cow-phone. They all did cartwheels in sequence and ended with the splits to the raucous applause of Tilly, the giant beach bum, the golden lady and the pharmacist. Blowing kisses and curtsying on their way out of the tearoom, they disappeared into the night.

"What the …?" said Mike.

"I'm obviously higher than I thought I was," said Jock.

Paul was grinning from ear to ear along with Melany, who declared, "I've never had so much fun in my life!"

Paul soon remembered his determination to get home so he could get to work on time, even though any hope of getting some sleep beforehand had gone out of the window. "Well, we need to get our car fixed, so I suggest we take a walk down the street and see if we can get a better signal for our phones."

"I'll go with you," said Melany linking his arm.

"And I'll go with you as well since I need to talk to them myself, don't I? Come on, Jock," said Mike.

"No, I'm staying here and getting myself a strong coffee."

"Okay, get one for me too while I'm gone."

"Get me a smoothie if they have them," said Melany.

"Make that two," said Paul.

"Give us your phone though," added Mike, "just in case ours don't work but yours does."

"Okay, I'll just get my bank card out of the cover."

"There's no need for that, bank cards are no good 'ere, we only take cash," interrupted Tilly.

Melany gave Jock a twenty, and Mike took Jock's phone. As Jock's three companions left the tearoom into the street, the pharmacist asked him, "Would you like to buy some pills?"

"Oh, no thank you."

"Why not?" he asked, looking offended.

"I'm just not interested, thanks."

"Are you sure? I've got uppers AND downers."

"I'm sure thanks! You've probably already noticed that I've had enough pills tonight already, so thanks anyway, but no thanks."

The beach bum stood up tall and interjected with, "**Fie** were you, I'd run away before you get into more trouble."

"And you're not taking me with you!" added the elderly, golden lady who had begun painting a box of eggs with gold paint.

Tilly interrupted with, "Stop harping on at him, you lot, leave him to settle down! What can I get you, young man?"

"Two espressos and two smoothies, please."

"Already done," she said, carrying them over to him on a tray. "There's your espressos and there's your smoothies - Melany and Mango."

"Thank you, how much is that?"

"It's all right, my love, you can pay when you leave. Would you like a piece of tiffin, you look like you need fattening up, you're so long and thin … like a beanstalk!"

"Well it's kind of you, but I don't think I have enough cash to cover it."

"No, no, no, it's on the 'ouse, I insist!" she said.

"Well, if you insist, I do fancy some tiffin."

"And here I was thinking you had a huge store of cash hidden away somewhere!" said the beach bum.

"And why would you say that?" asked Jock.

"Just heard it on the grapevine."

"You don't know anything about me," said Jock getting annoyed.

"I know you're a Jack-the-lad!"

"No I'm not! "

"**Fie** were you …"

"Look, can you just stop talking to me please while I have my coffee?" He took a slurp of his espresso and Tilly brought him a large piece of tiffin on a plate, which Jock wolfed down with a giant gulp. His throat felt a bit dry after the tiffin and the espresso, so he was tempted to drink one of the smoothies, but he resisted the temptation.

Suddenly the tearoom shuddered as though they were just struck by an earth tremor. It shook Jock up a bit too, "What was that?" he said, his heart pounding in his chest.

"Don't worry, just make yourself at home," said Tilly. "After all, an Englishman's home is his castle."

"Thanks." Jock was surprised at how light it was getting outside, and hoped his friends would come back soon.

There was a sudden loud thud, and Jock jumped out of his wits. But it was just a seagull flying into the tearoom window.

"Aw, poor little bird," said Tilly.

Two more seagulls flew into the window.

The beach bum said, "I told you he was a Jack-the-lad."

"What's that got to do with anything?" asked Jock.

"Well, that's why all the birds are after you, and you really do have your head in the clouds. **Fie** were you ..."

"JUST SHUT UP YOU FREAK!" yelled Jock and his voice echoed throughout the tearoom. At that moment, Jock's head started to spin and he knew it was nothing to do with anything he had taken at the beach party as that was already wearing off. "What have you done to me? You've spiked my drink, haven't you!"

"No I haven't," said Tilly looking offended.

Jock glowered at the pharmacist, "It was you, wasn't it! You've drugged me!"

The pharmacist shrugged his shoulders. "Don't you realise? All your drug taking has killed and maimed your fellow human beings!"

"How?"

"There's a long line of casualties leading up to you getting your so-called recreational supply; you and your friends are guilty."

"What people get up to in their own time is nothing to do with me, and what I get up to has absolutely nothing to do with you!"

"Of course, you're completely innocent," the beach bum added, sarcastically.

"Just shut up or I'll punch your lights out!"

"You want to give me a blind eye do you? You and your three friends are good at turning a blind eye to what's going on, but as long as you get your thrill it doesn't matter, does it?"

"Like I said, it's nothing to do with me what other people do, and I can do what I like with my life."

Beach bum continued, "Just think, ALL those people who are made into addicts by force, ALL the gang killings, ALL the people your age who die using illegal drugs, ALL the suicides, ALL the broken families, ALL the torture, abuse and murders among rival gangs, and you don't care, you snivelling little goose!"

"You're the snivelling little …goose! You drugged me!"

The pharmacist said, "No, you drugged yourself - again and again! Just join the dots … but no, you cover your eyes and pretend you are a decent, moral human being. Whenever you lot dance at a party, you are party to the dark world of crime. I know this is a bitter pill for you to swallow, but is it any wonder that you've been brought here?"

"What do you mean, 'brought here'? I crashed the car into a tree and we couldn't get a signal on our phones, so we came here for help, and all you do is spike my drink!"

"No, no, no, you're wrong!" insisted Tilly.

"You know it's true!"

"No, it's not true, we didn't put drugs in your coffee, we put them in the tiffin!"

"I've got to get out of here!" Jock tried to move, but his head and body felt so heavy.

"You need to get your head out of the clouds and come down to earth!" said Tilly, edging closer and pushing her face into his once more. "Ever heard of a man called Ted Biggar?"

"How do you know Mr Biggar?"

"Stole from him, didn't yer?" added the beach bum, "You wormed yourself into his home and just took what you liked, didn't yer? You seduced his daughter and she fell head over heels for yer, didn't she?"

"How do you know all this?"

The pharmacist added, "You told her you'd fallen for her as well, didn't yer?"

"It's not my fault she fell in love with me."

"And it was all just to get your hands on that cash wasn't it?" said the golden lady.

"Look, I don't know where you're getting all this information from, but …"

"But what? Go on!" said Tilly.

"Her suicide was nothing to do with me!"

"Just you keep telling yourself that, there's a good lad." Beach bum told Tilly, "**Fee** doesn't stop pretending, he deserves to be punished. **Fie** were him I'd confess."

"I agree," said Tilly.

"Look, I'm not confessing to anything!"

The beach bum continued, "**Foe**tunately, we can make it right for yer, if you want it, that is."

"Absolutely not!"

"Well then, you've had yer **Fum**, and now it's our turn!"

Jock just managed to get up out of his chair, and leaving the twenty pound note on the table, he headed for the door.

"Wait!" shouted the giant beach bum, and Jock turned momentarily to hear the giant add, "Say hi to Cliff for me!"

Jock ignored him and rushed out of the door, immediately falling down from a precipice atop the White Cliffs of Dover. His body splashed into the sea and onto the rocks beneath before he was washed out, dead and penniless.

"Well he did need a downer!" said the pharmacist.

DAILY TITBITS
by
Justin Caadfar Esquire

Life is full of mysteries! In the early hours of Monday morning, three young people from England, two men and one woman, were found by French police staggering along the Champs-Elysees screaming in agony. They had been the victims of an acid attack by robbers on scooters. They were immediately rushed to hospital.

The muggers on scooters had sprayed acid in the faces of the young English people, and they all received an eyeful of the caustic solution. They are all believed to be permanently blinded from the attack. All their cash and bank cards were stolen, but they escaped with their lives.

What police are confused about is their story of how they got there. They had been at a beach party on the Devon coast, in England, only a matter of a few hours earlier, and they have absolutely no recollection of how they ended up on the streets of Paris. In their statements they all said they had been in a car accident in Devon, visited a café at 2am, and left the café a little later to try and get a signal for their phones. They also said they had left their friend Jock Green in the café and were concerned for his welfare as his bank card and phone were in their possession before they were also stolen by the muggers. However, no one has been able to get in touch with Jock since the incident.

Unfortunately, it looks like the muggers on scooters will get away with the attack as there were no witnesses and the CCTV cameras were not working in that area at the time of the assault.

The three victims have been questioned several times and they have not changed their story about having been at a café in Devon at 2am that same morning. To add to the confusion, fellow partygoers have confirmed that the three victims and their friend Mr Green had left the party somewhere between twelve midnight and one o'clock in the morning, verifying their statements.

The only conclusion that the French police can come to is that as most of the revellers at the party were taking drugs, their accounts are unreliable. Blood samples taken from the victims verify the fact that they had used illegal drugs, so they must have travelled to France under the influence of potent chemicals and forgotten doing so. What also supports this theory is the young people's unlikely claim that a café was open at 2am in the morning with customers already inside. Cafes are never open at that time, anywhere in England!

The mystery continues!

A word of warning: Never end up in Tilly's Tearoom!

Chapter 3
The Meaning of Ug

The tearoom was being prepared and the walls were already festooned with portraits of stars. Tilly was dusting and arranging her knickknacks, novelties and curios on tiny shelves throughout the tearoom. On the shelves behind the counter, there was a space theme, including three globes of varying sizes, a 3D model of our solar system, and an empty mug with NASA written on the side. This latter object was a little unusual for Tilly as she did not have a particular liking for Americans - to say the least. On the uppermost shelf were two space rockets and a couple of astronauts. She had arranged them all in as attractive an order as she could, but it was not really her scene, so it did look a little like it had been randomly thrown together.

"I haven't got space for everything!" Tilly moaned. "I could go on forever with my no end of bits and pieces of bric-a-brac-ing knickerknackery and whatnot! Where am I going to put it all? I need shelves ad infinitum to put everything on. I need more space! Did you hear everyone? I NEED MORE SPACE! Well, perhaps it's no matter to you," she said. "All you do is drink endless cups of coffee, shove cakes down your worm-hole and make impossible demands on my time!" Everyone ignored her as usual, just as she expected them to. They had their occupations and responsibilities, and she had hers.

The big man disappeared into the back and suddenly the music to Elton John's timeless 'Rocket Man' came on and filled the room. At that moment, a man in his late fifties entered the tearoom from outside and headed towards one of the wall tables. The regular elderly lady, who was wearing round spectacles, squinted at the visitor, analysing every small step he took on the tiled floor before he sat down, the table next to his being occupied by the middle-aged man, this time dressed like a university professor. Tilly came to serve the new customer. "What can I get you?" she asked.

"Well I think I'll go with a nice traditional English tea!" the customer replied in a rich American accent while giving her a broad toothy-white smile.

"Please?"

"Excuse me?"

"Please!"

"Oh, I get it, please excuse my manners, I would like a nice traditional English tea PLEASE!" and his smile was wider and whiter than ever.

"That's what I like to see!"

"Don't you mean, 'That's what I like to hear,' haha?" the customer said to save face and lighten the mood at the same time.

But that did not work with Tilly who stared at him with her arms folded. "I said what I meant and I meant what I said," she said.

"Right."

"Travelled far, have you?" Tilly asked.

"I've come all the way from the United States of America just to visit your coffee shop!"

"Coffee shop?"

"Teashop?"

"Teashop?" said Tilly, sweating so much that steam began to rise from her head. "In our language it is called a 'Tearoom,' you know."

"Your language? Oh, never mind, I'm sorry if I offended you, I mean 'tearoom.'"

"That's more like it," said Tilly, "And how on earth did you hear about my tearoom?"

"I didn't, I was just being polite," the American said, realising his café experience was going to be something of a challenge.

"Who are you, exactly?" Tilly asked.

"Well, I couldn't tell you EXACTLY as I don't understand myself sometimes, haha, but I go by the name of Tom," he said.

"Cue the music!" shouted Tilly.

"Cue the music!" shouted the professor on the next table.

"CUE THE MUSIC!" screeched the elderly lady on the table against the opposite wall.

Just then, 'Space Oddity' by David Bowie came on and filled the tearoom.

"And what do you do, Tom?"

"I'm a senior professor of science at Boston University."

As soon as the American said this, the professor on the table beside him chirped up. "In that case, my friend, we have something very important to discuss."

"Well, what is it you'd like to discuss?" asked Tom. Tilly left to get the tea and the American continued talking to the professor who joined his table. The American continued, "Who are you, may I ask? I am sorry if it is rude to ask in this way, I'm not used to British manners."

"You may ask, my name is Professor Lawrence Ranger, and I studied Philosophy at Infinite Universe-ity."

"Well, I've not heard of that university before? Is it a famous one?"

"All British universities are famous!" he said proudly.

"Sorry, I've just never heard of it. Great to meet you, Professor Ranger." Tom held out his hand and the professor obliged. The American thought the professor's hand felt like jelly, and strange waves of energy crept up his arm.

Distracting the American from his weird experience, Ranger inquired about his educational background. "Did you study Rocket Science at university?"

"No, I was a Physics Major ...."

As the American waffled on to his debating partner, Tilly asked, "How do you like your tea?" But the American did not hear her. "Do you like it weak or strong, Tom?" Again he did not hear. "Can you hear me, Major Tom?" The American still did not hear. "CAN YOU HEAR ME MAJOR TOM? DO YOU LIKE IT WEAK OR STRONG!"

"Er, in the middle please," he finally replied.

"In the middle it is," Tilly said.

"So you'll know all about the Big Bang Theory then?" asked Ranger.

"Yes I can tell you all there is to know about the origins of the universe if you like," said Tom obligingly.

"No, I mean the TV programme."

"Oh, I see, I think we're on different wavelengths, haha."

"Is that a joke?"

"No, of course not."

"But you can tell me all about your faulty theory if you like," said Ranger, rudely.

"Faulty theory? You don't believe in the Big Bang theory, then?"

"No I don't," said Ranger.

"So, you want me to talk about the origin of the universe, not the TV programme?"

"Of course! Why would I want you to tell me about the TV programme? That would be ridiculous!"

"You're absolutely right," agreed Tom, feeling frustrated.

"So, sock it to me, man!"

"Right, the universe began from a small area of very high density and temperature at a finite time in the past. Basically, there was a singularity before the Big Bang. This prior spacetime singularity was a location where gravity was infinite. The Big Bang took place approximately 13.8 billion years ago from the aforementioned very small area of high density and temperature, causing it to expand and form the galaxies as we know them."

"Wow, you are so intelligent!"

"Thank you. After the expansion began, atoms formed, and the earliest stars and galaxies were formed mostly from hydrogen."

"Ooooh, I've got goose-bumps! It's like Mickey Mouse has grown up a cow!"

"What?"

"Cue the music!" shouted Tilly.

"Cue the music!" shouted the professor.

"CUE THE MUSIC!" screeched the elderly lady.

Just then, 'Life On Mars' by David Bowie came on and filled the tearoom, and Ranger urged the visitor to continue. "You were saying?"

"In fact most of the gravitational activity we observe is due to the effects of Dark Matter which surrounds galaxies. We don't know what it is, but we know it exists because of what we observe."

"Dark Matter?" Ranger asked with some suspicion in his voice.

"Yes, Dark Matter."

"DARK MATTER?" Ranger repeated a little louder.

"Yes, Dark Matter, what's the matter with that?"

"My point exactly!"

"Your point exactly?" asked Tom with some confusion in his voice.

"That's exactly my point, what's the matter with that? How can anything you said have anything to do with the origin of matter?"

"It's quite clear that this is how matter came into existence in the first place."

"Which place?"

"Well we don't know that."

"So, you see my point."

"No, I'm not sure I can see your point."

"And you have not taken into consideration the existence of spirituality!"

"I don't believe in spiritual things outside of observable or quantifiable energies."

"Yes you do!"

"No I don't!"

"YES YOU DO!" screeched the elderly lady on a table at the other side of the tearoom.

"Well if you say so." Tom responded sarcastically.

"We do say so!" responded Ranger, "How else could you be a person?"

"Actually, I do not believe my personality has anything to do with spiritual things."

"Whoa! That's a big lie!" exclaimed Ranger, "Just because your conscious mind refuses to believe it, that does not mean your inner spirit does not believe it! And just because you don't believe your spirit exists, does not mean it doesn't exist! You see my point?"

The elderly lady moved to the middle table in the tearoom and brought with her a keypad with two red buttons on it. She listened intently to the debate as her spindly and shaky hand hovered over the right hand side button because at that point she thought that Ranger was winning the debate. Ignoring the existence of the elderly lady, Tom the American continued to try to prove his point. "Everybody knows, and not only my students and I, that the Big Bang Theory is the most likely explanation for the universe in its present state." The elderly lady's spindly hand shivered back over to the left button on her keypad.

"That's a lie, and no doubt."

"No it is not!" insisted the American.

"Yes it is, lots of people don't believe in the Big Bang Theory."

"So?"

"You said that EVERYBODY knows the Big Band Theory is the most likely explanation for the universe, and that's not true, as you yourself know! Do you see my point?"

"Oh, I see what you mean, I wasn't being so literal, I was ..."

"Liar! And you should not lie to your students, either, it's mean!"

The elderly lady's spindly hand shivered back over the right button on her keypad.

"It's at least true for my students, they all definitely believe in the Big Bang Theory."

"That's because you lie to them and fool them into believing it!"

"Do you honestly expect me to believe that science doesn't provide the best chance we have of finding out the answers to our existence?"

"What I'm saying is your theories are based on a serious lack of evidence."

"There is more than enough evidence to support the Big Bang Theory."

"Please explain more about this amazing theory that is backed up by such reliable evidence," urged Ranger. "I'm quaking in my boots."

"Okay, I'll try, but you seem to find it difficult to comprehend."

"I comprehend all right. You said it all began with a very dense and very hot area, blah blah blah, which you did not actually see, and you said that most of the gravitational activity after the Big Bang is due to the effects of Dark Matter, which you have never seen - and you don't even know what Dark Matter is."

"Right."

"How can you tell your students to believe something that you don't know is true, especially when you have no tangible evidence of its existence?"

"But we have masses of scientific evidence of these things, and you can read all the science behind it in books and research papers; I will give you a book list if you want."

"Books, books, books."

"What's wrong with books?"

"Just because there are books does not prove the content is right. You are so simple minded."

"I find that quite insulting and I feel inclined to put an end to this ridiculous and offensive conversation."

"So you will only talk to me if I agree with you, then." said Ranger.

"That's not what I said. I just think you're not open to observable truth."

"It is not observable truth when you can't observe it; you are lying to me again! As you know, you did not observe the Big Bang and you have never observed Dark Matter, and neither have you met anyone else who has observed the Big Bang or Dark Matter. So, stop lying!"

"If you were more intellectual …"

"So you think you are more intelligent than me?" Ranger asked, looking surprised.

"Well, now that you've said it, yes, in science at least."

"You are the one who lacks intelligence and you seem to have a limited working memory. Either that, or you are just a compulsive liar! I have just proved you have spoken incorrectly, and you have refused to accept the truth, so how can anybody trust anything you say?"

"What you are forgetting is that these theories have been developed throughout history by the greatest scientific and mathematical geniuses of all time."

"There you go again!" said Ranger.

"What now?"

"You said that these theories have been developed by the greatest scientific and mathematical geniuses of all time."

"Yes."

"So you see my point!"

"NO, I DON'T!" said the American.

"Man, you aren't very intelligent, are you?"

"I think my university would disagree with you on that theory."

"Well that may be true, however, I know for a fact that your ideas do not come from the greatest scientific and mathematical geniuses of all time."

"And how do you work that out?"

"Because you have not taken into account the mathematical genius Zingerjaggybul from Planet Fling in the Squiltoid Solar System on the edge of Gladiator Galaxy, and you haven't even alluded to the provable research of Santander Gringolet of the twin planet Tip'nTop from the Pinpoint Solar System that orbits around the 5001st arm of the Squiggly Crayfish Spiral Galaxy."

"Now I know you're talking nonsense."

"You see, you refuse to believe the truth."

"Look, I don't know why I allowed this discussion to take place ..."

"Here's you tea," said Tilly, laying the cup and saucer on the table for the American customer.

"Thank you!" he said to Tilly with a broad smile before he continued his conversation with Ranger. "I would quite like to have my tea by myself, if you don't mind, as I have to leave soon."

"That's true!" Ranger responded.

"And I am well acquainted with the best scientific research, whatever you say."

"STOP LYING! You clearly do not even believe in the researchers I have mentioned to you. In fact I don't think you have read the research of even one zillionth of researchers in this universe."

"You are right, I have not read the works of research from other solar systems. There! End of conversation!"

"So you finally admit you have been lying to me and to your students."

The elderly lady's hand was hovering over the right hand side button, when she butted in with, "What about Heaven?"

"Heaven doesn't exist," said Tom.

"Doesn't exist?" she said, "And what about Hell then?"

"Hell doesn't exist."

"There! Lying again!" the elderly lady continued.

"Look, I've had enough, I am going to finish my drink and leave."

"You're not going anywhere until you admit your mistakes," she added in all seriousness.

"If you want to believe in Heaven or Hell, that's up to you, it's a matter of faith or hope, like a myth."

Ranger entered into the debate again, remaining at the American's table. "You are digging a black hole for yourself, Tom."

"Really?" he said nonchalantly.

"You lie to your students and you lie to us about the Big Bang Theory and Dark Matter because you expect everyone to believe what YOU believe even when YOU can't produce evidence, and you have insulted my friend over there for believing in Heaven and Hell, even though they do exist and she has seen them. You are a hypocrite!"

The elderly lady licks her lips as her hand continues to hover over the right hand button.

Tom was unable to restrain his desire to make Ranger see the light. "Well, at least my ideas are more tangible than your abstract ideas."

"It doesn't matter what YOUR ideas are, what obviously matters is the TRUTH," said Ranger.

"Philosophy is nothing but abstract ideas with no proof whatsoever!" shouted Tom.

"So prejudiced!" responded Ranger.

"Well, why don't you tell me what YOUR ideas are, then?"

Ranger took on the challenge, "I think you need to accept all the facts and possibilities, including those expressed by all professions, including philosophers. Philosophy is based on just as much truth as science."

"Rubbish!"

The elderly lady's hand hovered over the left hand side button.

"For example, you rely too much on trying to work out the origins of one physical universe, but that is only one tiny part of the puzzle."

"There may be other universes, you mean?"

"Precisely, and the word 'universe' is not enough to express all of these things. The 'universe' is so small a thing! There are so many other things, and even the word 'thing' is too limited. These 'things' include Heaven and Hell, not made up of quantifiable energies that have entered your head. There is also the significance of the numerous types of nothingness that exist outside the universe, and the effect of those nothingnesses on this universe; there is chaos; there is non-matter, and none of these things have been taken into account by you when considering the origin of this universe. And you have totally ignored the contrasts between existence and non-existence. This shows that you have to learn to respect the whole thinking of your own species at least. Science as you know it is only as large as a pin head in a thousand universes."

"Whatever," Tom said.

"And you think you know how this universe began? You fool!"

"Okay, I'm a fool," Tom said.

The elderly lady's hand then trembled over the right hand button.

"And here's a major point, Tom!"

Tom folded his arms and tried to ignore Ranger.

Ranger tried again, "This is major, Tom!"

"Cue the music!" shouted Tilly.

"Cue the music!" shouted the professor.

"CUE THE MUSIC!" screeched the elderly lady.

Just then, 'Space Oddity' by David Bowie came on again and filled the tearoom.

"And you have not even considered all of the universes inside your own body!" continued Ranger.

"What?"

"And you have made it clear that you are not willing to consider the human spirit inside you which is not the same as matter or energy in your academic repertoire. Yet you somehow think you know how the universe began? If you don't have a clue about existence and non-existence today, how can you arrogantly claim to understand what happened 13.8 billion years ago?"

"Right." he said, sarcastically.

"Consider the importance of reality and unreality."

"Fine," he said, yawning in boredom before taking a slurp of his tea.

"Your attitude makes you nothing more than a primitive being in a tiny universe, who believes with certainty only what he wants to believe, and who insists to everyone he meets that he is right."

"Yes you're right, of course," he said, again sarcastically.

"Like I said, the word 'universe' is not enough to describe everything, so the word that is generally used is:

*Univers'nparadise'nhellsgalloriumsimchaosadinfinitum**ug**interlocker yexfinity'ninfinity'nexternality'neternity*

"Well, of course you must be right," said Tom with a fake sincerity.

"And there's even a song to go with it," said Ranger as the tall guy in the back room turned off the music and entered the tearoom, along with creepy imp-man, who was playing a violin. Everyone except the American danced around the centre of the tearoom and sang one line each as follows:

Univers'nparadise'n

Hellsgalloriumsimchaos

Adinfinitum**ug**interlockery

exfinity'ninfinity'n

externality'neternity

"But that word is too long," said Ranger sitting down again, while the other singers returned to their positions, and creepy imp-man left through the back of the tearoom.

"Yes, that word is too long," agreed Tom, almost losing the will to live!

"So in short, it's called 'Ug.'"

"So cave men got it right then!" said Tom, being sarcastic for the last time.

"Absolutely!" said Ranger, and at that the elderly lady pressed her quivering hand down onto the right hand side button. The tiled tearoom floor underneath Tom's chair opened up directly beneath it and his body slipped into infinite spacetime, along with his chair.

"Well he needed to discover a bit more Ug!" said the elderly lady.

"He certainly did," added Ranger.

"It's gonna be a long, long time 'till touch down!" exclaimed Tilly.

The floor of the tearoom then went back to normal, and the imp-like, creepy man entered again from the back. "Shall I call the Sweepers?" he asked.

"No, not this time, thank you," said Tilly, and with that he exited the room with a disappointed look.

Tilly went to retrieve Tom's cup and saucer. "And he didn't even drink his tea! So rude!" she said.

Chapter 4
Venus

"What's that?" Tilly asked the creepy, nasal man who presented her with a six by six by six inch transparent cube.

"It's Major Tom."

"So he's not touched down yet then!"

"Of course not, and I thought it would make a nice memento for you."

"Absolutely, but why has it got a hole in the top?"

"Well, he's got to breathe, hasn't he?"

Tilly put the box on her serving counter and examined the contents. She could see Tom the American flailing about while falling through space. "Thank you," she said, "It will indeed prove to be a suitable decorative memento for my serving counter." Not many things interested Tilly, but this fascinated her. The creepy man edged away into his lair through the back as he could see that Tilly was preoccupied.

Meanwhile, Craig Watson and Molly Mason had parked in a small village and were strolling along Willington Lane in the Cheshire countryside. It was 7pm and the night was young. As daylight began to turn in, the sky darkened, leaving the shadows of trees and the occasional lights flickering from the country homes dotted along the distant roads. The air was fresh and the possibilities were endless. Craig did not want to think too deeply about what it all meant; he just wanted to enjoy the experience and did not worry about things getting too serious.

"What a beautiful evening!" said Craig, "Look at the twinkling stars, it's just like you can reach out and touch them." They both reached up to grab some. Then they looked at each other and giggled like little children. Molly stroked Craig's arm and her hand lingered a little longer than Craig had expected.

"I really like you," she said.

"Oh, thank you, it's nice to know you're not going to murder me along this dark country road, at least."

"Aw you found me out!" she said, and then she linked his arm and leant against him.

They continued in silence for a while along the road, but they were being followed by a dark figure at a distance.

"Let's have a coffee," Craig suggested.

"Coffee? Your place or mine?"

"Right there!" he said, pointing at a café 200 metres ahead of them.

"A café at this time? That's a surprise. Do you really think it'll be open?"

"Tilly's Tearoom, looks like it."

They looked through the windows as they got closer and noticed customers sat at tables. On reaching the door, Molly read the sign: 'Open for business,' and Craig held the door open for her as she entered at the sound of a tinkling bell.

The patrons could see them clearly under the bright lights. Craig was dressed smart-casual and looked like he was in his late 40s, while Molly was about 30 and dressed like she was going out to dinner, wearing a slim-fitting green dress.

"Don't they look sweet?" said a young woman to her husband as they drank tea together on one of the tables. The tearoom was quite full on this occasion, so Craig and Molly had to find a table at the back. Craig pulled out a chair for Molly, who sat with a big smile on her face. Craig's expression betrayed a new confidence in himself, veering on the side of smug, as he sat himself down opposite Molly.

"What do you fancy?" he asked, checking the menu.

While the two new customers cogitated, Tilly, the owner of the tearoom, tripped and stumbled onto the floor behind the counter. The customers did not realise, but she had tripped over a bloodied, severed human leg, which she had left lying around on the floor due to being fixated on her new Major Tom memento. The leg poked out at the side of the service area, but she quickly kicked it back behind the counter before anyone could see. "Stupid thing!" she said, and then she floated over to the door of the tearoom, locked it, and turned the sign round to 'Closed (for business).'

No sooner had Tilly returned to the service counter than the door rattled as someone tried to enter. But nobody noticed and the figure went away from the door.

Craig stepped up to the counter to order.

"Hello, sweetheart," said Tilly.

"Hi."

"And what can I get for you?"

"We would like a medium cappuccino and a large mocha, please."

"Certainly, my lovely, That will be four pounds sixty."

Craig gave Tilly a five pound note and Tilly gave Craig forty pence change. "Oh, is that a charity box?" he asked and immediately popped his change into the six by six by six cube. Tom was still falling through time and space when he saw a giant ten pence piece hurtling towards him. He squirmed about to avoid it hitting him, but it cracked his hip as it passed. Then a giant twenty pence piece, spinning out of control, cracked his right shin as it passed. In agony, he continued falling until another ten pence that was hurtling through the darkness and reflecting the light of heavenly bodies, struck his other shin, setting him spinning rapidly. Tilly was rivetted to this sight, but Craig just sat down to join his new companion.

"So, what are we doing?" asked Molly, resting her hand on his arm.

"We are sitting in a café, about to have a drink of coffee."

"I know, but what are we really doing?"

"I am enjoying spending time with you, just chatting."

Just then, Tilly arrived at the table with a tray from which she set down the cappuccino and the mocha.

"That was quick!" said Craig surprised. Tilly's eyes widened and gave Craig a knowing look as she put down the latter drink – that is, the mocha - on the table in a very decisive manner. Craig gave Tilly a puzzled look, and then Tilly suddenly did a seemingly random dancing jig beside him, before returning to her serving counter.

Craig smirked at his companion, "Strange woman!"

"She likes you."

"Does she?"

"Yes, in a very strange way." They both giggled. "Oops, here she comes again!"

Tilly enacted a strange dance as she came towards their table again while saying to Craig, "So sorry, I forgot to ask, do you take sugar?"

"Oh, no thank you."

"Very well, what about your wife?" asked Tilly.

"She's not my wife, she's just a friend," said Craig. "Do you take sugar, Molly?"

"No," she replied, trying to hide her annoyance.

"Right you are then," said Tilly as she floated back to her counter.

Molly got hold of Craig's hand. "Now, where were we?"

"I think we were trying to work out what we're doing," said Craig, and suddenly their bodies jerked up in their seats in shock, because the noise of the coffee machine was unpleasantly and unusually loud.

"She's doing it on purpose!" said Molly.

"Who?"

"The coffee lady, she's interfering."

"These coffee machines are a bit loud, aren't they?"

At that moment, Tilly tripped over the leg behind the counter again. She stood up and composed herself. Then she suddenly appeared beside Craig. "Here's some more hot milk for you, honey."

"Thank you," Craig said obligingly.

But Molly was not so obliging. "Could you leave us alone now please, thank you."

"Of course, I was just trying to make you feel welcome." Tilly moved back behind the counter and tripped again, but neither of them noticed because at that moment Molly got up from her seat and crouched beside Craig before grabbing his collar and kissing him full on the lips. She then immediately sat back down. Craig was pleasantly surprised, but was not sure this was a good idea. Just then a little happy girl danced up to their table with her hands behind her back.

"Hello?" said Molly.

The girl smiled and presented them with a teddy bear. "This is for you!" she said.

"Thank you," said Molly. "It's Winnie-the Pooh, isn't it? Isn't he sweet!" Craig smiled. "Here you are," Molly added, handing it back to the girl.

"No, it's really for you."

"Well, if you're sure."

"I'm very, very, very sure!"

"Well, I'll put it there in the middle of the table, so he can look after us, thank you so much!"

"He's thinking about honey," the girl said.

"That's right, he loves honey, doesn't he?"

"He's thinking, 'I wish bees didn't nest high up in trees because it's too difficult to climb up.' He wishes the bees' nests were at the bottom of trees, so he had more time to do things he wanted to do without getting too tired trying to climb up trees all the time," she said.

"And he wants to get to bees' nests to get his delicious honey, doesn't he?" said Craig.

"Of course." And with that, the girl skipped away to her mum, who smiled across at them.

Molly called over to her. "It's very kind of her, thank you."

"It's okay," replied her mother, walking over, "And I wanted to give you something too." The girl's mum held out a potted plant.

"Wow, so kind," said Craig, but Molly did not look too happy.

"It's the least I could do for such a happy couple." Looking directly at Craig, she added, "And she is indeed a real honey!"

"Yes, indeed she is," he said, smiling at Molly, wondering why she looked offended.

The woman edged away backwards with a sickly smile.

"Let's finish our drinks and go to my place," Molly suggested.

"Okay, we'll see, but I quite like it here."

Just then, Tilly tripped up again behind the counter, and the imp-like man appeared beside her. "Here, take this and put it where it belongs!" Tilly said, plonking the severed leg into his arms. The imp-man carried the leg into the back. Tilly watched Craig and Molly closely.

"Excuse me!" It was the mother with her child again; she had returned to Molly. "My husband would also like to present you with a gift."

"Thank you, but I think we have enough gifts now, so …"

"I promise you, this is the last gift, and then we will leave you alone; we just wanted to give you something you deserve." A sickly-smiling man popped out from behind his wife, holding out an ornament of some kind. He placed it gently on the table next to Pooh and the plant.

"Thank you very much," said Craig, "It looks like a troll with a cat fishing?"

"He got it right, he got it right!" said the little girl, jumping up and down in excitement.

"Not yet, honey," her mum said as all three of them tiptoed away backwards with a sickly smile on their faces.

"That's it!" shouted Molly, "We're going!"

"But why?"

"This was a mistake!"

"What was a mistake?"

"I shouldn't have agreed to it."

"I don't understand."

"Somebody's set me up!"

"Look, whatever it is, we can discuss it."

"No, we can't, don't you see?"

The plant on the table suddenly moved and distracted Craig who said, "It moved, did you see it move?"

"You don't know what it is, do you?"

"I think I've seen them on TV, but I've forgotten their name."

"It's a Venus Flytrap."

"That's it. When a fly gets too close, the plant traps it and the fly dissolves inside, poor thing. I wonder why the woman gave it to us."

"You are really stupid, aren't you, the plant is a trap and Pooh eats honey. Do the words 'honey' and 'trap' mean anything to you?" Suddenly, bees began to buzz around their table. "Get away!" Molly screamed, "Where are they all coming from?"

"Calm down and they will go away on their own; and by the way, I have absolutely no intention of trapping you into anything."

"Trapping ME?" she laughed, "As if I'd be interested in a man like you!"

"So, you're saying that you don't like me after all? You are the honey trap?"

"What do you think?"

"But why?"

"How do I know? I just take the money."

"So, where's the photographer?"

"Stop worrying about the photographer, just get these bees off me!"

Everyone in the tearoom got up to see if they could do something. "Go away!" Molly continued, waving her arms around as she stood up. She wanted to run out of the room, but the flapping patrons were blocking her in.

"Don't panic!" one said.

"It's your perfume!" said another, "That's why they like you the most."

"Well I don't like them!"

"We know, but you look too much like a flower," added someone else.

"Help me! Craig, don't just sit there!"

"She should have bee-hived better, shouldn't she?" said a man with a London accent.

"Get a bucket of water!" suggested Craig, so Tilly went to fill a bucket with cold water. By this time, Molly had flapped herself into a far corner of the tearoom, and the bees were all over her. The bees seemed to come from nowhere until her whole body was totally covered with them; not one single speck of skin or clothing was visible, from head to toe, even when she wriggled about.

Tilly arrived with the bucket of water and gave it to Craig, just as Molly stopped fighting for her life. The other patrons of the tearoom surrounded Craig and watched as he threw the water over Molly. She fell to the tiled floor and everyone cautiously leant forward to see what the bees had left behind as they swirled away from her and dispersed.

Craig crouched down, shielding his head under his jacket. As you can imagine, the café patrons could see Molly's head, arms, legs and face totally covered in deep red blisters. Tilly checked Molly's breathing and her pulse. "It's done," she said, and all of the patrons breathed a sigh of satisfaction and headed back to their tables, while Tilly unlocked the tearoom door and left it open.

Craig slowly peeped out from under his jacket and could not believe the horror of the sight. The woman he had brought into Tilly's Tearoom was slumped in the corner, her tongue bloated and hanging out of her mouth, and her eyes staring at him with red, swollen eyelids. In shock, he dashed for the door. He did not notice the severed leg on the floor at the entrance and tripped over it, falling forwards through the door and out onto the pavement, flat on his face. He staggered to his feet in a dizzy swirl, stumbled down Willington Lane to his car, and decided to keep the whole experience a secret if that was at all possible.

Tilly removed the leg and locked the tearoom door again. Just then the impish man emerged from the back and asked, "Shall I call the Sweepers?"

"No," said Tilly, "Better call Removals."

On his return to Liverpool, Private Eye Philip Scrounge uploaded his photos to see what evidence he could present to his client, Mrs Felicity Watson. He wished he had taken photos prior to the couple's time in the café as he could not for the life of him see a clear image of her husband Craig Watson. Every time he had taken a photo through the window of the tearoom to obtain proof of an inappropriate liaison, there was a waitress obscuring the man. There was one photo that showed the man's arm in contact with the woman's arm, and that was the only part of his body visible in the picture. What was particularly strange though was that the head, arms and shins of the waitress obscuring the man were not visible, only her clothing was. There was a photograph of the moment Ms Mason kissed Mr Watson, but Ms Mason was obscuring the man in that one. As for when the disaster with the bees occurred, there were plenty of pictures of Ms Mason, and what a terrible sight it was! There was even a good one of the water splashing towards her when Mr Watson dispersed the bees, but again only his arm and hand were visible, as the rest of his body was obscured by the mass of café patrons. And again, the only face that was visible was that of the scarred dead body of the woman, because the only parts of the café patrons visible on the photographs was their clothing; wherever their hair, heads or hands should have been on the picture, there was only the tearoom beyond them, and Mr Watson was surrounded by the clothing of the patrons anyway. What I mean to say is, the flesh of Craig and Molly were visible in the photos, except Craig's face was always obscured, but the flesh of the café patrons was absent where they were present, if you know what I mean. PI Scrounge even returned to the café after he and Mr Watson had scarpered in their respective directions, just to see what the café patrons were going to do with Molly, and to see if she had survived the tragedy, but he could not for the life of him find Tilly's Tearoom.

"This is all I've got," said PI Scrounge to Mrs Watson, handing her an envelope with enlarged copies of the photographs inside, when they met later in Liverpool's Sefton Park.

"What's this? All I can see is an unrecognisable dead body in a corner surrounded by a load of clothes. Is this a joke?"

"No joke."

"Do you think I'm stupid?"

"I don't know what happened, honestly, he was there all the time."

"If he was there, you would have had pictures of him, and who's the woman anyway?"

"Er, actually I don't know."

"How can you not know? If you think you're getting paid, you're off your head!"

"Well, someone has to pay my expenses."

"Expenses for what? I said I would pay you if you brought me proof."

"This is it, he was there the whole time."

"Where is this café, anyway?"

"Now, that's the strange thing, it's disappeared."

"You're a conman! My husband told me he was working late like he normally does, and you have no proof to the contrary, now go and leave me alone, you're fired!"

Philip Scrounge grabbed the photographs off her and walked away. He was going to throw the photographs away, but then thought he would keep hold of them just in case he could somehow cash in if and when a dead body was discovered.

DAILY TITBITS
by
Justin Caadfar Esquire

The body of a woman has been discovered by ramblers who were walking in Delamere Forest, Cheshire, last week. She was half buried, and it looked like she had been stung all over her body by bees, but no bees' nests could be found nearby. Police are baffled. Detective Gordon Fairweather said, "This is a very puzzling case, as the victim was obviously very seriously attacked by bees, and stung thousands of times, which we believe was the cause of her death. But as to why her body was half buried in the middle of Delamere Forest, we have no idea. It is possible that she was trying to escape being stung by the bees, so she tried to cover herself up with soil to protect herself, but we don't think that is likely from the evidence available."

The police are treating the case as suspicious and have come into possession of photographs that show a woman matching the victim's appearance, slumped in the corner of a café, already severely stung and looking dead. That would mean a person or persons must have moved her body to hide vital evidence. The photographs include a group of people, but they cannot be identified as their faces have been airbrushed out. Experts are analysing the images to see if they are authentic.

It was the popular paper, 'Daily Watchdog,' that supplied police with the photographs, but the paper insists they have no idea who sent them to their offices. Whoever took the photographs would very likely have witnessed how the woman died, and police are urging the anonymous photographer to come forward and give evidence.

> *DNA tests have confirmed the victim as a Ms Catherine Kilroy who worked for an escort agency under a number of pseudonyms. So far, nobody connected with the agency who has been questioned can shed any light on where Ms Kilroy was at the time of her death.*

Private Investigator Philip Scrounge had no intention of ever admitting to taking the photos. He had been paid by the Daily Watchdog with the promise of anonymity should police investigate. So far they had not given him away and had lied on his behalf, saying that the photos had been received by post.

But that was not the end of the story for Scrounge as this had given him a taste for adventure, and he was determined to understand the mystery of the disappearing café called Tilly's Tearoom.

Chapter 5
Alison

Walking through the forest, the cool breeze blowing against her face, Alison, a nineteen year old student from Cambridge University, tilted her head to listen to the wood pigeons cooing, and her big blue eyes moved around in delight as she watched the sun's rays flickering through the tree branches. She was alone yet happy, loved by her friends yet content without them, hardworking yet carefree, energetic and confident. She was also a bit adventurous, yet never in danger ... until now!

Her imagination ran wild in an innocent kind of way, and it was in fact that imagination that had fuelled her fascination for life in all its facets. It was not too hot outside, and neither was it too cold, yet she had her very long, multi-coloured scarf swung around her neck; this scarf was special to her as her mum had made it for her before she left home for university.

Alison was picturing white rabbits hopping in and out of the trees and the Cheshire Cat swooning above her from a tree branch as she strolled through the forest. She smiled a trusting smile back at the cat. Then, she heard singing from a small group of people nearby who were sat having a picnic in a clearing in the woods. They sounded so happy that she was curious to meet them.

Coming into the clearing, she saw three people sat on a large table cloth, drinking tea and eating biscuits. They were just her kind of imaginary people as one was dressed like the Mad Hatter, one like the March Hare, and another like a mouse, just like in Lewis Carrol's *Alice's Adventures in Wonderland*. This gathering of people aroused her curiosity even more; after all, why would normal people dress up like this in a public place just to have a picnic in the forest? She edged closer and at first they ignored her and continued with their conversation.

The Mad Hatter stood up on the table cloth, and boy was he tall! He held up a teacup, "A toast to Alison!" and then he sat down again, cross-legged.

Next, the person dressed as a mouse stood up, and boy was he small! "A toast to Alison!" he said in a nasally voice before crumpling to the table cloth in a deep sleep.

Alison, who was stood not too far away, suddenly realised that they were toasting someone with the same name as her. "Surely they can't be toasting me, how would they know me? And how would they know I was here since they haven't even looked at me yet?" she asked herself. She was fascinated to know the answer to her questions, infatuated in fact.

Just then, to Alison's surprise, the March Hare bounded up to her, and it gave her quite a shock, I can tell you. "Welcome to our tea party," he said. By the look of his eyes, Alison thought he must be a middle-aged man.

"Well thank you, but why are you dressed like a hare?" asked Alison, not able to resist the chance to find out what all of this entertaining and fascinating nonsense was about.

"I am not dressed up like a hare, I am a hare!"

Giggling, Alison said "Well, if you say so."

Escorted by the March Hare, she approached the table cloth on which the Mad Hatter was sat and the mouse was asleep. She could not see a flask in the middle of the table cloth, but she did see a very large teapot. "What are you all doing?"

"Shush!" said the Mad Hatter with a bulbous finger over his lips, and pointing to the mouse with his other hand, "He's dreaping."

"Dreaping? Don't you mean sleeping?"

"Haven't you ever heard of dreaping before? You must have had a very poor education."

"No, actually …"

March Hare opened a small notebook. "The official definition of 'dreaping' is 'dreaming while you are sleeping during a deep sleep.'"

"That's a very good word," said Alison, "I think I'll use it in the future."

"Oh no, you can't do that," March Hare added, "As it says in my book, only Mad Hatters, hares and other amphibians can use the words 'dreaping,' 'pingwit,' and 'phripple.' It says it right here, it's law!"

"Well that's not very sharing."

"You are only saying that because you like breaking the law!"

"Why would you say such a thing? And I haven't even used the word 'dreaping' yet!"

"There you go again, breaking the law, exactly like I said; that's why creatures like you are not supposed to say those words."

"Fair enough," said Alison, not because she agreed with him, but because she had no intention of going round in circles. "But I feel I should mention, by way of information, that Mad Hatters and hares are not amphibians."

"Amphibians! How dare you call us amphibians!"

"Er, I didn't."

"You are always using words you shouldn't use!" said March Hare.

"Whatever you say, anyway, what's the special occasion?"

"Occasion?" screeched the Mad Hatter. It was rather strange hearing such a giant of a man screeching.

"Yes, the occasion that you're celebrating."

"Who wants to celebrate an occasion? I'd much rather celebrate a creature!"

"A creature! Absolutely!" said the mouse, waking up from his dreap momentarily and speaking in his nasally voice.

"Well, that's what I mean," said Alison.

"Well if that's what you mean, why didn't you just say so?" added the Hatter.

"I did, well, in a manner of speaking."

"Your manner of speaking is extremely vicious if you ask me," he continued.

"I think you'll find I'm anything but vicious," said Alison, quite puzzled.

"Well that remains to be seen," said the mouse, yawning.

The Mad Hatter looked concerned and squinted at Alison in a suspicious manner, "You are just like the Studge in the song of the same name, I'm sure you'll agree."

"I have never heard of that song."

The mouse stood poised to speak, and melodiously sang the following folk song:

The Stirline Studge

'Twas phripple, and the leglongdales,
Did bludge and dreap in the fronds;
All melanchlad were the timtam tales,
And the pingwits fried the pronds.

Beware the Stirline Studge my girl!
The teeth that crunch, the hands that snatch,
Beware the jawning Breaph, and curl
The firlrite Patterstatch!

Alison listened respectfully as the song was very tuneful, but she was baffled by the lyrics: "To be honest, I don't have the faintest idea what that song is about."

"That's because you're not listening with your eyes," said the Mad Hatter.

"How can you listen with your eyes?"

"Easy, just open them when you hear a song."

"Okay, I'll remember that next time."

"Good, I'm glad we have THAT issue sorted out!"

"I am curious, by the way, why did you propose a toast to someone called Alison?"

"Alison? Who's Alison?" screeched the Mad Hatter.

"I am Alison!" said Alison.

"We don't know you from Alan!" exclaimed the Mad Hatter.

"Don't you mean Adam?"

"Adam? Who's Adam?" he replied. "Why do you keep saying unknown people's names?"

"It's a saying, you said …"

"You know too many people, it's not fair for everyone else!" Mad Hatter said slamming his teacup down and folding his arms in a grump.

"Oh dear, I seem to be getting nowhere. Thank you for inviting me Mr Hare, but I'm afraid I'm going to have to leave," said Alison waving as she moved away from the group.

"Afraid? You should be afraid!" said the March Hare, holding onto Alison's arm firmly and dragging her back and onto the table cloth with a thud. "There's danger in the forest! Just look, can't you see it?"

Alison looked but all she could see were the beautiful trees swaying in the breeze. "I can't see any danger," she said.

"That's because you're not looking," said the Mad Hatter. March Hare gripped Alison's arm tightly while the Hatter poured her a cup of tea from the huge teapot. "Here, have a drink of tea."

"Thank you."

"You're welcome."

Alison took a slurp of the tea.

"Where's my wibbly wand?" asked the Mad Hatter, taking off his top hat and pulling white rabbits out of it in his search. "Oh, here it is!" He pulled out a crooked shaped stick and dropped his hat on the ground from which shot out a hundred more white rabbits. "Right, I have to remember how to make us all bigger before it comes."

"Before what comes?" asked Alison, taking another slurp, "This tea's delicious!"

"Never fear my dear, whatever comes, it will be too small to bother us."

"I sincerely hope so," Alison said, staring into her teacup in curiosity. "There's a storm in my teacup!"

The Hatter stood tall and shook his wand around, "If I could just get my wand to work!"

"It's spinning round and round, and a walrus, surrounded by oysters, is swirling round and round and round, down into the bottom of my teacup," said Alison.

The Mad Hatter put one foot forward, held out his wibbly wand and spoke a spell:

*"Make us big and make them small,
For this is not her fault at all!"*

There was a whoosh and the Red Queen appeared, looking remarkably like the picture of a queen that you get in a deck of cards. She was shorter than the Mad Hatter, but much plumper. Her face was stern and angry. Pointing her finger at Alison she screamed, "OFF WITH HER HEAD!"

"I beg your pardon!" said Alison, quite offended at such an idea, wondering why a person of such superior status would suggest someone should do such a savage thing.

"But what has this girl done wrong?" asked the mouse, cringing in fear.

"How dare you ask me that question!" shouted the Red Queen.

"I'm sorry, your majesty, I was just thinking that if a creature had not done anything wrong – and I am very sorry, your majesty, if this sounds a little rude - why should that creature have his or her or its head removed from his or her or its body, if he, she or it is innocent?"

"WHAT!" screamed the Red Queen, "She stole my flowers!"

"Excuse me, your majesty," said Alison, standing up and curtsying, "Begging your pardon …"

"Get on with it!"

"With all due respect, I have not stolen ANY flowers."

"I've seen them!"

"Oh, yes I do have some red roses at home which were sent by a secret admirer," admitted Alison.

"That's what I mean! All red roses are mine!"

"But I did not steal them."

"But you did not give them back to me did you! Off with her head!"

"No, I want to keep my head on my shoulders!" protested Alison.

The Mad Hatter said, "It had better work this time!" He poised himself to utter the spell again:

> *"Make us big and make them small,*
> *For this is not her fault at all!"*

Suddenly, the 'real' Alice in Wonderland appeared, lying down in the middle of the table cloth on her back, but she looked old. The curious thing was, she was wearing Alison's multi-coloured scarf.

"How dare you!" shouted the March Hare, who jumped on top of the elderly Alice and began strangling her with the scarf.

"Stop it! Stop it!" screamed Alison, watching from the side. "Leave her alone!"

The March Hare scowled back at Alison while continuing to strangle Alice. "It's all your fault!"

"What's my fault?"

"I wouldn't be doing this if it wasn't for you!" the March Hare screamed with his twisted face oozing venom.

"I don't know what you're talking about, let her go!"

"I can't, it's all your fault!"

"GET OFF HER!" shouted Alison as she could see the life had nearly gone from the elderly Alice's face.

At that moment, the trees began to bend and break, and from the midst of the woods emerged a huge, terrifying beast with red roses being spat out from between its teeth. The monster, which resembled a green, scaly dragon, the size of a detached house, had fiery eyes and spittle poured from its mouth as it roared. Even the Red Queen looked scared and shouted, "OFF WITH ITS HEAD!" her huge voice barely audible over the horrendous noise of the monster.

Meanwhile, the March Hare continued to strangle Alice with the scarf. In spite of the imminent danger from the monster, Alison grabbed hold of the March Hare and tried to pull him away from Alice. The Queen continued to command the demise of the monster which was now directly above them all, pouring saliva over the tea party. The Hare, the Hatter, Alice, the mouse and the Queen were drenched with drool.

"OFF WITH ITS HEAD!" the Red Queen screamed, and the mouse pulled out a chain saw from the top hat. Strapping it on tight, the mouse scurried up the tough scales of the dragon to its neck, and then the mouse jumped into the air, bringing the spinning saw-blade down between its vertebrae, severing the neck. As the head of the dragon spun in the air, Alison succeeded in pulling the Hare way from the elderly Alice. The Queen held out her arms to catch the dragon's giant head, and the Hatter caught the falling mouse in his top hat. Blood, like an immense blanket was heading to earth, with the massive severed head close behind it, and they were all in for a drenching, so Alison ran away from the table cloth and into the trees for cover; but she did not stop to see what happened next, she just kept running.

In a state of shock, Alison stumbled over shrubs and plants, along paths and streams under the shade of the forest, for about an hour, until she bumped into three of her local friends; they were Michael, Toby and Matty. Matty shared student lodgings with Alison during term time at Cambridge as they were old school friends, but they were not due to head back to university for another two weeks. She was the first to recognise Alison in the distance. "Look, there's Alison, she looks as if she's in some kind of trouble."

They all jogged towards her to see. "Alison!" they all called.

"Help me!" she said in her exhaustion.

"What's happened?" Matty asked.

"I don't know where to begin."

Putting her arm around her, Matty said, "Come on, we'll take you back home."

"No, I'm okay."

"You're not, you need to sit down and wrap yourself in a blanket."

"I need to go back, a woman's life is in danger."

"What woman?" asked Michael.

"An old woman, she was being strangled and I managed to pull the Hare off her."

"Pull the hair off her? Why on earth would you pull the hair off an old woman?"

"No, you don't understand!"

"Look, calm down, Alison, we love you and want to help," said Toby.

"Then come with me and I'll show you; there's probably been a murder by now; hurry!"

All four of them followed Alison and they covered the distance in half the time as Toby supported Alison's weight. On the way, Alison explained everything to them and as you would expect, they thought she had taken some kind of drug; either that or she was suffering delusions after some kind of shock or mental breakdown. Either way, they needed to get to the bottom of it all.

Just before they reached the spot from where Alison had fled, she described the part about the mouse chopping off the head of the dragon.

"It's strange you should say that!" said Matty, "We have some sad news for you; our personal tutor Professor Henry has been murdered."

"What? That's terrible! When?"

"His wife saw him leave the house in Cambridge this morning, so he must have been murdered today."

"Today? Where? How?"

"His body was found in his uni office; there was blood everywhere, apparently."

"That's dreadful, who would want to kill him? He was a bit weird, but even so…"

"Someone chopped his head off!"

"What! I can't believe it."

"I can," said Matty.

"Matty!"

"He was a bit of a perv to all intents and purposes."

"How do you know?"

"Just things I've heard."

"Actually, I think it was him who sent me those roses," said Alison.

"Quite likely," said Matty.

"But he never said anything directly, I just got that impression somehow, and I didn't want to give him the chance to bring it up."

"That would have been very awkward!" said Toby.

"Yes, how do you say 'no' to your tutor and go on as normal? Any idea who killed him then?" asked Alison again.

"No idea, he was only found about an hour before we bumped into you," he added. "Someone heard a man's scream and found him there with his head cut off!"

"How awful!" said Alison. "News travels fast."

"It does," said Matty, "It went straight onto social media."

They arrived at the clearing and Alison could not believe her eyes. There was no blood, no dragon's head, no tea party or table cloth, only her multi-coloured scarf was there, coiled up beneath a small bush close to where she had been sat.

Matty recognised the scarf. "That's your favourite scarf, Alison."

"Yes, I left it here when I ran away, but there's no blood on the ground and no dragon's head, I don't understand."

"Don't you think you were just high on something."

"No, you know me, I wouldn't take anything like that, although, they did give me a cup of tea – they might have put something in it!"

"Let's go," said Michael, deeply concerned about her mental state.

Alison picked up her scarf – which was spotlessly clean - and slowly headed home with her friends. On arriving home, Alison promised she would call her friends later to reassure them that she was all right. She lay down on her bed alone, clutching her favourite multi-coloured scarf. "Who would want to murder Professor Henry?" she asked herself.

As she continued to fondle her scarf, she felt an object fall from it. It rolled off her bed and onto the floor. She leant over the edge of her bed to retrieve it. Lying on her back on her bed again she held the curious object close to examine it. It was decorated in a complex manner and felt quite heavy and metallic; it depicted various colours and shapes. She treasured it, whatever it was, as it reminded her that she had genuinely experienced something peculiar, even if she could not explain it or prove it to anyone.

DAILY TITBITS
by
Justin Caadfar Esquire

Some progress has been made in the case of Professor Benedict Henry, a senior lecturer from Cambridge, who was found beheaded in his university office last month. He was a well-respected member of staff, but he had a secret side to his personality, as the police found what they have called 'extremely disturbing images' on his personal computer. We have been informed by a reliable source that Professor Henry had hundreds of pictures of young adults being strangled. Police are trying to identify the people in the pictures to see if they are known strangulation victims or among recorded missing persons.

As far as the identity of his murderer is concerned, there are no reliable witnesses, but police have been questioning some of his students again this week to try to gather evidence. It is believed that the professor was also in possession of compromising pictures of his students, but no one has come forward with an accusation of assault.

The case continues.

Chapter 6
The Keeper

He was the Keeper of the Castle Keep, that is, the strongest tower within the castle. The Castle Keep was the Keeper's last defence against the world around him. He was determined to keep everyone and everything out that would not be of benefit to the castle and its inhabitants. The castle was situated in Wales in a place where many would not dare to venture in those days.

The Castle Keeper had an associate known as the Fiend of Forest Dell. He lived in the valley among the trees where feet feared to tread. He was once a friend of the Keeper of the Castle, but now they were enemies. In spite of their differences, they both had the same occupation, and that was to protect their environment and keep out undesirables; and as they were no longer friends, their occupation included keeping each other out.

This was difficult for the Fiend and the Keeper, because they relied so much on each other's resources. The Castle Keep contained the last remaining store of wheat and barley, along with other foodstuffs, and Forest Dell had the only remaining constant source of drinking water in the area by way of a stream. They needed each other but neither trusted the other.

Tilly the Storyteller: So, what was the solution? How could they solve this problem?

Amelia: They could just become friends again.

Tilly: Yes, you're right, that's what they should do, but they've had so many disagreements about so many things, so many times, that they were not in the right frame of mind to try.

Amelia: Grown-ups should know how to be good friends to help children to know how to be good friends.

Tilly: Another good point. You're a very clever girl. What's your name?

Amelia: Amelia.

Tilly: Amelia, you can learn a lot from this story, even though you already have good answers.
Amelia: (Coyly) It's a good story.
Jack: My mummy and daddy aren't friends anymore.
Jack's Mum: (From among the group of parents standing and sitting to the side while watching their children who were sat with the Storyteller) Jack! I don't think the Storyteller's interested in your mummy and daddy's problems.
Tilly: It's okay, he can say whatever he likes, I don't mind.
(Jack's mum looked at her fellow-parents and carers with a concerned grimace.)

The world in which the Keeper and the Fiend lived was difficult, and the weather could be cruel too. The inhabitants of the castle relied on their two protectors – the Keeper and the Fiend - to help them. The two protectors were in charge of everything, and while they were enemies, the castle inhabitants were in danger of death.

Jack: Like my mummy and daddy.
Jack's Mum: We're not in danger of dying, Jack, we've got plenty to eat and drink, and you have loads of wonderful toys and computer games.
Tilly: I think what he means is his mummy and daddy are enemies and that puts him at risk.
Jack's Mum: My child is not at risk!
(Amongst the other parents, half were embarrassed on behalf of Jack's Mum, and the other half were being judgemental about her.)
Tilly: What clever children I have in my Storyland today! (Jack smiled, but his mum looked even more concerned.)
Mandy: Will they all die?
Tilly: Yes (The parents at the side were aghast).
Mandy: (Looking tearful) I want a story with a happy ending.
Tilly: It is a happy ending.
Mandy: But you said they're all going to die!
Tilly: Of course they will die because, as you know, everyone dies.

Graham: (To Mandy) I think the Storyteller means everybody dies eventually, when they should do, like, when they're old.
Tilly: What intelligent children I have with me today!
(All of the children smiled proudly) It was a happy ending and they all died when they grew older, a long time later - and it was all a long time ago anyway.
Doris: (Doris began to cry and Doris' Mum giggled nervously) I don't like it when people leave me (At that, Doris' Mum stopped giggling).
Jack: Don't cry, it's okay, it's only a story.
Tilly: Oh no, it's not ONLY a story.
Doris: My daddy's left me! (Doris' Mum came to remove Doris) No mummy, I want to stay!
Doris' Mum: But you're upset.
Tilly: (With sincerity) It's okay to be upset when you're learning something important, isn't it?
Doris' Mum: Could you be careful please,? They are only children, after all.
Tilly: I will (Doris' Mum moved back to the side with the other parents). As I was saying, it's a true story, but it happened a LONG, LONG time ago (Tilly gave Doris' Mum a wink). So back to my original question, how can they get enough food and water to live on so that they can be happy again and live as friends until they are old?
Billie: The people who live with the Keeper can sneak down and get water from the stream.
Tilly: So clever!

The inhabitants of the castle tried to sneak down into the dell, but the Fiend had built a high fence alongside the stream and laid out so many traps that the inhabitants of the castle got seriously hurt and had to go back.

(By this point, some of the parents were beginning to agree amongst themselves that the story and the Storyteller's questions were more appropriate for teenagers rather than Primary School age children.)

Fred: (Intelligently) Can't they go farther along the stream away from the fence, and away from the traps, to get water, and then they can bring it back to the castle?
Tilly: They tried it and decided not to do that again:

Many inhabitants had already tried to go farther along the stream, away from the fence and the traps to get water and bring it back to the castle, but it was treacherous in those areas, making the stream inaccessible.

Fred: What does 'inaccessible' mean?
Tilly: It means it would be impossible to get the water and even more difficult to get it back to the castle if they could collect some from the stream.

Some people tried this and never returned because something dreadful happened to them.

(Some of the parents were saying things like: 'She's making it up as she goes along …' And: 'She's letting the children develop the story instead of telling them one that's already been written!')

Chris: If I was the Fiend, I'd just sneak into the castle and get some food.
Tilly: He tried this:

The Fiend, on many occasions, tried to sneak into the castle to get some food, but he didn't have anyone to help him and the inhabitants of the castle were always on the lookout for him. They always chased him away by shooting sharp arrows; he had to run away to save his life.

Mark: Why couldn't the Fiend just eat fruit and animals from the forest?
Tilly: So intelligent!!

The Fiend was actually in the best situation because his resource was water, and the squirrels in the forest were edible. However, the squirrels had been warned about it, and were packing up for another home, where they wouldn't get eaten to extinction – and the fruit in the dell wasn't edible.

Kelsey: I think the Fiend and the Keeper are silly; they should just be friends. If they became friends they'd have enough food and enough water.
Tilly: That's right! But how could they become friends when they didn't trust each other anymore?
Minnie: AND they should think about all the other people who will die in the castle. The Fiend and the Keeper are just being selfish; they are only thinking of themselves.
Tilly: Good point! Wow, you children are amazing, you understand sooo much! (The parents at the side gave each other a proud smile.)

It wasn't only the Fiend and the Keeper who were suffering from hunger or thirst, it was the people who lived in the castle too. Without water they would die. All of the other water supplies had either just dried up or been sabotaged by the Fiend.

Andrew: Well, I think they should sit down together and have a nice long conversation over a cup of tea.
Bartholomew: And perhaps someone from the castle could sit with them to stop them fighting.
Tilly: The problem is the Fiend and the Keeper couldn't contact each other very easily because there were no phones or computers in those days. Today, it's much easier to contact someone and arrange to meet them because most people have a phone and they can take that phone outside too.
Tina: Did they have a TV?
Tilly: No.

Fred: I know, everyone who lives in the castle can stand on top of the highest bit and shout together: 'COME TO THE CASTLE, WE WANT TO TALK TO YOU AND BE YOUR FRIEND!'
Tilly: Well done, young man.

On a couple of occasions everyone who lived in the castle stood on top of the highest wall of the castle and shouted down to the Fiend saying, 'COME TO THE CASTLE, WE WANT TO TALK TO YOU AND BE YOUR FRIEND!' But the Fiend was too afraid to go to the castle as he thought the people were tricking him so they could kill him and get water from the stream with nobody to stop them.

Annie's Mum: (To the other parents) She is absolutely letting the children make up the story as she goes along!
Andrew: They can shout: 'WE ARE SORRY, WE WILL NOT HURT YOU. PLEASE COME AND WE CAN SHARE EVERYTHING TOGETHER!'
Tilly: I like the sound of that one. I think you are all absolutely amazing; you understand everything!
Andrew: (Jumping up and down) We understand everything! We are absolutely amazing!
Tilly: Even though it's a wonderful idea, they had already tried it:

On the second occasion they shouted from the wall, adding, 'WE ARE SORRY, WE WILL NOT HURT YOU. PLEASE COME AND WE CAN SHARE EVERYTHING TOGETHER!' But it didn't make any difference.

Sophia: Why didn't it work?
Tilly: For the same reason as before.

The Fiend didn't believe them, and he had nobody to give him good advice.
The castle was on a hill just above the dell and there were no trees or traps on the slope. The trees started at the bottom of Castle Hill and

they continued down into the dell. Sometimes the castle inhabitants would walk around Castle Hill, looking down into the dell, longing for something to drink. They were so sad.

Has anyone here ever been sad like that?
Annie: I'm sad like that every day because my mummy and daddy aren't friends anymore. (Annie's Mum went red.)
Tilly: Sometimes when people stop being friends, it's not only themselves that are unhappy, is it?
Gus: My mum and dad are like the Fiend and the Keeper as well. I wanted them to stay together as a family, but dad said they're happier living in different houses; but me and my sister aren't happy.
(Gus' Dad blushed.)
Tilly: Exactly! They should stop thinking about themselves and think about their children, shouldn't they? (All of the children nodded sincerely. The parents didn't know whether to be angry or ashamed.)
Annie's Mum: (Taking Annie by the hand) It's time to go, Annie.
Tilly: Bye bye Annie, it was great to meet you (all of the other children said goodbye and waved).
Annie: (Shouting) I don't want to leave!
Annie's Mum: Come on, the story's going to finish soon, anyway.
Annie: Can I listen to the end, mummy, please; I want to know how the Fiend and the Keeper became friends again.
Annie's Mum: (To Tilly) Can you see what you're doing?
Tilly: Yes, I am so pleased Annie has enjoyed the story.
Annie's Mum: That's the problem, I don't know what you're trying to do?
Tilly: I'm trying to tell the story, I think the children are enjoying it. (All of the children nodded enthusiastically.)
Annie: (To her mum) I need to learn how to get you and daddy to love each other again so we can all live together as a happy family.
Annie's Mum: Things like that just don't happen.
Annie: Why? Why do you and daddy have to live apart? I want my daddy and mummy to live together!

Annie's Mum: Well, I think you're very lucky, you have two daddies; you have Michael AND daddy.
Annie: I want my real daddy to live with us, I don't want Michael.
Annie's Mum: That's not very kind, Michael has done lots of things for you, and he doesn't have to.
Annie: I didn't choose him.
Annie's Mum: Your mummy needs to be happy too!
Annie: But I'm not happy, and Michael makes me more unhappy! It's not fair!
Gus: Yeh, how come Michael gets to live in Annie's house but Annie's Dad isn't allowed to?
Gus' Dad: You'll understand when you're older.
Annie: I'm never going to be happy!
Gus: It's the same as me and my sister.
Kelsey: Same here!
Bartholomew: Me too! Mums and dads should think more about their children, and stop wanting different boyfriends and girlfriends.
Tilly: Truly amazing, you know everything!
Gus' Dad: (To Gus) You'll eventually learn that life isn't that simple.
Gus: (Out loud) But you're always telling me and my sister to be good and kind to each other, and me and my sister are! And when we argue, we always make friends again. So why can't you and mum be nice to each other? You're grown-ups! If grown-ups can't be friends, how can you expect your children to be good friends all the time?
Gus' Dad: When you're older we'll teach you what life's really like. (Most children started to cry at the thought that growing up means you don't stay friends with people and you don't stay together and love each other) (To Tilly) You really need training on how to deal with children!
Tilly: Anyway, shall we carry on with the story?
(All of the children cheered. Gus' Dad and Annie's Mum decided to risk letting their children hear the ending to the story.)
Annie's Mum: (Attempting a last minute justification, she crept up to Annie and whispered) Your mummy and daddy both show you how much we love you all the time; we take you to the zoo, we buy you ice

creams, computer games ... (Annie ignored her to listen to the Storyteller).

The inhabitants of the castle were very unhappy and frightened, and they became very angry with the Keeper. They said: 'Why did you have to fall out with the Fiend - you used to be best friends?' And: 'Why did you let things get this bad?' And: 'We are suffering so much, don't you care?' And: 'If you really cared about us you would make a bigger effort to become friends again with the Fiend of Forest Dell.' And: 'We used to be happy together. It's your selfishness that got us into this mess!' And: 'Why did you promise to look after us as the Keeper of the Castle if you were going ruin our lives like this?' And: 'We're going to die and you don't care!'

Liz: (To Gus and Annie) Perhaps your mummy and daddy left you because you were naughty.
Liz's Mum: (Aghast) Liz, that's so rude!
Liz: Well, daddy told me that our family's not working, and I was naughty that day.
Liz's Mum: He didn't mean it was because you were naughty.
Liz: He did, he said it. I'm not lying!
Liz's Mum: I'm not accusing you of lying. Daddy didn't mean it was YOUR fault, it was probably mine and your daddy's fault.
Liz: So why don't you say sorry and become friends again so we can be a family like before?
Liz's Mum: I think everyone here (meaning her fellow-parents) would agree that life isn't as simple as that, just like we keep telling you.
Andrew: I think that's another way of parents saying they want what they want, even if it means taking a mummy or daddy away from their children.
Tilly: Wow! So perceptive!
Andrew: (To the parents) How can you possibly force your children to live together and care about each other and then – being more 'mature' – you decide whenever you like to dump your husband or wife,

and the children have to live without their mummy or daddy? Anyone can see that's not right!
Tilly: Amazing!
Liz's Mum: Clearly, this story has got a bit out of hand and we should all call it a day.
All children: NO! NO! NO!
Andrew: Why do grown-ups try to take us away whenever we speak the truth?
Tilly: Because parents are too embarrassed or selfish to admit they're wrong.
Annie's Mum: That's enough!
Andrew: You see! We have to just shut up when our parents fall out and split everyone up, even when we're hurting inside and we need to tell someone.
Annie's Mum: (To Andrew) I don't want to speak out of turn, because I don't know if your mummy or daddy are here, but it's only the mummy and daddy who are splitting up, it's not about the children; it's the mum and dad that made the promises to love each other, so if they stop loving each other it's up to them if they prefer to separate and find another partner. Then the children have two homes, two bedrooms, and they go out to lots of places.
Andrew: Like a guilt offering! Just because you have money, you think that can replace a mum or a dad. Do you think money is the solution to everything? You see, she doesn't see it, just like all the other mums and dads who split their families apart.
Annie's Mum: (Offended) This is getting ridiculous!
Tilly: She's right, it is getting ridiculous, because she does see it, and so does everyone else here.
Annie's Mum: Excuse me! How can you possibly claim to know our lives and what we think and what we don't think?
Tilly: You know how much it hurts; that's why you try to make up for it with gifts and treats. But it doesn't replace what the children have lost, does it? They don't feel as safe, they don't feel as secure, and they no longer believe love is forever.

(Tears welled up in some of the parents' eyes and some of the children cried when they heard that 'love is not forever.')

Andrew: They tell us to forgive people all the time and make up, but they can just throw each other out of the house, even if it makes their children unhappy for the rest of their lives!

Tilly: That's right.

Annie's Mum: That is totally not true!

Gus' Dad: The children don't need to be unhappy for the rest of their lives.

Tilly: But they so often are! They have sorrow in their heart for the rest of their lives, even if they learn how to put on a brave face.

Gus' Dad: But they need to learn that life is hard and they can't always have what they want. We need to teach them grit!

Andrew: There you go again! If you're telling the truth, why are children - at home and at school - taught to love and care for each other and to be friendly with everyone?

Gus' Dad: It's just what we do, but it's not real life.

Liz's Mum: I take exception to that. We teach them the ideals, but they will find there are always exceptions.

Tilly: It does take grit and determination and forgiveness to make relationships work.

Andrew: But he's telling us to learn grit so we can accept breaking up families.

Tilly: Clever boy.

(Annie's Mum felt very offended by all this and anger filled her eyes as the debate continued)

Gus' Dad: If I didn't have grit, my children wouldn't have all of the lovely things that I've provided for them.

Andrew: If you had grit, you would find a way to keep your family together?

(Annie's Mum then broke down in tears of guilt)

Gus' Dad: That's not about grit, it's about love. And people fall out of love.

Andrew: Love is forgiveness, sacrifice and commitment, even when it is difficult, and love has responsibilities that come with it.

Tilly: (Standing to congratulate Andrew) Give him a round of applause! (All of the children and two parents stood clapping their hands)

Andrew: You split up children from their mummy or their daddy and put a different man or woman in their place and you don't care how much it hurts us!

Tilly: (Sitting down in her Storytelling chair again, and the children sitting back down on the floor) That's amazing, you are so right.

Annie's Mum: (Grabbing Annie angrily by the arm) Come on, we're going!"

Annie: You're hurting me!

Tilly: Please be gentle with your daughter.

Annie's Mum: You just shut up or I'll punch your lights out!

(All of the children gasped)

Tilly: But I don't have any lights.

Liz's Mum: You're poisoning their minds, you crazy lady.

Tilly: I don't think so, I've only spoken the truth, and the children have only spoken according to their own experiences.

Gus' Dad: But you keep praising them when they are disrespectful to their parents.

Tilly: I'm only telling them a story and asking them to think of ideas to get two people to make friends again. It's not as if the Fiend and the Keeper weren't good friends before. There's no reason why they can't forgive each other, if only for the sake of the people that the Keeper has to look after. He has a duty of care.

Andrew's Dad: She's right. We could ALL do with listening to this and learning from it.

Gus' Dad: You're actually supporting this woman?

Andrew's Dad: As far as I can see, she's only telling the story and the children are sharing from their hearts. It's about time we listened to our children if they're hurting so much.

Annie's Mum: (With a very angry voice) My daughter wasn't hurting until she started listening to this rubbish.

Annie: I was, I have always been unhappy since daddy left home.

Gus: Me too, since my mum left. I cry every night when I go to bed; I've kept it a secret because I don't want my dad to think I'm a baby, and I don't want to upset my mum, so I don't let them hear me crying.
Tilly: That's a shame, isn't it.
Gus: They said they don't love each other anymore, but why don't they try harder?
Tilly: Selfish isn't it? We should all make an effort to get on well with each other.
All of the children: YES!
Andrew: And if children fight at school, teachers always tell them to make up and be friends, and they do, because they believe it's right.
All of the children: (All nodding) Yes!
Tilly: I can tell you the end of the story now, it will only take two minutes.
Andrew: I want to hear it. Let's all stay and listen to the end of the story (all of the children agreed).

The Fiend was very lonely and he had nobody to talk to, but that didn't stop him saying to himself all day, every day: 'It's all the Keeper's fault, he's so greedy and selfish!'

The Keeper wasn't lonely, but he was asked by someone every day: 'Why have you caused us to suffer so much?' And he would always blame the Fiend: 'It's all the Fiend's fault, he's so noisy and bossy!'

Liz's Mum: Can you get to the point, please?
Tilly: Yes.

The inhabitants of the castle realised that the Keeper couldn't help them to be happy or safe, so they had a meeting without him and worked out a way to help themselves. They decided to try harder to get help from outside of that district; it seemed to be their only hope.

Nine trusted volunteers were chosen to go in three parties, each trying a different route to ensure at least one group was likely to make it out of the area alive. They took with them plenty of gold to pay people to come and save them from a horrendous death. The plan was for at least one of the groups to find a safe route so that healthy, strong people from outside the region could transport into the area water and other essentials by donkey, horse and cart, or by any other method that may be deemed safe and secure. Then they were hoping that someone, with an ability to mediate between people who once loved each other deeply but have since fallen apart, would be willing and able to come and help the Keeper and the Fiend to become friends again. This was vitally important as sooner or later the inhabitants of the castle would need to access the stream in the dell freely.

This they did and it was a success. However, only one group survived the journey; the six other brave volunteers died during their attempt to leave the area. But within three days, supplies were beginning to be transported into the castle from the outside world for the desperate inhabitants, and a couple of days after that, Melchizedek the mediator arrived to help the Fiend and the Keeper to be reconciled.

The first thing that Melchizedek told the Keeper to do was to carefully package up lots and lots of food and shoot it into the Forest Dell using their powerful catapult with a note attached. Everyone was sad to risk throwing away so much good food, but it was a risk they had to take to stand any chance of a reconciliation between the Keeper and the Fiend, which was far more valuable.

This is the note that the Keeper wrote (and it was signed by all of the castle inhabitants and their guests):

Tilly: I wonder if one of the parents would be willing to read the letter? I was going to ask one of the children, but I don't want to make them feel uncomfortable.
Andrew's Dad: (Stepping forward) I will.
Tilly: Thank you so much.
Andrew's Dad: You're welcome:

Dear Fiend,
I know we have had a falling out, but we used to be dear friends. We have both caused a rift between us and I think it is time we were

reconciled. We need to try to trust one another again. I know it may take some time, but I am willing to try, and I hope you are too.

Although we may disagree about who started the break down in our relationship, I am willing to forgive everything you have done and said that hurt me, and I will not insist on discussing it (unless we are both able and willing to do so after we have regained our trust in one another). For my part, I am truly sorry for everything I have said and done that hurt you. I know words are not enough to repair the damage but I hope we can heal each other by meeting again and building up our trust.

I am hoping you will somehow believe my message, but whether you do or not, I am sending you this food package as you must be close to starving now. Don't worry about us not having water as we have enough to last us all for another three weeks now. But I do hope we can be reconciled before that so that we can not only be friends again, but also so we can provide for one another and so the inhabitants of the castle can be saved from death and given a secure life. I am not doing this just so the castle inhabitants can have access to the stream, but also so they can be looked after and protected within a happy, peaceful and caring environment, where their protectors are committed to them and each other.

(All of the parents shed a tear or two at hearing this letter being read out, and their children were surprised at how much the adults were beginning to appreciate the story at last. Andrew's Dad continued:)

We have put away our bows and arrows and promise not to shoot at you whether you come up Castle Hill today or even two weeks from now. Among the visitors who have brought water and other provisions, we have Melchizedek, a mediator. He will be here for a week and is willing to sit with us to air any differences we may have to help us to be reconciled. I would prefer us to be reconciled without him, but he is here in case we need him.

I am aware that you may still not trust me even though we have sent this package of food to you, but I am hoping from the heart that you

will take that step of faith and come to the castle where we can feast together with the castle inhabitants and our guests.
Welcome!
The Keeper.

Tilly: (To Andrew's Dad) Thank you so much for reading the Keeper's letter to everybody.
Gus: So, what did the Fiend do in the end?
Tilly: Well, the story ends like this:

The Fiend ate a pie and some fruit from the package, and washed it all down with fresh water from the stream. Then he waited for a few hours to make sure there was no poison in his body. Nothing untoward happened to him, so he took the final risk and set off through the trees to Castle Hill. As he emerged from the trees at the bottom of the hill, he held up a wooden shield with the following words on the front of it in big letters in their own language:

I COME IN PEACE.

The castle lookout saw him and called out to the Castle Keeper that the Fiend was at the bottom of Castle Hill with a sign saying 'I come in peace.'

The Castle Keeper was so happy, and he quickly gathered the three inhabitants who had successfully brought help to them and a handful of his guests. They all walked out of the castle with their hands in the air, and waited at the castle wall to see what the Fiend might do. The Fiend could not see anyone on top of the castle wall with bows and arrows, but he was aware that they might be hiding somewhere.

The Castle Keeper called out: 'We have come out to welcome you; you are safe.'

The Fiend slowly walked up the hill. Seeing this, the Keeper told everyone to stay in their positions so as not to frighten the Fiend, while he walked down the hill alone towards the Fiend with his arms outstretched, even though he was afraid the Fiend might be concealing a weapon behind his shield.

The Fiend and the Keeper met half way up the hill and the Fiend dropped his shield at the last moment. Then they embraced to the cheers of everyone in and around the castle. The two reconciled friends walked up Castle Hill together and everyone welcomed the Fiend into the castle. That night there was a huge celebration full of feasting.

Andrew's Dad: (To Tilly) Thank you for that moving story.
Tilly: You're welcome.
(All of the children began to stand up to leave with their parents, and every parent – including the ones who had been angry with Tilly - thanked the Storyteller with a sincere, emotional smile. This story changed a lot of attitudes, and time would prove that it would have long term positive effects. It would be this very story told by Tilly that would begin the process of reconciliation for a handful of the adults who had listened to it, and in this way, it would also bring more happiness and security to an even bigger handful of children.)

Andrew and his dad stayed behind after the children left with their parents. Andrew morphed back into the middle-aged man, and Andrew's Dad morphed back into Tilly's giant colleague.

Chapter 7
The Pattering of Eight Little Legs

PI Scrounge was tossing and turning in bed; he could not rest; he needed to understand why the café he had stood outside of had disappeared. He knew it had been there, he knew the photographs he had taken were real – as he still had the originals – and he knew that he had witnessed the death of the woman he had hired for the honey trap.

He was usually only motivated by money, but this was different; it was a mystery nobody had ever investigated before. It was unique and of huge significance. Scrounge was a realist and had considered every possible way in which he could have been mistaken about it all, but there was no rational explanation for such an irrational fact. He had taken the photos himself, printed them and sold them. He had witnessed a death, and that cause of death – confirmed by his photographs – had also been confirmed by forensic scientists, but - and it was a big but - the café had disappeared! Even though the scenario was impossible, it happened, and nothing could change that fact.

For the Private Investigator there was a HUGE 'why' to investigate, and that was: Why was the woman killed and moved to that particular place in Delamere Forest and left only half buried? There was also a HUGER 'who' to investigate, and that was: Who were the people in the café, especially as their faces and hands were invisible on photographs? There was also a HUGERER 'where' to investigate, and that was: Where is the café now? But the HUGEREREST thing to investigate was 'how.' How was it possible for a whole café to disappear overnight, never to be seen again in that place in the future, and never to have ever been seen in that place before the day it disappeared? This was now Philip Scrounge's obsession and he was willing to spend his entire life and last remaining slither of sanity fulfilling his quest for answers – and if there was some money in it by the end of it, then that couldn't hurt!

His obvious first step was to visit the site where the café called 'Tilly's Tearoom' had been located for those few hours when the incident happened. Scrounge would drive there again go look around. Then he would talk to the residents in the neighbourhood to find out if they had seen or heard anything on the night in question, that is without allowing anyone to suspect he had anything to do with the dead woman's demise, thereby arousing suspicion from the police!

Tilly was wiping down the surfaces of her tearoom, awaiting customers. She turned the 'Open for business' sign round on the door and returned to the serving counter on all fours, stopping and starting, glancing around as she went. The three regulars in the café did not bat a teapot lid as she crawled, and they simply did not care, not even an itsy bitsy or even an incy wincy bit! On arriving behind the serving counter, Tilly climbed to her feet and started pouring several cups of tea from the spout while spluttering instructions at the tearoom patrons.

"Now, I know you are all busy spinning a web of deceit today, and that is fine, but don't go moaning to me if you don't get your curd tarts; I am busy too, after all!" She waited for their response but there was not even a teensy weensy, itty bitty, tiny winy scrap of a twitch, but that was usual.

The regular giant of a man towards the back of the tearoom was going to play the part of Reginald Candyfloss; the old woman was sat on a tuffet in the corner eating cheese; and the middle-aged man was reading a book on arachnids.

Yes, I'm sure you've got a good idea what this one's all about, but hang on in there and you might enjoy it anyway!

The young couple who entered the tearoom this time looked normal to all intents and purposes. Jordan had tidy light brown hair, and was dressed smart casual; his friend Maddie was dressed casual smart. They sat at a table in the sparsely populated tearoom, thinking it was quite quaint yet seriously lacking cool. They only wanted a frothy coffee anyway before Jordan was off for his interview. The plan was for Maddie, who was sat facing the door, to wait for him to get back, unless she got bored.

Tilly crept up, "What can I get you, me darlin's?"

"Just two frothy coffees please," said Jordan.

"Right you are, lovey."

Jordan smiled at Maddie, "Thanks for coming to support me."

"What are friends for? Thanks for the coffee."

"It's the least I could do."

Tilly eventually brought the two cups of coffee, carrying them in a very strange manner. She held one cup in each hand, her thumbs closest to her body, gripping the saucers from underneath, while four fingers from each hand emerged from below the saucers facing Jordan and Maddie, like eight fingers wiggling together. "Here's your frothy coffees, my little sweethearts."

"Thanks," said Jordan.

"Thank you," said Maddie.

Maddie used her teaspoon to scoop the froth from her cup into her mouth, looking pensive yet serene. Jordan was more anxious due to his forthcoming likely job-related rejection and was wanting Maddie to liven up a bit to get his mind off it, and he got what he wished for. It started from the welcome mat adjoining the door of the tearoom; from the mat, then along the tiled floor, came a spider with the intention of sitting beside Maddie, but she spied it in advance.

"Arrrrrrrrr!" she cried, running to the back of the tearoom.

Jordan popped up to comfort her. "What's wrong?"

"Can't you see it?"

"What?"

"There's a spider over there!"

"Thank goodness for that, I thought someone was being murdered!"

"Get rid of it, it's coming closer!"

"Okay, okay, me darlin', I'll get rid of it for yer; don't want yer deafening everybody with yer screamin' do we," said Tilly, floating round the service counter with a clean cup and saucer in her hand. Jordan looked around at the patrons of the tearoom. They had not even flinched; instead they simply stared directly at Maddie with no emotion on their faces. Maddie watched Tilly scoop up the spider onto the saucer and place the teacup over it before taking it to the door to release the monster. Maddie felt reluctant to drink her coffee now as it made her think there was a spider in her own cup.

Anyway, she eventually calmed down a little. "Thank you, I'm so sorry everyone, I just have a big fear of spiders. So sorry to disturb your drinks."

The giant man, the middle-aged man and the old lady did not stir. But Tilly did. "It's all right deary, just sit back down and I'll top up your coffee from the pot."

"Thank you," said Maddie again as Jordan escorted her back to her seat with his arm around her.

"I thought you would have grown out of your fear of spiders by now; I thought it was just something you suffered in your childhood."

"That's when it started, but I've suffered all my life. It's the long wiggly legs!"

"How did it start anyway?"

"It was when I was at Cannon Hill Park in Birmingham with my family. I got a spider in my candyfloss and nearly ate it. It was wiggling about on top of it; it just made me feel like I had hundreds of spiders wriggling around in my body." She shuddered. "It was horrible!"

"Perhaps you should get some help."

"I've tried, nothing works. Anyway, I should let you think through your answers to the interview questions."

"I don't think I can think of anything new."

Maddie's breathing settled once more but she kept looking around nervously, worried that another spider might jump up at her. She was about to ask Jordan if he was nervous about his interview when she suddenly noticed pictures of spiders on the book that one of the patrons was reading. "OH!" she exclaimed as her body shivered.

"What's wrong?" asked Jordan.

"He's reading about spiders!"

Jordan looked. "I see you're enjoying a book about spiders."

"Yes," said the man, "You should let your friend have a read, she will find out that most spiders are innocent little creatures that would never harm anyone."

"Oh no thank you," said Jordan, glancing at his friend reassuringly, "She is well acquainted with all things spider."

"Thank you," she mouthed to Jordan shuddering, but his attention was being drawn to the strange old lady dressed like a little girl wolfing down wedges of cheese while sat on a tuffet in the corner.

"I wonder why she's not sat at a table?" he said, and Maddie turned round. Her head turned back immediately.

"Everything's just reminding me of spiders all the time!"

"Don't worry!"

"Anyway, we should be more concerned about your interview."

"Don't worry about that, it'll be just another rejection to add to my collection!"

"Don't say that, you'd be great for the job."

"Will they realise that though?"

"They will, and if they don't, they're stupid."

"Thanks for your support."

Reginald Candyfloss put a pink wig on his head and got up from his table. He walked over to the guests' table and asked if he could give Jordan some tips for doing a good interview.

"May I offer my services. I would be delighted to give you some tips before you go for your interview."

The man was too tall for Jordan to notice the wig on his head at first, but as he answered the giant, he looked up and laughed involuntarily. "That's very kind of you but ... ha ha ... oh sorry!"

Reginald Canyfloss bowed his head to the centre of the table between Jordan and Maddie. "Do you like my hair?"

Maddie screamed as his hair looked just like the candyfloss she had been eating as a child when her arachnophobia began. Not only was it like her candyfloss, but there was also a spider in the wig. Maddie got up from the table, her heart pounding. "THAT IS SO CRUEL!" she shouted at the man.

"She's right, I think you should apologise to my friend," demanded Jordan.

Tilly interjected: "Absolutely not, he's leaving before he utters another word!" And looking over at the man who was reading the book about spiders, she said, "Mr Webster, we're going to need your help to remove this rude man!" Mr Webster helped Tilly to escort Reginald Candyfloss outside.

"I am so sorry dearest, that must have been so upsetting for you, here let me pour you that coffee I promised," said Tilly, disappearing behind the serving counter.

Jordan helped Maddie back to her seat. "I think I want to leave," she said.

"I don't blame you, but there's nowhere else to go and wait."

"But I don't know what I'll do if something else happens while you're at your interview."

"Look, I'm only going to be twenty minutes, an hour at the most. The café owner looks nice and she's going to pour you another nice cup of hot coffee, she'll look after you."

"But what about that weird woman in the corner and Mr Webster with his book of spiders?" Her body shuddered at the mention of the word 'spiders.'

"It's just all a really bizarre coincidence. The chance of anything else weird happening is one in ten thousand billion. Don't worry."

"I'm sorry, I should be concentrating on you, not you concentrating on my stupid phobia."

"Look, I'm going now, enjoy your hot coffee and I'll be back in less than an hour, and hopefully we'll have something to celebrate together."

"I'm looking forward to that!"

"Good, so am I!"

Jordan said goodbye and thanked Tilly, who replied, "Don't worry, we'll look after her."

After Jordan left the café, Tilly crept up behind Maddie on all fours with the coffee pot on her back, but Maddie didn't notice. Standing up again beside her at the table, catching the coffee pot with her flexible arms as she did so, she said, "Here, enjoy your hot coffee."

"Oh, thanks."

Tilly tipped the coffee pot and out poured hundreds of spiders that saturated the table top and spilled to the floor around Maddie's ankles. She screamed hysterically and jumped up and down on the spot before she could think of a way to overcome her shock well enough to escape from the terror. She finally ran to the door to leave, but a large vertical stick plunged downwards in front of the door to block her path. She decided to head around the pool of spiders to access the back door of the tearoom, but she noticed another vertical pole had appeared. Glancing around the walls, her panoramic view revealed the existence of eight such narrow poles. All that was left for her to do was look upwards and as she did so she noticed the ceiling had gone, and in its place was a vertical tunnel stretching up as far as the eye could see, with huge spider webs stretching across the tunnel at every point. But the worst thing was the body of a giant spider which was attached to the poles around the room. The poles were the gangly legs of this super-sized arachnid. It wasn't like a tarantula with a fat body, but rather a spindly spider with a relatively small body that wobbled and swayed around atop its immensely long thin legs. The shock was more than she could bear, so she fell to the tiles, unconscious.

Creepy imp entered the tearoom from the back. "Shall I call the Sweepers?"

"Deliveries please."

"Right you are."

PI Scrounge drove to the village of Willington in Cheshire, close to where the events of the honey trap had taken place. He parked in a little car park beside a post box and a little bus shelter.

He tried to retrace the steps he took on that fateful night and eventually reached the place where he was certain the café had been. It was a field. Between the field and the narrow pavement on which he was stood, mature bushes stretched alongside it as a border. He continued another sixty or so metres until he reached a gate; he climbed over and walked back to the exact spot where the café had been. There was nothing, not one thing to betray the fact that a fully functioning café-building had once stood there.

He supposed it was rather stupid of him to think that a disappearing café might leave some kind of evidence behind it, but he considered that one might have expected some kind of imprint in the soil or grass.

He scrutinised the ground with his eyes and his feet, and examined each and every interesting stone and groove, until eventually a metallic-looking object caught his eye. It was sticking out of the ground, half buried, a bit like a thick, misshapen disc, the size of his hand. It felt heavy. "What on earth is this?" he asked himself, but of course there was no answer. Who could he ask? How could he find out what this mystery object was, and did it have anything to do with Tilly's Tearoom? "I know," he said to himself, "I'll show it to people in the village." And that is what he endeavoured to do. But before that, he took plenty of photographs of the object and its resting place, just in case he lost the mysterious object, broke it or got it stolen.

Meanwhile, Maddie woke up to her phone ringing as she was sleeping on her settee at home. It was Jordan.
"Where are you?"
"Who's this?" she asked, rubbing her eyes and yawning.
"It's Jordan, where are you? I got the job, by the way."
"Oh, that's brilliant, I … I …"
"It's all right, I understand why you left the café, with all that spider stuff going on."
"Yes, that's right, I … I must have left."
"I spoke to the owner, Tilly she's called, she said you were feeling a little under the weather."
"You could say that."
"Where are you now? Do you want me to come and meet you?"
"Yes, yes please, I would definitely like to see you."
"Where are you?"
"At home."
"Okay, see you in twenty."
"Great, and congratulations by the way."
"Cheers, see you soon."
Maddie could not remember how she had got home. All she could remember was seeing a giant gangly spider above her head in the cafe. Everything after that was a blur. She made herself a mug of coffee and sat down at her coffee table, when suddenly she spied a creepy you-

know-what crawling towards her. She jumped, but surprisingly, the coffee mug in her hand did not spill; usually, coffee would end up on the carpet, the ceiling, the walls and on her clothes, but not this time!

In Cheshire, PI Scrounge strode up the driveway of one of the large houses, and what a beautiful garden it had! The house was named Chocolate Box. He used the lion-head door knocker to get the owners' attention. A simply dressed tall man opened the door and stared at Scrounge.

"Sorry to bother you, I'm a detective working on the case of a mysterious disappearance, nothing to be alarmed about."

"Okay, how can I help?"

"I wondered whether you'd ever seen a café being constructed in the field just down the road there."

"A café? On Willington Lane?"

"Yes."

"No."

"Oh, I guess that's a 'no' then."

"Yes."

"Oh."

"You could ask the farmer who owns the land, he would know, wouldn't he?"

"Of course, you're right." Scrounge suddenly held out the mysterious object in front of him. "Have you ever seen this before?"

"What is it?"

"That's what I'm asking you," said the private detective holding his head high and squinting his eyes.

"I've no idea, where did you get it from?"

"We have reason to believe it belonged to the missing ... thing."

"The missing 'thing'? I thought you were asking me about a missing person."

"I am."

"Who's missing?"

"Someone called Tilly ... Steerum."

"Never heard of her, sorry I can't help you," said the house owner closing the door.

Scrounge dropped the mysterious object on the step by accident. He picked it up quickly to check he hadn't chipped it. He hadn't, but this gave him an idea. He descended the driveway with his gaze fixed on the strange object. He was so distracted by it that he didn't hear some of the loud comments between the man and woman in the house as he left their property:

"I think he's impersonating a policeman."

"You should report it."

"No, I wouldn't bother, he's probably down and out and docsn't have anything better to do."

Outside the house's property, Scrounge could be seen jumping up and down.

"Look at him, he's a bit of a weirdo!" said the Chocolate Box woman loudly while watching him through the window. "We should phone the police."

"Okay, keep your eye on him and I'll give them a ring if he doesn't go away."

Scrounge picked up the object and couldn't see even a minute scratch after having jumped on it twenty times. He decided he would go home and try to break it open with his power drill. After all, the strange object looked remarkably like some kind of ornamental box that might contain something even more valuable than the box itself.

Maddie did not run away from the spider in her house, and her body was strangely calm as she stood there sipping her coffee, following the spider's progress as it crept towards her. Normally she would be going berserk, screaming for the nearest person to get rid of the creature, and if no one was near, she would run out of the house to get help. This time, she just stood there watching it, unafraid.

When the spider had just about reached her bare foot, she felt a twinge of discomfort in her stomach, but not enough to make her run and scream. When the spider was only an inch from her foot, she stamped on it and squelched it into her carpet.

Just then, the doorbell rang, so she hopped to the door to let Jordan in.

"Hi," said Maddie.

"Hi, are you okay? You sounded funny on the phone."

"I'm over the moon," she said, hopping back to the settee to sit down. "And look," she said, holding her bare foot in the air.

"What is it?"

"Take a good look and guess!"

"Er, there's something a bit revolting on the bottom of your foot."

"Oh is there?" she said sarcastically. "Come on, what do you think it is?"

"A squashed insect of some sort ... no! It's not a spider!"

"It is, and I squashed it deliberately."

"How? You're terrified of spiders!"

"I know. I was. But since I've been to Tilly's Tearoom, my life has changed."

"But how?"

"It was the giant spider ... in the tearoom."

"None of the spiders were that big really, you can get them this big," Jordan said, showing the size with his hands.

"No, this one was bigger than the tearoom itself."

Looking a bit puzzled. "Bigger than the actual tearoom?"

"Don't you believe me?"

"Well I believe you believe it, because I know you wouldn't lie to me, but do you honestly expect me to believe there was a spider in a café that was bigger than the café itself? It's impossible for something bigger than something to be inside that something, isn't it?"

"Not if it's squashed up."

"Was it squashed up?"

"No. I know, I must be going mad, and I don't know how I got home either. But it must all be true otherwise I wouldn't have got over my arachnophobia."

"Well ... I have no idea, but I'm glad you've got over your fear."

"So am I!" she said. Hopping up to the kettle, "Want a coffee?"

"Yes please, I wouldn't mind."

Clanking around, "Anyway, how was your interview?"

"It went great. They offered me the job there and then; in fact I've got to go back there in a couple of hours for them to show me the ropes."

"I'll go with you so I can thank Tilly on the way."

Jordan and Maddie eventually set off together, and when they reached the place where they had been in the café, Tilly's Tearoom was gone, and there was no sign of it. They even asked some passers-by and they just looked at them like they were crazy.

So, there we have it, yet again Tilly's Tearoom has disappeared. How does that happen? Perhaps PI Scrounge will find out. Let's wait and see. Oh and by the way, no spiders were harmed when all this took place ... except for the last one that is!

Chapter 8
The Criminalist

However hard he tried, PI Scrounge could not open, dent, or even scratch the nameless object he found on Willington Lane. He needed a team to work with. He actually needed friends, as no one seemed to take to him for some reason. I suppose that's no surprise with his scruffy coat, his windswept hair, scuffed black (now grey) shoes and his shifty eye, always on the lookout for a bob or two. The police didn't take to him either and in fact saw him as a bit of a looser. It didn't help that he had no steady income, so that he felt he had no choice but to grab whatever cash he could, whenever he could.

Actually, the object he was in possession of could be of importance to national security for all he knew, but sharing his story with MI5 might open him up to being a murder suspect in the bee-woman case. He thought his best chance of cashing in was to make rich collectors or even criminals aware of the strange object's existence, to drum up some interest. He was determined to think of a way to disseminate the information in as safe a way as possible.

In the back room of the tearoom, Tilly was sat astride what was once an incredibly beautiful woman, but now she had lots of stab wounds in her torso. "Forty," Tilly said, pulling the knife out again, spraying blood up into the air, having already created thirty-nine wounds. "How many more do I have to do?"

The nasally imp answered her with, "Just nineteen more to go."

"Work, work, work! There's never a break is there? Why do I have to do it anyway? Why don't one of the Sweepers do it?"

The Sweepers were stood behind her watching intently.

"Forty-one, forty-two, forty-three," said Tilly as she continued stabbing with her knife. "I do have other things to do you know."

"And number fifty goes through the neck, remember," said the imp.

"Forty-four, forty-five, okay, I will do number fifty through the neck."

Tilly continued until she had finished all of the stabbings in retaliation for the people this now deceased beautiful woman had killed. Tilly was upset about it all because her own clothes were now caked in blood - not ideal if you want to keep Tilly in a good mood! She liked everything to be nice and clean.

After the final stab, Tilly squelched herself off the body, "Right, I'll go and clean myself up. Don't be long you lot, we've got other things to do."

"Of course dear," said the imp, who ordered the three Sweepers to dispose of the body.

Elsewhere-ish, the stocky Ricky Crabstick practised his robbing poses in the mirror in his mother's dingy flat. His mother knew he was on the way out soon, so she gave him a last minute order: "Don't forget to buy me some fags while you're out!" she shouted.

"Right mam, I won't forget," he said, swinging his baseball bat around with a menacing face. "Give me your money!" he snarled at his own reflection, "Or I'll beat the brains out of your skull!"

The car horn he was waiting for blurted out, so Ricky left with his Batman mask, a bag and his baseball bat. "Bye mam." As usual he slammed the door.

"And don't slam the door!"

The driver was Frog, Ricky's big-eyed friendly thug. His job was to drop Rick off at a shop, drive round the block, and then pick him up again with the cash before they made their getaway and ditched the stolen car.

"I saw a new café on the way here called Tilly's Tearoom, how about doing that one?" suggested Frog.

"Wha'ever!" said Batman, swaying side to side with the rhythm pounding through the car body.

Meanwhile, the Sweepers had finished disposing of the beautiful, now completely mutilated, body of the woman, and were near the back door to the tearoom, taking off their hooded cloaks. One was the giant man, one was the middle-aged man and the other was the elderly woman, all of whom were the most regular patrons of the tearoom. The creepy imp-man took away the three cloaks for washing and the three tearoom patrons took their positions at tables where Tilly was floating around with a cloth. "It never stops, always cleaning up after people, I need a holiday! It's all right for you lot, you just follow orders, but I've got to think of everything; you know, I should be a special guest on TV, or there should be a film about my life; then they'd see just how hard it is to do my job, then everybody will appreciate me. I can see it now:

THE UNFATHOMABLE PATIENCE AND COMMITMENT OF TILLY THE WONDER WORKER

Or perhaps:

TILLY'S TERRIFIC TEMPERAMENT, A WOMAN OF DISTINCT WISDOM AND ETHICAL STATURE

Or maybe even:

TILLY, THE ONE TO TRUST!"

While Tilly was musing, the tearoom door burst open and in strode Ricky Crabstick with the Batman mask over his face and baseball bat in hand. The three patrons of the tearoom cowered down to their knees beneath their tables. Tilly ducked behind her counter shivering. Out in the street, Frog, who had dropped Batman off, screeched away in the stolen car, and everyone in the tearoom could hear it crash into a lamppost - except for the numb-skull who had just entered Tilly's tearoom. Frog's beady eyes had been watching his 'cool' friend enter the tearoom while he sped off quickly, the collision making its back wheels leap into the air, causing Frog's eyes to pop out of their sockets.

"Hand over your money!" said Batman to Tilly behind the till.

"Please, please don't hurt me!" Tilly begged, and the elderly woman wailed in distress under her table.

"Do as I say now! Give me all the money in' till!"

"Tilly."

"What?"

"My name's Tilly."

"Don't play games with me, give it all to me from your tilly!"

"From my tilly?"

"Pardon?"

"You said 'give it all to me from your tilly.'"

"No I didn't, I said give it to me from your tilly, or I'll slam you with my bat!"

"You see!"

"Do it, or I'll bash your head in and that's a promise!"

"All right, all right," said Tilly shaking. "Please don't hurt me, I beg you for mercy."

"Nooooo, please don't hurt her," begged the big guy from under his table, speaking in a serious yet shaky voice.

"Please, please, please, don't hurt any of us," begged the middle-aged man from under his table, and the elderly woman wailed.

"Shut up! I'll hurt whoever I like, whenever I like, and I'll be as bad as I want to be and you can't stop me!"

"Yes, of course," said Tilly, trembling with her hands in the air. "You should be allowed to do whatever you want to, even if it hurts other people."

"Yes, that's right, I should be able to hurt whoever I like, whenever I like. So, give me all your money!"

"I was just wondering …"

"Hurry up! Give it to me now, before I break your head with my bat."

"Give it all to Batman, Tilly!" shouted the middle-aged man, trembling on his knees.

"Yea, do what he says," said the tall guy trembling on his knees under his table.

The elderly woman just wailed some more.

"Okay, okay, I just need to find the key," said Tilly.

"You don't need a key, I've done this before you know," said Batman.

"Such a clever little boy with a bat," said Tilly.

"Hey! Less of the little boy, I'm Batman! I mean, I'm Rick, Ricky Crabstick! Oh, I shouldn't have told you that, now give me all the money!"

"No, I can't," sobbed Tilly.

"You have three seconds, and if you don't give me the money after three, I'll hit you with my batman ... my bat!"

"NO!" said Tilly standing with her hands in the air, looking terrified. This infuriated Batman, so he swung the baseball bat round his head and began to slam it downwards, directly onto Tilly's head, but just before the bat struck her head, Tilly clicked her fingers twice, and the bat disappeared from Batman's hands, causing his hands to crash hard against the serving counter, breaking two fingers on his left hand. His trousers also disappeared.

"Arrgh! What did you do with my bat?" Batman screamed, nursing his hand in agony.

Tilly offered to help. "Oh, my poor love, let me help you."

"No, give me the money or I'll kill the lot of you."

"Give him the money!" shouted the tall chap from under his table.

"All right, all right!" said Tilly, opening the till and handing about one thousand pounds in cash to Batman. Batman grabbed it off her quickly and shoved it into his bag, before heading towards the door with it in his hand. He turned round threateningly saying, "If any of you tell the cops or anyone else about this, I'll come back and kill you all, and your families." Tilly couldn't stop herself from bursting into laughter as she stared at his bare legs.

"Where's my trousers!" shouted Batman. "Right ..."

At that moment, Tilly clicked her fingers twice again and the bag of money disappeared from his hands before he himself collapsed on the floor in agony, unable to get up.

"Ow, ow, ow, argh! What's happened to me?" he shouted, as he writhed around in agony. The two male patrons of the tearoom walked towards Batman, picked him up by his arms and dragged him into the back of the tearoom.

"You asked what's happened to you, so now we're going to show you. We can watch it on a film together; you're actually starring in a film with Tilly!"

"What are you talking about? I'm going to kill you!"

"I know, there there," said Tilly while the two men strapped him into a chair in the back room, facing a portable screen. The elderly lady set the projector going, and this was what they saw:

Tilly and Batman were standing on opposite sides of the till at the serving counter and Batman was about to bring his baseball bat down hard, directly onto Tilly's head, but before that could happen, Tilly clicked her fingers once. Batman then froze and the tearoom patrons set to work. Tilly removed the baseball bat from his hands and left it on the counter. The tall man pulled down Batman's trousers and threw them behind the counter, and the middle-aged man removed the Batman mask and put it on himself. Then Tilly joined the two men in putting the robber's body into strange poses, so that the elderly woman could get interesting video footage with her camera. One pose was a replica of the thinking man, another was Pinocchio, as Tilly held the baseball bat against his nose; the tall man made him point at it, and the middle-aged man adjusted the robber's lips and eyes to look surprised at the size of his nose, and all of this was accompanied by audience laughter on the video.

While Batman watched his own humiliation, he screamed curses at them, threatening again and again to kill them, but eventually the imp man came along with duct tape and covered his mouth with it under his Batman mask to keep him quiet – after all, they didn't want the movie to be ruined. After this they continued to watch the film together:

Tilly and the men then repositioned Batman, replaced his mask, and lifted his empty hands into the air as though they were holding an invisible bat. Tilly stood back behind the counter in exactly the same position she had been in before the robber's humiliation took place, again looking terrified. The two men hid under their tables again and

Tilly clicked her fingers once, at which point, the robber banged his hands onto the counter, breaking his fingers.

As the robber watched this from his chair he wriggled and wriggled.

The robber headed towards the tearoom door with the money bag, and turning around, he threatened everybody, before looking down to see his bare legs, and the audience laughed again. From behind the counter, Tilly clicked her fingers once more, and Batman's body froze. Then the tearoom patrons got to work a second time. Tilly took the money bag off the robber and put the money back into the till, before picking up the baseball bat once more. The two men lifted Batman's body onto one of the tables on his back, his head flopped backwards and his legs dangling. Tilly moved towards Batman with the baseball bat and there was a sudden cheer from baseball spectators in the background as Tilly then slammed the bat down onto the robber's left kneecap.

"Strike one!" shouted the tall man.

Then Tilly swung the baseball bat again and slammed it down onto the robber's right kneecap.

"Strike two!" shouted the tall man. The crowd on the video roared.

The robber's body was then dragged back into position again four metres from the door. They had to cleverly balance his body as his legs were buckled. Tilly walked back behind the serving counter and the two men hid back under their tables.

Tilly clicked her fingers and then Batman fell to the ground without his money bag and screamed in pain.

Sweat poured from under Batman's mask as he saw himself being dragged screaming to the seat on which he was still sat. The elderly woman turned the projector off.

"Have you learnt your lesson yet?" asked Tilly after she ripped the duct tape from his mouth.

"I'll kill you, I'll destroy you!" screamed Batman in agony.

"Oh dear!" said Tilly, and the two men carried the robber back to the place where he had fallen before, very close to the tearoom door. Batman wriggled around on the floor in pain, "I promise you, I promise you all, you are all going to die!"

The middle-aged man calmly stepped over Batman and opened the tearoom door, while Tilly stood over the squirming criminal with the baseball bat. She slammed it down hard onto his right elbow, shattering the bone.

"Strike three!" shouted the tall man, and Batman screeeeeeeamed louder than he had ever screamed since he was a baby, as he fled from them on his belly like a scorched worm.

"And you're OUT!" declared the middle-aged man as he shut the door after the worm.

Honestly, who in their right mind would try to rob Tilly's Tearoom?

Outside the tearoom, there was a commotion by the lamppost where Frog's stolen car had crashed. Frog's eyes had been popped back into place by paramedics, and police were talking to him.

"It was his idea!" Frog said, pointing at Batman who was writhing along the concrete like a worm.

"And who is he?" asked Police Constable Dawn Sturdy.

"It's Ricky Crabstick."

"Are you sure?"

"Absolutely, he did most of it."

"We've been wanting to talk to Crabstick for a long time, haven't we PC Holden?"

"We certainly have, looks like he's been in the wars though, doesn't he?"

One of the paramedics on the scene rushed over to Batman and removed his mask before examining his hands, arm and legs.

"Arrest her, she's evil!" Crabstick shouted at the police in the distance, while pointing in the direction from which he had crawled.

"Who's evil?" asked the paramedic.

"Tilly."

"Okay, I'm sure the police will come over and ask you for more information in a moment. What's your name, by the way?"

"I'm Batman, you need to get her arrested, she's just beaten me up."

"Who are you pointing at? Where is this Tilly?"

"Are you stupid, can't you see the sign, Tilly's Tearoom! Ow, ow!" he shouted.

"Well, all I can see is a shop called Terry's Sports."

"What? Are you blind?"

"Just stay calm, sir."

The two police officers approached Ricky Crabstick and were horrified by his wounds.

"It looks like he's been beaten up!" said the paramedic.

"Are you Ricky Crabstick?" asked PC Holden.

"What's it to you?" he replied.

The paramedic defended Ricky's aggressive response. "He's in a lot of pain and suffering from concussion, so I don't think you'll get much out of him until he's been seen to in hospital."

"Right, Dawn, will you go with him in the ambulance?"

"I don't want to travel with a pig!" shouted Batman. "Anyway, you need to arrest the woman who beat me up!"

"Who is she?" asked Dawn.

"I've told this idiot already, it's Tilly! She owns Tilly's Tearoom, there!" he insisted, pointing.

"He is a bit delirious isn't he?" said Dawn, "Come on, let's have you in the ambulance."

"Okay," said the paramedic.

"No pigs!"

"I'm coming with you whether you like it or not, so just calm down and we'll talk when you're feeling a bit better, all right?" said Dawn.

A stretcher was brought and as Batman was put on it, he kept shouting about Tilly's Tearoom.

P C Holden returned to Frog, "Do you know anything about Tilly's Tearoom?"

"Yea, that's it over there, stupid!" Frog said pointing towards Terry's Sports. "Where's it gone?"

"I think you're both messing us about, you'll need to come to the police station, we want to talk to you about a spate of robberies."

Batman and his Frog had robbed ten homes together and caused grievous bodily harm to more people than you could imagine, many of whom were extremely vulnerable and terrified.

Crabstick's mam was not sympathetic towards her son in his present distress as he had failed to get her some fags. When he finally went to prison, his mam could no longer use him to do everything for her. The circumstances forced her to move from her sofa.

ADVERTS

Has anyone seen this object? It might be exactly the same as this picture or slightly different. Either way, please contact: Cris Pounge, on 07956782126. No fools or freaks please, only sincere respondents are welcome. All witness claims will need to be verified. This is a very sincere and important request, so please do not hesitate. This may be your lucky day!

The UK Daily

PI Scrounge hoped nobody would be able to work out the anagram of his name on the advert – it hadn't occurred to him he could have used a completely different name.

Chapter 9
Let's Have Some Happy!

One day, Tilly discovered that one thing she loved was a nice park, one with plenty of play, jolly, exuberant, flowers of pink, purple, yellow, red, orange and blooming. She was in a peculiarly expressive mood on this occasion, having been treated to a tap into a world of natural, receiving a glimpse of human, an impression of global, no longer satisfied with her usual, which was rather dull. During her existence, she usually simply followed instructions, often not understanding the ins and outs. Now she was experiencing 'normal' dressed in pretty. Oh these experiences! She just revelled in them. The powers at be had decided to give her some free and a little relief from crazy for a change. In her usual, Tilly didn't understand the difference between upper class, lower class, middle class, working class, down and out, up and down, in and out, up to the neck, free and easy, us and them, cool, hip, horrid or harried. These were not in her experience or even her vocabulary. But, as I intermated, the powers at be had decided to give her some posh, just for a change.

As one would expect, Tilly was not alone in the park – there were ducks! And these were not the only feathery! There were also children with their caring; there were long green, and trees with their thick and wrinkly, their many-coloured rustling in the gentle. Oh these experiences! Tilly felt like she would explode! In the park, there was a winding, a wiggly that took you all over the picturesque and undulating. Humming as she walked, her spirit was free, her mind filled with colourful and her heart throbbing. Her face could not avoid brandishing a happy, so much so that nature joined in with her beaming.

After what seemed a beautified lifetime - as long as infinite yet short as a flash – Tilly encountered a character, a two-legged variety. It hobbled along with a walking stick. They were heading towards one another. As the man came into view, Tilly could see his hair flap from side to side like an elephant. His eyes were unusually large and his nose was far bigger than you are imagining right now – seriously! It was so long that he had to tie it in a knot around his belly. He had the beard of a goat which wiggled about in the breeze where it was free to do so, being partly trapped by the secured nose; oh, and his brown cassock flapped about excitedly. This strange looking chap could have taken a detour down any of the winding paths, but instead he followed a line of bees that were heading for Tilly.

Once he was only ten metres away, Tilly could finally discern his complexion; his face was grey with pinkish cheeks. His hands were wrinkly, but his fingers were stubby grey. The thing that stood out the most to Tilly, however, were those gigantic blue eyes. When he and Tilly were only several metres apart, the bees heading for Tilly caught her attention with the backdrop of those eyes that now looked like dark blue waterfalls. The bees skimmed over Tilly's head and disappeared when the strange man spoke to her.

"How do you do?" he said, with a deep, gentlemanly voice.

"How do you?" responded Tilly standing still.

The man came to a halt too and held out his wrinkly stubs. They shook - and it was not only their hands that shook! This was a meeting and a half! Actually, that's not quite right, it was a meeting and fifty thousand halves, but there isn't time to explain all of that stuff.

"It is with great sincerity," he said, sincerely, "that I have this dialogue with you."

"I am at your service."

"You are in danger of understanding."

"I am?" said Tilly.

"Understanding is a multifaceted function that requires the correct facilities and faculties."

"Is it?"

"Your work is exemplary."

"Thank you."

"We can't let you understand any more than is acceptable to your facilities and faculties."

"Right."

"Keep up the good work!"

"I will."

At that, the strange man put his hood over his head and the bees returned to lead him back along the wiggly path. Bang goes Tilly's taste of natural beauty, human emotions and global understanding! Never mind, at least she could still do her pretending – it was her duty!

Now that she couldn't appreciate the wonders of creation in the way that she was starting to do so during her time at the park, she awaited her instructions from … (just too amazingly wonderful to describe). These instructions typically involved something that looked quite mundane or too usual to make a song and dance about, from a human point of view, but isn't life just teeming with such usuality? "As a wise being once said," Tilly said out loud to herself as she walked, "It is with the usual usuality that normal normality flourishes and finds its home in the everyday human's humanality." I must admit it sounds better in the antipawthenticasional tongue. Another one is 'Fluidity is more fluid than fluency.' And conversely, 'Fluid is the cause of frequent fluicide.' Tilly had no idea what the adage about 'usuality' meant, but in fact she was a prime example of a being that was living it out, unbeknown to her – but she didn't have the emotions to concern herself too much about it. In spite of these regular events seeming to scream "USUALITY!" it was quite a deceptive description as it did not begin to describe those fifty thousand halves that I referred to earlier, and therein is the mysterious miracle of LIFE.

Anyhow, Tilly's elongated day in the park was not over yet as she had some other characters to meet. There was a jovial encounter with Armadillo Man, a flapping frenzy with Jellybean Fairy and a cuddly rescue on behalf of Baby Freckles. But in this limited recount of events, we are focusing on two figures of apparent normality - Mr and Mrs Cottage, who were visiting the park with their enormously intelligent children, Tickle and Beetroot.

Mrs Cottage was a plump, rural woman who always wore a country dress, and a shepherd's pie for hair. Mr Cottage had a bulbous nose that dripped dew every time he moved. He was a little taller than his wife, and as thin as a stick. He was a chatterbox; he was the sort that wouldn't stop talking even if he was inadvertently squashed by a steam roller, covered in tar and then sat on by an elephant. His wife however would hum between every well-thought-out sentence, few as they were. She was partial to chewing toffee too, while her husband would simply wiggle a stalk of straw in his mouth. It stuck to his lip as though it was part of him, whereas in fact he replaced it with a new stalk every week.

Tickle looked like his dad. His body was spindly, and that included his hands which would stick out and tickle everyone and everything in front of him. He always wore his dad's black hat, which covered his eyes and made him look a little bit like a young scarecrow. His sister, Beetroot, was as red as a pickled beetroot all over her body, and she tried unsuccessfully to hide that fact by dressing up in multi-coloured dresses with frills galore. Her mum's complexion was rosy-pink, but when positioned side by side with Beetroot, Mrs Cottage's face looked ghostly pale.

This meeting with Tilly was prearranged, but the Cottage family had no idea about that fact – and neither did Tilly, until she came across them in a section of the park called Dragonfly Rose Garden.

"Come back Tickle!" ordered Mrs Cottage, but in a kindly manner, "and don't let your sister deceive you into venturing into places you're not allowed to venture into!"

"All right, mummy!" said Tickle, running back to his mummy to give her a big tickle on her tummy.

"Stop it, Tickle, you know you're not allowed to tickle every time you go near someone."

Tickle just wriggled with a giggle. "But mummy, you said I could tickle twenty times a day, and each time a tickle must take no longer than 20 seconds, and I've not had my quota yet." Having spoken again, his body wriggled in a tickly manner – again; this was in fact why he was named Tickle, including the fact that when he was a baby he would wriggle about and giggle as though he was being tickled every single time he cooed or said 'Gagga,' 'Dadda' or 'Mamma.'

"Yes I did give you a quota, but you're going to have to grow out of your obsessive tickly nature sometime."

"You can't grow out of wriggles, tickles and giggles – ever!" And he couldn't stop wriggling while he said it!

"Well you're going to have to try!"

"All right mummy," he agreed while giggling and wiggling.

"ARE YOU LOOKING FOR ME OR NOT?" shouted Beetroot.

"Coming ready or not!" obliged Tickle.

"You've already said that!" snapped his sister, getting annoyed.

Tickle pretended he couldn't find Beetroot who had covered her multicoloured dress with a mono-coloured blanket especially for this game to avoid being seen.

"I'm among the roses!" she cried.

"But I've looked everywhere among the roses!" Tickle said, his body rippling with a giggle.

Beetroot got angrier and angrier, her face becoming deeper and deeper red. She thought she was being clever hiding among red roses, but she hadn't considered how annoyed she would get waiting to be found, especially if her brother was messing her around. Tickle did indeed have a plan. He knew Beetroot would hide among the red roses, so he did his utmost to make her angry so that her face would become a deeper red than the petals, thereby making her face stand out, since he knew she would not bother to hide her face in the circumstances and still just revel in her ability to stay camouflaged. This was one of many attempts by Tickle to make his sister redder than ever. Tickle thought it was hilarious when he saw her face among the flowers going deeper and deeper red while her expression grew angrier and angrier. He pointed at her, "Found you! Found you!" his body wriggling.

Beetroot popped up from the rose bed. "That's not fair, you tricked me! I know what you did!"

"Now now, you two! Come on it's time to go!" said Mrs Cottage.

"Hello!" said Tilly, arriving on the scene and almost bumping into Mrs Cottage.

"Hello, I see you've come to see the roses," said Mrs Cottage a little awkwardly, as she couldn't understand why someone would nearly bump into her when there was so much space around her and there was hardly anyone else in Dragonfly Rose Garden.

"Yes, lovely aren't they?" said Tilly, not having any idea what she was talking about. The encounter Tilly had had prior to this with the hobbling character had shaken her up a little. Tilly could usually fulfil her pretending duties with considerable ease, but on this occasion her faculties were a little dislocated. Anyway, she kept doing the best she could.

Meanwhile, Beetroot, holding her blanket like a cloak in the breeze, was running around the rose beds in order to escape her brother who could barely run due to his constant giggles. And not far away, Mr Cottage was talking twenty to the dozen with a gardener.

The gardener's fingers were quite green as he had been clearing freshly cut grass and pulling up weeds. Like Mr Cottage, he too had a stalk of straw dangling from his lip and it looked quite comical to see them chatting, as though it was their stalks talking to each other rather than their mouths. They were both wearing dungarees too, but one thing that was not the same was in connection with bodily fluids: While Mr Cottage dripped dew from his nose, the gardener sprayed saliva like a garden sprinkler every time the straw in his mouth moved, rather like a sophisticated water pump. It didn't bother Mr Cottage too much as he was an outdoorsy type and felt he was in need of a wash anyway. Mrs Cottage had no idea what her husband was talking about, but was quite happy to be out of earshot from his incessant talking.

"As I was saying," said Tilly, "this is a beautiful park, isn't it?"

"Yes it is, do you come here often?"

"Not as often as I would like to," said Tilly who adjusted her position a little. She had already done this craftily several times during their awkward conversation. Mrs Cottage felt as though she was on a swing in a roundabout way, and didn't understand the fact that Tilly was trying to avert her gaze away from seeing her husband. With this new position, Mrs Cottage was even more distracted by Tickle and Beetroot who were still dancing around the rose beds in fits of laughter.

"You have lovely children, don't you?" said Tilly, and Mrs Cottage nodded in agreement, but then wondered why Tilly's piercing eyes were staring straight into hers like screwdrivers.

Mrs Cottage had exceptionally good eyesight (unlike her hearing); she could see a pin drop a mile away! But while facing away from her husband, she had no idea what the gardener was saying or doing to him. What the gardener was actually doing was finding out just how much Mr Cottage valued his children.

"So, like I said, I'm an unusually rich gardener," said the gardener.

"Prove it!" said Mr Cottage drooling dew drops from his nose.

"I have heard you are willing to part with your children, for the right price, of course."

"Where did you hear that?"

"Oh, here and there on the grapevine."

"It's not common knowledge, so I'm curious to know how you know."

"Oh, I have a very reliable source."

"Okay, so what's it to you?"

"Well, I think you'll find me very generous, in fact so generous you could pay your debts a thousand times over."

"That much?"

"Yes."

"Like I said, what's it to you?"

"Let's just say, I know a Mr Freak who would be very interested in meeting your son with his unusually long fingers and your daughter with her unusual red skin."

"I don't want to send my children to a freak."

"Well, that's ten million pounds down the drain, then."

"Wait a minute, did you say ten million?"

"Ten million pounds, yes. But you don't want that. An alternative would be …"

"Wait a minute, I haven't decided I don't want the ten million yet."

"Of course, but like I said, there are alternatives, such as five million from a Miss Tambourine, who would love them and bring them up as her own."

"Yes, but she's only paying five million."

"Yes, but five million would be enough to pay your debt off five hundred times over. And it would be reassuring to know that your children would be cared for."

"How do I know you're not lying to me?" asked Mr Cottage, suspiciously.

"I'll give you a deposit. If you change your mind, you can keep the deposit and we can forget all about it."

"I will not change my mind."

"But they are your children, after all ..."

"How much is the deposit?"

"Ten thousand pounds."

"How do I know you will keep your end of the bargain?"

"I will give you the deposit now."

"But YOU might change YOUR mind later!"

"Mr Cottage, the deposit alone is enough to pay off your debt that you are so anxious about, and like I said, if you change your mind, you can keep the deposit anyway."

"I won't change my mind."

"Well if you insist."

"I bet you're going to trick me last minute, aren't you?"

"Here's the deposit," said the gardener, handing him a black folder. Mr Cottage snatched it quicker than a cobra bites a person that tries to kiss it or a scorpion stings a foot that stands upon it. He ripped the folder in his impatience to count the money. Meanwhile, his wife was still chatting to Tilly, when Mrs Cottage noticed she could see her husband with the gardener through the reflection in Tilly's glossy eyeballs. She thought she could see him opening a package of some sort. Mrs Cottage turned to look, but then Tilly grabbed her arm and began to escort her further away, but still within Dragonfly Rose Garden; they continued with their conversation while Mr Cottage made a home for the cash in his roomy inside jacket pocket where nobody would look.

"Well it's nice doing business with you!" said Mr Cottage with a smile.

"I will call your mobile tomorrow morning to give you the details how we will pay you the balance and collect the children."

"Right you are. Eight o'clock should do it. Mrs Cottage will be busy making breakfast at that time and we can discuss arrangements without being disturbed."

"No problem."

They shook hands and bodily fluids from Mr Cottage's nose and from the gardener's mouth flew everywhere!

After exchanging a few niceties, the gardener left Dragonfly Rose Garden. "Right children, it's time to leave!" shouted Mr Cottage.

Tilly also said goodbye to Mrs Cottage and added, "It was nice meeting you, and perhaps we'll meet again in the rose garden one day."

"Indeed we might, goodbye."

As they walked home, Mrs Cottage asked her husband about the package she saw.

"You must be mistaken," he said.

"I distinctly saw you holding a package of some sort."

"Oh yes, the gardener was just showing me some bulbs he was going to plant in the park, that's all."

"That's all right then. Tickle! Beetroot! Don't run off? Walk together and stay close to mummy and daddy!"

"Tickle's crying!" said Beetroot.

"Why?"

"Because he's not allowed to do any more tickling today, he's fulfilled his quota."

"Control yourself, Tickle, you can do it! Mummy and daddy control themselves all the time, don't we daddy?"

"Er ... yes, absolutely. You'll never get on in life if you don't learn to control yourself."

"Like gambling," said mummy, "People who gamble their savings away get into all kinds of trouble don't they daddy?"

Daddy backed up the statement, but his face became almost as red as Beetroot's.

"Our children are wonderful, aren't they?" added Mrs Cottage to her husband.

"Yes they are, we are very lucky." Mr Cottage folded his arms, hugging the folder close to his chest.

"You won't ever let anything bad happen to our children will you?"

"Of course not. They belong to us, how could I ever let anything bad happen to them? I'll protect them at all costs." The colour of his face grew as deep red as Beetroot's was at the height of her frustration during the game of hide and seek. Again, he hugged the folder close to his heart.

That evening, Mr Cottage was careful not to allow the folder of cash to fall out of his jacket pocket when he hung it up beside the front door. Every time he walked through the hallway, he would check his jacket to ensure it still contained the cash.

That night in bed, Mr Cottage did not toss and turn as you would expect; he didn't dream about screaming children calling for mummy and daddy either; neither did he feel any dread at the prospect of his wife's descent into mental decay. Instead, he slept like a baby.

The Cottages got up reasonably early as a rule, and that morning was no exception. The children were playing in the lounge, Mr Cottage's wife was cooking in the kitchen, while he was in the hallway waiting for the eight o'clock call. It came, and the decision was made to trade his children for cash from Mr Freak. Mr Cottage was to take the children to their local play park for twelve noon where the exchange would take place.

As a rule, at the weekend, they all sat down together for breakfast, and this weekend was a typical one in that respect, except that Mrs Cottage was unusually quiet because she was thinking back to her conversation with Tilly in the Dragonfly Rose Garden - that is the conversation they had just after Mrs Cottage noticed the folder of cash in her husband's hands:

Holding Mrs Cottage by the hand, Tilly said, "This is going to be hard for you to hear, my dear, but your husband is planning to sell your children to a Mr Freak tomorrow at your local park, but our people are going to protect the children."

Mrs Cottage's body began to shake. But she didn't say, 'No way!' or 'My husband would never do such a wicked thing, he loves his children!' Instead she said, "I suppose you would expect me to say that he wasn't capable of such a thing, but I know him, he has a wicked side, and he has gambling debts."

"Well that is what he is planning to do, and you will not be able to persuade him not to – you can try if you like!"

"No, if what you're saying is true, I want to play it out and see how far he is willing to go. I guess you're from the police then."

"No, nothing like that."

"So, how do you know all of this? And if you're a good person, why haven't you called the police or stopped it in some other way?"

"I haven't called the police because I know your husband will sell your children one day; if you stop him by yourself today, he will do it later and find ever deepening ways of covering his tracks. It needs to be dealt with now. If he is arrested by the police now, he will try again when he leaves prison."

"Are you a fortune teller or something?"

"No."

"Then how do you know?"

"Well, you know it too!"

"Yes, I think I do."

"So it is little surprise that I know."

"I get the impression you're avoiding answering my question."

"Your impression is right. Your husband has accepted some cash as a deposit."

"The black folder?"

"Yes."

"Your husband will take your children to the local play park tomorrow for twelve noon, where he is expecting to receive a further 9,990,000 pounds. He will then hand over the children. There will be three removers ..."

"Removers?"

"Don't worry, they belong to me. Your husband will expect the transaction to go smoothly, and he is fully expecting people to take your children away. But, don't worry, the three removers and the gardener will take your husband instead."

"What's wrong mummy?" asked Beetroot.

"Oh, nothing darling, eat up your porridge."

Mr Cottage said, "I thought I would take the children to the play park at noon while you cook dinner."

"Yippee!" cried Tickle, wriggling and giggling on his seat.

"Isn't there something you want to tell me, daddy?" asked Mrs Cottage.

"Such as?"

"Why are you going to the play park?"

"So the children can play on the swings, roundabout and slide."

"And then?"

"Mummy, why are you behaving in a strange way?" asked Beetroot.

"Yeh!" added a wiggling Tickle, "Why are you being so serious?"

"I just want to make sure you're safe."

"Of course they're safe, they're with me," said daddy.

"Are they?" Mrs Cottage thought back to two o'clock in the morning when she sneaked a look in her husband's jacket pocket to see the black folder containing more money than she had ever seen in one place before in her life.

"You know me, of course they're safe! Why wouldn't they be?" he said, going redder and redder.

"Haha, daddy, you look like Beetroot!" giggled Tickle pointing at his daddy's face with his wiggly fingers.

"Why are you blushing?" asked Mrs Cottage, "Have you got something to hide?"

"No, it's just very hot in here, that's all."

Mrs Cottage began to prepare the vegetables at 11.30, and five minutes later, Mr Cottage and the children said goodbye to her, as they left the house. As soon as she saw them disappear round the corner, she rushed her coat and shoes on and followed them at a distance. She had her phone ready to call the police in an emergency. She hoped against all hopes that her husband would not go through with it.

Finally, she stopped at a distance and watched her children as they played on the swings and the slide. Mr Cottage put his jacket lovingly over some railings as it was quite a warm day.

"Hello again," said a friendly voice beside Mrs Cottage. It was Tilly.

"Hello again."

"Can you see the gardener approaching your husband?" she said, pointing to the right side of the park.

"Yes."

"That package contains the money, far more than the money you saw in the middle of the night."

"How did ...?"

"Look over there," she said pointing to some bushes at the other side of the park. Mrs Cottage could see three people, two men and a woman. "These people will take your husband away."

"How do I know they won't actually take my children away?"

"I will come with you. Look the gardener is handing your husband the cash now."

Tilly and Mrs Cottage strode towards Mr Cottage and the gardener just as a larger package than the one her husband was given yesterday had dropped into his hand. Tickle saw his mother. "MUMMY! You came!"

"Hi mummy!" said Beetroot.

"Hello my darlings," she said as she suddenly rushed forward and snatched the package from her husband's hands, ripping it open, allowing fifties to fly everywhere in the wind. "What's all this for?"

"Oh, this kind man wanted to give us a special gift. Er...he knows that things are financially tight for us at the moment."

"Twice in two days, that's amazing. And what do you have to do in return?"

"Nothing! Absolutely nothing! It's a gift."

"No, that's not true," said the gardener calmly and looking confused. "You said we could have your children. Have you changed your mind?"

"No ... er ... yes."

"It's too late!" exclaimed Mrs Cottage, as she saw the three 'removers' making a beeline for him.

"Oh dear, oh dear, Mr Freak is going to be very disappointed," added the gardener. "Never mind I will give Mr Cottage to him for free to sweeten him up."

"Good idea!" said Mrs Cottage. And as soon as she spoke those words, Mr Cottage was grabbed and led away wriggling and screaming. Meanwhile, the children had been giggling and chasing the fifty pound notes to help their mummy and daddy, but when they heard their daddy scream, they dropped it all and ran to their mummy who held them tight in her arms.

"What's happening to daddy?" they cried.

"It's okay, he just has to go and say sorry to someone. He might not be back for a while though."

"I want my daddy!" said Beetroot.

"And me!" said Tickle, but this time he didn't giggle when he spoke. A terrible seriousness came over them all. The gardener, the three 'removers' and Mr Cottage disappeared behind the bushes; Tilly said goodbye too and disappeared in the other direction.

Mrs Cottage took her two precious children home, and the children were quietly puzzled, because as they left the park, they noticed the money they had been trying to collect had all disappeared.

It took some weeks before they could all talk things through in more detail without being halted by uncontrollable tears, but eventually Mrs Cottage managed to have a serious talk with Tickle and Beetroot. She explained the dangers of gambling and the dangers of greed. "And your father owes ten thousand pounds," she said. "I don't know how we're going to pay it, but I'll find a way."

"Ten thousand pounds!" exclaimed Tickle.

"But nothing, and I mean NOTHING, is going to pull us three apart!"

The second Mrs Cottage spoke that last sentence, there was a knock at their cottage door. She went to answer it as her children sat contemplating. It was that strange Tilly!

"Hello, my love!"

"Oh hello, have you got any news?"

"No, I'm afraid not, I'm not on the case now."

"Oh. Er ... did you want to come in?"

"No thank you, I'm just returning something that belongs to you."

"Oh?"

"Mr Cottage left his jacket at the park. I looked after it for a while to give you some time to grieve your loss."

"Oh, that was kind of you, but to be honest I have plenty of things to remember him by. Actually, I don't know whether I want it or not."

"Believe me, you will want it."

"Well, if you say so."

Tilly smiled and walked away down the cottage path. Mrs Cottage hung the jacket up on the peg beside the door. It felt heavier than it should have done, and then she suddenly remembered the black folder.

Sure enough, the folder was there full of cash, just like it had been in the early hours of that fateful day.

Meanwhile, Mr Cottage was trying to get used to being in a basement with no windows in Mr Freak's house. He would be brought food three times a day, but apart from that he had nothing except a filthy toilet and a sink with a tiny mirror. The only clothes he had were the ones he was wearing when he was given into Mr Freak's care. Every time Mr Freak's assistant brought food to him, there was the threat of a taser. It had already been used on Mr Cottage several times. Every other time he would ask the same question: "When are you going to let me out of here?"

The assistant would always say, "One day," until after a couple of months had passed, the answer was, "Today."

Mr Cottage was delighted to know he was going to be set free, and about four hours later, his door was suddenly opened and fresh clothes thrown at him. The door closed again while he got dressed. He tried his hardest to smarten his hair up in the little mirror.

Eventually, Mr Cottage was collected by the three 'heavies' from the play park and their companion, the gardener. The assistant and Mr Freak were nowhere to be seen as he was escorted out of the house and into its immense grounds. There was an outhouse on the grounds, as big as a small dance hall, and a car park containing cars of numerous sizes and descriptions. "I thought you were setting me free," said Mr Cottage. Among the four, there was no word, not even from the gardener. "What are you going to do with me?" The three 'heavies' gripped more tightly onto his arms while the gardener put a gag over his mouth. He wriggled but it was hopeless. They took him into the building where there were about fifty people sat in chairs, all staring at him with curious faces as he was led onto a stage and forced to stand between his escorts.

There was a strange 'Ah' sound from the audience, and Mr Cottage looked around to see if he recognised anybody. But they were all weird, like exaggerated humans, more like characters from a child's animation. Among them was Armadillo Man with a scaly-looking scalp, like a shield in place of hair. He had big ears and a long nose. His tongue kept sliding in an out of his mouth like it was searching for ants.

Jellybean Fairy was shuffling about in her seat looking a little like an elfin princess with a tiara on her head. She had a cute little nose and a gleaming-wide smile. Baby Freckles was an interesting sight. He was the size of a six year old, but the shape of a baby. But it was his freckles that stood out more than anything. These were just three of the strange-looking members of the audience with exaggerated features and wearing a variety of styles of clothing - like 'fancy dress' costumes.

"One thousand pounds?" called out the gardener with his verbal sprinkler full on. A hand went up in the audience, but Mr Cottage couldn't see the body it extended from.

"Two thousand pounds?" The same hand went up again, but from between different members of the audience. Again Mr Cottage couldn't see the body from which the arm extended.

"Will anyone offer me three thousand pounds?" The same arm went up, but again from a totally different area, and so it went on until the gardener reached a call for ten thousand pounds. Up until that point, all of the weird characters in the audience just sat still and seemed to stare through Mr Cottage. But on the call for ten thousand pounds, Jellybean Fairy raised a dainty, gloved arm holding a wand.

"Any advance on ten thousand pounds … second time of asking … third time of asking … SOLD to Jellybean Fairy!" Jellybean Fairy stood up and bounced around in delight while all of the weird characters in the audience smiled and clapped.

The gardener removed the gag from the mouth of the merchandise as Mr Cottage was trying to ask the gardener a question while he was being dragged away again: "What's she going to do with me?"

"I don't know, all I know is she's famous for her taxidermy. People travel thousands of miles to see her work." Mr Cottage tried to wriggle free to do a runner, but the removers were just too strong.

Mr Cottage was desperate now, "What's going to happen to me!"

"Relax, it's just a business transaction."

"But this is all against my will, I'm not a slave, and I'm not an animal, either!"

"Don't be silly," said the gardener, "nobody is suggesting such a thing; we just know that this is the type of thing you approve of."

"What! Doing something against a person's own will? Being forced to live with someone dangerous?"

"Yes."

Tickle and Beetroot found life difficult not having their father and not knowing whether they would ever see him again. Mrs Cottage had the additional problem of explaining to people where her husband had gone. All they had told people so far was that he was away on business. As it happened, the likely scenario would turn out as follows (but I can't divulge how I know this):

Mr Cottage would appear again, but he would not end up as part of the family - well not to the same extent as before, anyway – and he would wander around aimlessly, unable to change his character. His children, Tickle and Beetroot, would grow up with their loving mother, but they would always be scarred. However, instead of moping around feeling sorry for themselves (which they would have every right to do), they would turn their trauma into healing, as they would fight for love, justice and equality for the millions of downtrodden people in the world; and they would do so knowing they themselves were loved by one another. And this love was the most precious thing in the world to them!

Chapter 10
Firestone Village

Rees and Shauna had enjoyed their picnic in the fields of Devon, in Dartmoor National Park. They were actually a little lost and found themselves wandering along a village lane on a little jaunt. They passed a sign depicting a wicker man in a field with villagers dancing around it. The name on the sign was Firestone Village, which they had never heard of. They began to get an uneasy feeling as they walked past the houses. The villagers all seemed to be out in their gardens. It was as though they were waiting for nothing more than to slowly turn their heads and gawp at visitors as soon as they were close enough to give them an excuse. From young to old they stopped their play, their gardening or their conversations about flowers, just to stop and stare over their privet hedges at Rees and Shauna, who tried smiling and saying hello, but they received no response. They didn't know whether to giggle or tell them off for being so rude. The faces of the villagers were emotionless and their eyes unusually large. Rees and Shauna must have passed more than thirty individuals before they found a sign pointing off the road to a visitors centre; it was a brown sign so it was obviously a bona fide place for tourists! They might have a gift shop and a café which would be nice! They entered the pristine glass doors into one big room festooned with tables around a central fireplace with a flue stretching above it. The fire wasn't lit as it was warm weather outside.

"This is nice," said Shauna seeing how popular it was and admiring the ambience.

Along the edges of the café were tables and shelves with memorabilia to buy. They hovered around those for a while. While Shauna was admiring a selection of ornate mirrors dangling from a frame, she thought she noticed lots of café patrons staring at her, so she immediately turned round and was surprised to see that they were all getting on with their own business, chatting, eating and drinking. "The villagers outside have obviously spooked me," she said to herself.

Rees signalled for Shauna to come to him. "Look, does this remind you of anything?" The object was a little cottage with two children beside it, a girl and a boy.

"Hansel and Gretel," observed Shauna.

"Shall I buy it for you?"

"No, it'll just keep reminding me. I know why you want it, though."

Rees just stared at the object longingly.

Shauna tried to get her brother away from the ornament of the witch's cottage. "Come on, let's find a table."

They sat a couple of tables away from the fireplace and studied the perspex menu card. Amongst the words and the pictures of cakes and scones, Shauna thought she could see the reflection of all the café patrons behind her staring right at her with curious faces. She turned as quickly as possible this time but again saw that everyone was getting on with their own business, chatting, eating and drinking. She shook her head to come to her senses and her body shivered with it too.

"Will you get me a chocolate cake and a drink of Tilly's tea?" asked Shauna. "What are you having?"

"I'll get myself a gingerbread man and share a pot of Tilly's tea with you."

"There's bread crumbs all over this table, ask them for a cloth as well."

Rees got in the queue, and as he waited, he thought back to the thing that dominated his mind every day.

Shauna and Rees were only eight years old at the time:

"I'm sorry to say your mummy is dying, there's nothing the doctors can do," said their daddy.

The children were twins, and they looked after each other well. They were also best friends. They loved their mummy, but they did not love mummy and daddy's friend Rita. She seemed to be always hanging around their daddy! The children sobbed as they listened to their daddy attempting to prepare them.

"Mummy doesn't trust Rita," said Shauna, "She thinks you're in love with her instead of mummy."

"That's not true," said daddy, "Come here," he added, hugging the two children together.

This situation was hurting the twins deeply; not just their mummy's imminent death, but also the fact that their mummy was going to die feeling betrayed. Rees bottled it all up, but deep down he was wondering if Rita was poisoning his mummy.

"If mummy dies, I hope Rita doesn't live here," said Rees.
"No, there's no reason for Rita to live here," daddy replied.
"But she's always here!" Rees insisted.
"That's just because she's helping me to look after mummy."
"I don't want mummy to die!" cried Shauna.
"I don't either, but she'll be going to a better place," said their daddy.
Daddy hugged them tight, but the twins knew something was not right. The only thing that made them doubt their suspicions was that their father didn't appear to suspect that anything untoward was happening.

Finally, the queue had reduced in size and it was Rees' turn to order their food and drinks. "A pot of Tilly's tea for two, a chocolate cake and a gingerbread man, please."
"Right you are."
"Oh, and throw in a brownie if you don't mind."
Smiling at Rees, "So it's a case of having your cake and eating it."
"I wish!" said Rees.
"Well, wishes do come true to those who are true."
"I've not heard that one before," said Rees.
"Ever a true word spoken in jest."
"Well wouldn't that be a fine thing."
Rees paid the money and took the tray. Meanwhile, Shauna had been looking at the reflection of staring café patrons in the perspex menu again and again, then turning quickly again and again only to find them continuing as normal - again and again. She was disturbingly baffled.
"Here's your cake," said Rees.
"Oh, you got a brownie as well, we've not eaten brownies since just before mummy died. I don't know if I want to eat it."
"Come on, we've got to get over it sometime."

"But what if Rita killed mummy … and then it might have been her that killed daddy ten years later!"

"The police didn't suspect her, so we should just assume that she's innocent. Anyway, we've no idea where she is now, so there's nothing we can do about it, and there's probably a statute of limitations anyway."

"If she's guilty, she shouldn't be allowed to get away with it."

"Honestly, leave it, there's nothing we can do, Shauna."

"I'll never get over it if I don't do something."

"You will, just give it time. Oh, sorry, I forgot to get a cloth."

"It's all right, the crumbs have gone."

"That's strange!"

"Rita was just like that witch in Hansel and Gretel, deceiving us, controlling us and trapping us, not giving us enough food, squandering daddy's money!"

"A very, very evil witch!"

"I would love to throw her into that fireplace in the centre of the café, just like Gretel did to the witch in the story when she pushed her into the oven and closed the door."

"I would love to as well, but it's never going to happen."

They both watched as what looked like a team of pixies flocked to the centre of the café and removed the fireplace, leaving the flue behind, so that a pole was left stretching from the floor right up into the rafters of the very high ceiling.

Shauna was excited. "I wonder what's going to happen?"

"Look, someone's coming down the pole!"

Rees and Shauna could not believe their eyes as a middle-aged, chubby lady swung down the pole doing classic pole-dancing poses on the way as loud music suddenly blurted out from the walls. The pole-dancer was dressed like a circus acrobat.

"What on earth!" said Shauna, laughing.

"HURRAY FOR TILLY!" shouted the audience as they clapped their hands to the music.

Every time she spun round, Tilly the pole-dancer would smile at Rees and Shauna. "I'm sure she keeps staring at us and nobody else," said Rees.

"She is!" agreed Shauna, and she glanced into the perspex menu's reflection again, and again she saw the café patrons staring at her, but exactly like before, they were not staring at her when she turned round to look.

Then the music stopped, and Tilly the pole-dancer made an announcement:

"Ladies and gentlemen, it is my great honour to welcome our star guest, and boy is she hot!" The audience cheered. Tilly looked up to the ceiling. "And here she is now! Give her a round of applause!" The audience clapped and cheered as a woman descended the pole slowly and in fits and starts. The woman was tied with her back to the pole, so that her limbs were unable to move. She was obviously desperate to escape, and as she wriggled, she slipped lower and lower until her feet eventually hit the floor where Tilly had been stood.

"Let me go!" she screamed.

Tilly stood back and shouted, "Give it up for Rita!" Everyone stood to their feet, clapped and cheered louder than before.

Rees and Shauna were dumbfounded. "It's our stepmother!" said Rees to Shauna.

"What on earth is going on?" said Shauna to Rees.

At that moment, Rita recognised her two stepchildren whom she had abused, and whose real mother and father she had killed to get hold of their money.

Tilly spun round on the spot with a flourish, "Here is a woman who poisoned another man's wife!"

Everyone booed.

"Not only that, she did it SLOWLY!"

Everyone gasped.

"Then ... then she married the widower."

Everyone tutted.

"And the man did not know he was marrying his wife's murderer!"

Everyone twittered disapprovingly.

"Then, she murdered him as well!"

Gasps of horror all round.

"Then she kept all the money for herself and abandoned her stepchildren, how could she do that?"

"SHE'S A WITCH!" shouted the audience.

"Who does she think she is?"

"A WITCH!"

"Disgusting behaviour! Did she really believe she was going to get away with it!"

"SURELY NOT!"

Rees and Shauna's hearts were pounding, at last having their suspicions confirmed, at last feeling people were on their side, and at last feeling there may be justice in the world after all.

"What should her sentence be?" Tilly asked the onlookers.

"BURN HER!" shouted the onlookers. "BURN HER TO ASHES!"

Shauna joined in, "BURN HER!"

In desperation, Rita called out to her stepchildren, "Shauna, Rees, she's lying! Don't listen to what she's saying!"

"I don't believe you!" shouted Shauna.

Everyone, including Rees and Shauna, chanted, "BURN HER! BURN HER! BURN HER!"

The pixies returned as long ribbons swung down to the sides of the pole. Each pixie held a ribbon and spread equidistant from each other and from what was now a maypole with Rita tied onto it in the midst of the pixies. Several other café patrons grabbed a ribbon, and a huge green man emerged from a corner of the room playing a fiddle. Those holding the ribbons danced and sang, in and out of each other, round and round the maypole to the music, until beautiful weaved patterns covered both the maypole and Rita's body. She was now unable to even wriggle. The only power she had was her ability to scream for help, but that was barely audible over the music and laughter.

Suddenly, the music stopped. The pixies stood back, and the giant green man, who was playing the fiddle, put it down and strode over to a pulley system. He activated it, slowly lowering a larger than life wicker woman, which covered both the pillar and Rita on descent. There was a sense of awe in the room, and Rita knew her fate was sealed. She screamed some more, even though she knew it was fruitless;

her sins had found her out in the end. Rita looked around at the wicker woman as it enveloped her: "NO! NO! YOU CAN'T DO THIS!" she cried. Once the wicker woman had completely surrounded Rita, the café patrons then looked intently at Rees and Shauna; Tilly walked up to them holding out a fire-lighting stick. Rees and Shauna took the stick from Tilly, and held it together. Then they walked towards the wicker woman with their hearts pounding, holding the lighter in front of them. Everyone quietly watched them as they stepped ever closer, determined in their actions in spite of the pleas for help from within the wicker woman.

The twins then triggered the flame on the stick and Shauna said, "This is for my mummy and daddy." They both then set the straw on fire with the stick and stepped back. The fire did not hesitate. Rita did not immediately feel the effects of the fire and tried one last time to reason with the twins, "Shauna and Rees, I shouldn't have done what I did, but I didn't have any money, it was the only way I could help myself."

"Yes, you did help yourself, and yourself alone."

"I don't mean that. Look, let me go and I'll give you all the money back!"

Rees and Shauna didn't bother responding.

Then the fire became Rita's only close friend as the smoke choked her screams and the heat seared her body. Soon the wicker woman became a voiceless raging inferno, and the café patrons started to sing and dance to the green man's fiddle once more.

At that moment the pixies ushered Rees and Shauna out of the café. "Go, go quickly, nobody will know what happened here today. Be happy that justice has been served and enjoy your lives."

Shauna and Rees did as they were told and they left the visitors centre. They hurried back through the village and nobody was in the gardens of the cottages and houses anymore. They kept going until they passed the Firestone Village sign. Then they looked back and saw smoke rising in the distance. They felt a pang of guilt, but more than that, they felt warmer, more confident and free.

Several days later, after the shock, Rees and Shauna finally talked in depth about their experience. They checked maps online and off, and could not find any mention of a Firestone Village in the area. So they decided to return to the site of their picnic and retrace their steps. The only thing they could see was field after field. They spent the whole day trying different routes to find the village where they had set fire to their wicked stepmother, but the village did not exist. However, they did pick up a strange metallic object during their search for the village and decided to keep it as a secret memento of their victory over their evil stepmother.

The twins were in a dilemma though while trying to make sense of it all. If they believed it had all happened as they remembered it, then how could a whole village disappear? If it did not happen, then how come they both remembered it happening in exactly the same way, identical in every detail.

Sometime later, they read of their stepmother's death in the newspaper. She had burnt to death, not in Firestone Village, but in her own beautiful cottage many miles away in Wales. They finally found out where she had been living all those years, and more importantly, they knew for certain that she had truly died, and somehow, in some miraculous way, they had caused that death, but nobody would ever find any evidence that they had visited her cottage as they had never been there. It was all over.

DAILY TITBITS
by
Justin Caadfar Esquire

DEATH OF A LONELY LADY

This month, the charred remains of a body that was found in a burnt out cottage in Wales, was confirmed to be that of Rita Thorn, the widow of Marcus Thorn from Devon. After her husband's death, she is believed to have lived as a recluse in her beautiful cottage. According to locals, she was a bit of a hermit.

"She always kept herself to herself, and she didn't have a dog, so she was never out and about in the community. We hardly ever saw her," said one neighbour.

Another neighbour said, "Whenever she was in her garden as I walked past, I would shout hello, but she sometimes didn't even answer. She often had a glass of wine in her hand, even in the morning."

Several villagers said she was also a chain smoker. "She always had a cigarette in her mouth, so it wouldn't surprise me if she just fell asleep with a lit cigarette in her hand," said Freya Wilson who lived next door.

That is also the official conclusion. Rita Thorn may have fallen asleep with a cigarette in her hand while she was in bed, and the fire took hold too quickly for her to wake up in time to call for help.

After investigation, it has been identified as an accidental death; there is no evidence of foul play. Chief Constable Edwards said, "This is a sad tale of a lonely woman, a bit of a recluse, being vulnerable in her solitude. She was a heavy drinker and a chain smoker according to her local community, so it was a tragedy waiting to happen. She had no friends to speak of and no work colleagues as she lived off her inheritance after her husband's death. It is a tragedy for the local community as they wanted to get alongside Ms Thorn, but that was not reciprocated."

One of the firefighters who was on the scene had this to say:

"The fire took hold so quickly, so by the time we arrived it was too late to save the occupant. All the neighbours in the village said it seemed to happen incredibly fast. It happened about two in the morning, so that didn't help either as people were in their own beds asleep, and Ms Thorn didn't have an alarm system to automatically call the emergency services. We have cooperated with the investigation team into the cause of the fire, and no evidence of unusual combustibles were found. It is a very tragic event. So as a fire service, we would just like to remind people never to smoke in bed, as there's always the risk that you will fall asleep and another tragedy like this one could easily happen again."

There was no will in existence declaring who was to inherit Ms Thorn's fortune, and if she had one in the cottage, it was totally destroyed in the fire. The only known heirs are her stepchildren from her late husband's first marriage.

The investigation is now closed, but we must remind everyone: Never play with fire!

Chapter 11
Tilly Goes AWOL

An upcoming visitation was of particular significance to Jeremy Nostril, who was determined to get everything right. He knew the visitor he was expecting could be a little unpredictable, but if he just got the balance between social interaction and business ambience right, he believed he could clinch the deal. He had been told by many not to be so worried as he, that is, Jeremy, was set to be an immensely successful businessman, but he just considered this to be polite banter and believed this outward display of confidence in his abilities was likely to be fake and people's real opinions were shared behind his back.

However and whatever, this important business meeting was going to take place soon, so Jeremy tried to prepare himself by predicting a likely scenario in his mind's eye:

There is a knock on his office door. "Please come in," says Jeremy in a friendly manner, yet having a spoonful of importance in his tone.

The door opens and a grinning businessman's elongated face emerges ahead of his body. "Terry!" exclaims Jeremy, greeting his potential business partner, who looks rather like a chameleon on stilts and for some unknown reason is wearing a black tuxedo. "Jeremy!" exclaims the lizard-like work colleague. Jeremy stands to shake the lizard's hand and they both make their way to the leather sofas where a bottle of champagne is stood on the coffee table, waiting to quench the thirst of two tall glasses.

"I really appreciate this Terry, you won't regret it."

"Well, I'm sure I won't, but lay it all out for me anyway, then there's no chance of a misunderstanding," responds Terry, his tongue unable to resist a rotating taste of his own drooling lips. This strange habit doesn't concern Jeremy; he has known Terry for a long time and has personally witnessed some of his seemingly unlikely projects succeed, so who cares? Jeremy is in fact jealous of Terry's successes, and wants to tap into this success somehow; he needs to get this meeting right.

"Well of course, but you have read my proposals, haven't you?" (Not too strong, Jeremy, you don't want to get his back up!)

"What do YOU think?" asks Terry on the defensive.

Jeremy thinks for a while ... "So what do you think?"

Terry stares at him for a while as Jeremy has not laid it out for him like he asked.

Nervous at this uncomfortable pause and sensing he has unwittingly done something wrong, Jeremy adds, "Have a glass of champagne!" He shakily proceeds to fill two glasses anyway and hands one of the glasses to Terry who takes it obligingly. They both take a sip.

"So?" hints Terry.

"So, I'm ready to sign," says Jeremy excitedly, "over to you ... ." In his nervousness, Jeremy spills a little champagne from his glass.

"I'm waiting," hints the chameleon, licking his lips.

Knowing something is amiss, but not quite sure what, "You're ready to sign? Marvellous, I'll just get the papers." Jeremy's body emerges from the sofa and rifles around on his desk. As he does so, he suddenly realises he has not responded properly to Terry's request for him to lay it all out for him. A feeling of dread suddenly drenches him from top to bottom. 'That's why he seems to be a bit obstinate!' he thought to himself. 'I've blown it!'

Just then, the door slams and the chameleon is nowhere to be seen.

This was just one possible scenario, and Jeremy learnt from his own imagination. He knew he should not allow nerves to take over, otherwise he would miss some very important elements in this interaction that was due to take place in approximately 15 minutes' time. He also had to get the right balance between trying not to sound too desperate and trying not to sound too laid back. 'This is going to be difficult,' he thought, 'but I shouldn't worry, the deal is great, so the only thing I need to do is get the interaction right. How difficult can it be?' He imagined another scenario:

There is a more decisive knock at the door and the chameleon opens the door before he is invited in. "Jeremy, just the man I want to see!"

A little taken aback, Jeremy stands to shake Terry's hand. "Come in, how's it all going?" *asks Jeremy.*

"Oh, good, good. I'm afraid I'm in a bit of a hurry."

"No problem."

"I wanted to make sure I discussed your project before I headed out."

"Great, no problem, but do you want to reschedule if you're in such a hurry?"

"No, no, I just wanted to say I think you have a sound proposal there, and we should go for it."

"Excellent. D...d...do you want to sign now?"

"Er ..."

"Time is of the essence!" *says Jeremy with a little desperate chuckle.*

"Absolutely, but if you could just give me a few days ... as you can see I'm in a bit of a hurry!"

"Of course, but sooner rather than later," *Jeremy says with another little chuckle (cringing at his own desperate tone).*

"You're right of course, send the contract over to my office and I'll get right on it."

"Is tomorrow possible?"

"I'm really sorry, I'm going to be out of town for a week."

"A WEEK? But the deal will be dead and buried by then!"

"Sorry, send it to my office and I really will sign it if I get back early."

"You don't want to sign it do you?"

"Yes, of course I do."

"But you don't seem to realise the urgency."

"Look, to be honest," *says Terry*, "it is a bit rubbish."

"What! No it isn't, it's the best proposal you've had in ages."

"Well, er ..."

"So you were lying when you said you were going to sign it."

"No, I said I would sign it if I had the time."

"You're messing me about!" *says Jeremy angrily.*

"Look, I have to go, bye."

"Get out of my office!"

Terry leaves and Jeremy throws his paperweight at the closed door.

'What's wrong with me?' Jeremy thought to himself. 'I've got to get my head straight or I am well and truly going to muck this up. I am NOT desperate and the proposal IS indeed the best he's had in a long time. It should be plain sailing. Just be friendly yet professional and get to the point!'

Jeremy Nostril hid the champagne and glasses under the coffee table as he concluded it was too presumptuous and that Terry didn't deserve champagne anyway. He decided he really didn't trust Terry - he was just a slimy lizard - and Jeremy was only trying to get Terry on board to gain from his expertise and contacts anyway. He imagined another scenario:

There is a knock at the door. Jeremy gets up to open the door and greets Terry with a firm handshake. "Terry! Come in, take a seat."

With a friendly smile, "Cheers. No champagne?"

"Oh, yes of course," says Jeremy pulling the bottle and glasses from under the table.

"That's a funny place to keep them!"

"I know ... anyway ... what do you think of my proposal?"

"Looks good, let me see the contract."

"Are you sure? I mean, yes of course." Jeremy hunts for the contract at his desk and his heart sinks as he can't find it.

"Come on man, you can't have lost it already." Terry moves over to the desk and grabs some paper from it. "Here it is."

"Oh, you've found it, well done!" says Jeremy relieved, yet sweating profusely.

It takes Terry three glasses of champagne to read the contract, after which he suddenly blurts out, "I can't sign this!"

"What? Why?"

"Because it's drivel!"

"No it's not!" says Jeremy, almost about to cry.

Suddenly, Terry signs the contract, laughing. "Did you honestly think I wasn't going to sign it?"

"No, of course not."

"It's a brilliant proposal, why wouldn't I?"

"Thanks Terry, it'll be great for both of us."

"Thanks for the champagne, I'm not going to be able to concentrate for the rest of the day now," Terry says, handing back the contract. "I'm in party mood."

"Me too!" says Jeremy, seeing Terry out.

'That's how it should go! Perfect!' said Jeremy to himself after that scenario had played out. He wandered over to the window to see if Terry's car had arrived. 'He will sign whatever, because it's an excellent proposal. Why wouldn't he sign? However things play out in this room, it doesn't matter because he's going to sign the contract anyway. It's been five years in the making, and my sweat and blood have gone into it - he'd better sign it - in fact if he doesn't sign it, I'll eat my hat!'

Jeremy's confidence had grown and he felt ready for anything. Jeremy's office door opened and his secretary's head popped in. "Terry Winshore is here to see you."

"Send him in please Marjorie."

Terry strode in with a stern face. Jeremy was taken aback. He hadn't anticipated the initial greeting to be so awkward. "Hi Terry!" said Jeremy, shaking a wet fish of a hand before leading the chameleon to the coffee table.

"Right Jeremy, what do you want? I'll give you three minutes of my time."

"You know what I want, I want you to sign the contract because you think the proposal is marvellous."

"Oh, I wouldn't say that."

Jeremy had to remind himself that this was not just a possible scenario – it was in fact reality, and reality was reality and there could be no alternative sequence of events; this knocked his confidence.

"What don't you like about the proposal?"

"What I'd like to say is, 'What do you think you're playing at?' Do you really think you can do this to me?"

"I'm terribly sorry, Terry," Jeremy said, beginning to get a little confused. "What exactly am I doing to you? If you think I'm being a little presumptuous, then I'm sorry, it is of course your choice."

"It certainly is!"

"What is it about the proposal exactly that makes you hesitate?"

"Well, all of it actually," said Terry, accidentally kicking something under the coffee table. "What the…?"

"Oh it's just the champagne."

"What have you got champagne under the coffee table for?"

Jeremy picked up the bottle and glasses and arranged them neatly on the coffee table and Terry stood up and hovered towards the door. "Are you leaving?" asked Jeremy.

"Why would I do that?" said Terry, at that point wandering away from the door and towards the desk. On the way, Terry banged his leg against the coffee table, knocking the glasses over. He stood them back up again before continuing to the desk.

"What are you doing?" asked Jeremy.

"Signing the contract of course," responded Terry, picking up the contract: "Here it is!"

"Well, that's wonderful news, I thought for a minute there you were going to refuse!" said Jeremy, feeling dizzy from the stress of it all (and not dismissing the possibility in his mind that Terry was on cocaine or something similar). While Terry was signing the contract, Jeremy poured two glasses of champagne.

"You know what the problem is with you, Jeremy? You can't tell when someone's joking."

"Cheers Terry," said Jeremy, handing Terry a glass.

"We're in business!" shouted Terry, ignoring the glass and heading to the door, "Yabber dabber doo!"

"Yabber dabber doo!" But surprised at Terry's quick exit, he inquired, "What? No champagne?"

"No, I've got a lot of papers to wade through."

"Well, we'll have to meet for a drink sometime to celebrate."

"We will, give me a call next week," Terry suggested with a friendly smile, returning briefly to Jeremy to shake his hand firmly.

"Indeed I will," said Jeremy.
"Enjoy your champagne!"
"I will."
"I'm just delighted it's official at last!"
"It certainly is, yabber dabber doo!" They both laughed. Jeremy added, "Thank you, you won't regret it!"
"I certainly hope not! Yabber dabber doo!"
"Yabber dabber doo!" repeated Jeremy, seeing him out of the door.

After Terry had left the office, Jeremy couldn't contain himself. He frantically checked his face and body with his hands. Satisfied he was not dreaming, he couldn't stop smiling to himself. 'All that worry ... and doubt ... and sweat and blood! It's finally clinched!' He looked down from his office window and saw Terry get into his pink Bentley and drive away. "You did it Jeremy! YABBER DABBER DOO!" he shouted to himself, throwing his arms into the air.

Marjorie, his secretary, popped her head into the office. "Is everything all right Mr Nostril?"

"Everything is wonderful, here have a glass of champagne with me; I've already poured an extra one."

Marjorie obliged but before she finished the glass, she apologised, "Please don't get me drunk Mr Nostril, I have piles of work to do."

"Of course you do, Marjorie, off you go."

"Thank you Mr Nostril, and congratulations!"

"Yabber dabber doo!" said Jeremy raising his glass to her as she left.

Still smiling to himself, Jeremy picked up the signed contract just so he could see it with his own eyes. Then to his surprise, instead of it having Terry Winshore's signature, the contract had been signed 'Fred Flintstone.'

Jeremy started to feel seriously ill. He became extremely dizzy and began gasping for air. He staggered to the door of his office, opened it and squinted at his secretary's desk to ask her to call an ambulance. Everything became extremely blurry. "Marjorie? Marjorie?" He staggered to his secretary's desk and could see her lying on the carpet. "Marjorie, what are you doing on the floor? Marjorie ... the champagne! He must have ...!" Jeremy fell unconscious to the floor beside his secretary.

Meanwhile, Tilly had gone AWOL that day to do some shopping. She was trying on fancy dress costumes in a new shop called *Fantasy Frills*. She tried on a vampire outfit, a police woman's uniform and many others. The one she settled for was a Tarzan outfit. After paying the money (which was a bit embarrassing actually, as she initially tried to pay using dinosaur cards before she found a few tenners), Tilly left *Fantasy Frills* and threw her bag into the back of her roofless safari jeep before leaping in beside the steering wheel. It started to pour down with rain as soon as she got going, and the wind was making the jeep sway. She was still wearing her Tarzan costume that she'd tried out in the shop! "How am I expected to get through this concrete jungle in the middle of monsoon season!" In spite of this, Tilly weaved in and out of the heavy traffic, ignoring the car horns blurting out at her in disapproval. Red lights didn't stop her either; she knew where she was going and nothing would stand in her way. She zoomed through a river of water on the highway, sending tidal waves over passers-by. "Yeh! I'm a surfing babe!" she shouted, her hair looking like a giant water rat. The jeep continued to sway and swerve at top speed until she found herself blocked behind a pink Bentley travelling at eighty miles per hour. She didn't hesitate bumping into the back of the Bentley.

Meanwhile, Tilly's elderly friend had been looking for her. Tilly's friend was presently sitting on the head of a huge water monster which was swimming at tremendous speed along the River Mersey, its head poking out of the water so the elderly lady could see where she was going - she was holding tight onto the reins to steer the monster in the right direction. Eventually, the Mersey Gateway Bridge came into view as the monster drew closer.

On the bridge, the cars stopped to see the strange sight of a monster's head coming closer and closer. The pink Bentley had to stop too and Tilly jumped out of the jeep, leaping into the air and somersaulting forward onto the bonnet of the Bentley. So, stood on the bonnet facing the business chameleon was Tilly in her Tarzan outfit, brandishing a large, thick tree branch.

"Get off my Bentley!" shouted the chameleon.

"BAM!" shouted Tilly as she thrust the thick tree branch down onto the bonnet.

"No! Stop!"

"BAM!"

"STOP! STOP! STOP!"

"BAM! BAM! BAM!"

"You're insane, you need to go to a mental hospital!"

"Let's talk about this over a bottle of champagne!" shouted Tilly.

"What are you talking about? Get off my Bentley!"

"Let's make a deal."

"A deal? What kind of deal? What on earth are you talking about you freak of nature!"

"You know, a deal, over a glass of champagne; I'm dying to spend some time with you."

"No deal, get off my car!"

"BAM! BAM! BAM!" Tilly shouted as she whacked the windscreen of the pink Bentley with the tree branch."

"If you think you can break through my windscreen you are deluding yourself, it's reinforced glass."

"Don't worry, I've brought my own reinforcements."

"Reinforcements?"

As they chatted, the cars on the Mersey Gateway Bridge began to disperse on seeing that the great water monster was about to mount the bridge.

"If you don't get off my car I am going to drive with you on the bonnet," said the chameleon with desperation in his voice.

"That would be fun!"

The chameleon's car started to move and Tilly somersaulted off the bonnet onto the concrete. But before the Bentley could move even 5 metres, the giant water monster's flipper flopped down onto the Bentley, flattening the entire vehicle with the chameleon inside it. "BAM!" shouted the elderly lady from the head of the monster before navigating it round to head back to Tilly's Tearoom. "Are you coming?" she shouted to Tilly.

"Yes, but I need to return my costume first."

"Right you are then, we can stop on the way."

Nobody had noticed Tilly's altercation with Terry Winshore, as the cars were not inhabited by what you thought when you read this account. In fact, to everyone in existence, the bridge was still closed off due to urgent repairs. The cars faded away as Tilly climbed up onto the water monster's head which had lowered itself to rest on the bridge.

Back at the office - or should I say just outside Jeremy Nostril's office - lay two poisoned employees.

These events may be of concern to you as I imagine you are thinking, 'If Tilly was in-the-know about this event, why didn't she do anything to prevent the poisoning from taking place?' I wondered the same thing. But first of all, Tilly is just following instructions; she only knows what she is allowed to know so she can do her job. However, as it happens, this is a happy ending, as a paramedic turned up and administered life-saving medical treatment to Marjorie and Jeremy. Don't tell anyone, but the emergency services were actually called by Tilly, or so I heard. She did not have permission to do this, but as she had had no instructions to the contrary, she used this absence of instructions as her excuse to do something she was perhaps not allowed to do. There may be consequences, and those consequences may even be catastrophic; who knows? I certainly don't know.

Fortunately, before they were well enough to report the poisoning to the police, Jeremy and Marjorie saw a news item on the office TV showing a picture of a mysteriously squashed pink Bentley on the Gateway Bridge, with the mangled body of its occupant blanked out of the shot. This was a mystery as there was no access to the bridge due to repairs taking place and there was no evidence of anything that could have squashed a car.

After seeing this, Jeremy and Marjorie decided not to mention to the police that they had been poisoned; neither did they mention the contract signed 'Fred Flintstone,' as they might have been investigated over a revenge killing – although who knows how they could have flattened a car in the middle of the Gateway Bridge, especially as the bridge was closed off! The only other problem was the paramedic who knew they had been poisoned; however, that all depends on who the paramedic was!!

Chapter 12
A Saw Point

They were a lovely couple, he, dressed smartly and sporting a pristine haircut, his girlfriend at his side with a fluffy coat and designer handbag. It is true, they lived in a cloud of cash, and they were proud to display that fact. However, it was difficult for them to come across as good, upstanding citizens, as that stereotypical fake persona eluded them. They only knew one, and that was to clad themselves with expensive tackiness. But that issue did not matter to them as they had their own powerful kingdom – not the usual one that involved the well-hidden stab-you-in-the-back legal loop-holy type of powerful with its own self-assured, smiley, serene friendly manner. This was a different kind of 'I'll get you when you're not looking' sort of smug.

You could almost pity the man – Daniel Duckers was his name – as his eyes had that hurt, innocent look, like butter wouldn't melt. Indeed, he did have a good side - like a wolf does on a full stomach. Women fell at his feet for the privileged opportunity to try and change him, and he kept them right there on the floor; but that did not stop them going back for more.

Daniel's girl was called Cindy Poppers, a slim model-type, one that had been airbrushed before the photo was taken. Her eye-lashes were so long they collected spider webs as she strode along the path she had chosen for herself, one which was not quite as easy as one would expect. She was only indispensable to her man as long as she remained as young as possible and at the same time she performed like Daniel's long-lost mummy. In fact, Daniel had not literally lost his mother, she just had no idea how to engage with her boy who could have been fathered by any of a hundred men. In fact, his mother's lovers were all cut from the same cloth, and that cloth was so ripped and caked in filth that you would describe it as something you might find in a lavatory. That is a very different image to the one that Daniel wanted to portray; he preferred to look like a famous footballer.

Daniel loved football as a child, but his skills evolved from kicking footballs to kicking skulls, you know, the ones that are already on the ground due to having already been pounded by his noble followers. Well, it did make him a fortune after all!

Cindy's father was unknown too, and she mourned the absence of a daddy who cared. Her mother had unashamedly sought to be 'looked after' by a string of wealthy businessmen and gentrified wasters. This left a huge gap in Cindy's soul. The only skill Cindy knew was to sleep her way into some sense of significance, and the only type of men that would put up with her beyond a couple of months were the broken ones who had resorted to crime, and the only way she felt she could ensure her man's faithfulness was to – by his side - faithfully abuse, scratch and maim that man's enemies. She was now an expert - she had reached the pinnacle of her career, one that required her to watch her back at every moment.

Daniel and Cindy needed each other too much, so much so that they would argue from dawn till dusk, each day beating each other and then making up in bed. This was their routine. On top of this, there was always their dismal day-job with a steady stream of spilled intestines. Such is life! Well, it's a livin' innit? Their position was hopeless; the lives they had created for themselves had trapped them, and the only hope for their survival was to continue to destroy individuals and families - and shower themselves in lavish living to supress the guilt.

One such typical day, Daniel and Cindy parked up and entered Tilly's Tearoom. Daniel checked his bling watch - 11:05 - just two hours before a scheduled meeting with Jimmy Rotter who had to be taken down a peg or two with a machete. But that was a world away at that moment, as Daniel wanted to experience some normality, to have a drink in peaceful, non-violent surroundings with his partner, speaking about mundane things, not how to cripple his opponents or to plan which unbelievably expensive holiday to go on next month in order to arrange illegal meetings with his rich sponsors, and then how to blackmail them into coughing up the lot. He just wanted to experience true serenity for a brief moment at least. A tearoom was harmless, no drunkards, no drug barons, no competition between lovers, no corrupt coppers, no blood and gore. He didn't know whether he could achieve it or not, but perhaps he could speak in a civilised and normal way to a couple of strangers without it turning into a fight. How hard could it be? The chances of bumping into his criminal rivals in this innocent building were extremely minimal. He had actually had this almost insatiable desire for normality come over him on two previous occasions recently, but he had swept it under his mental rug; that made this occasion unprecedented, and it was a scary yet somehow pleasant surprise to himself. Perhaps it was a long shot, but he might just pull it off.

Daniel's eyes looked even more innocent than usual as he stepped inside Tilly's Tearoom, perhaps this was because he felt some assurance that he had no bad motives and did not have to be tough for a change. There was a sparkle of hope in a heart he thought he did not have.

On entry to 'normality,' the couple turned a few heads, which was not surprising since they looked like celebrities and oozed importance, as though they were in some way rich and influential, which they in some way were. They both sensed they were being ogled at but Daniel was more concerned about having his time out. His heart and mind were harbouring a whole package of burdens that could spill at any moment, but Cindy's burden at that moment was to ensure her partner got what he had come for, whatever that ended up being. She didn't like upsetting her man if she could help it as the results could be pretty dramatic; however, she was curious to understand why he was so set on going to a benign tearoom. She did wonder if there was some clandestine event or meeting in the offing that he had not informed her about, but she had not picked up those vibes. This allayed her fears a little, and for some reason she didn't feel the usual urgency to ask. Meanwhile she decided to use the conveniences while Daniel ordered a drink of tea.

"I'm just going to powder my nose," said Cindy.

Somebody in the tearoom sniggered. This surprised Daniel who looked around to see where it came from. He didn't know – and at that moment he didn't want to know - so he shrugged his shoulders and studied the menu some more.

"Where's Fluffy gone!" asked a middle-aged man who was sitting at a table by himself.

"Didn't you here? She's gone to the lavatory to powder her nose," said an elderly lady in a fake posh voice - also sitting at a table by herself, but on the opposite side of the room; for Daniel, it was like listening to stereo. He now got the impression this was deliberately aimed at his girlfriend, but he stayed uncannily calm as he reasoned to himself, 'People just don't take risks like this when I'm around; they usually seem to know what'll happen to them. Who in their right mind would risk getting me worked up? And these people are just normal, boring people who don't want a fight!'

"Did she really say that?" asked the middle-aged man, chuckling.

The elderly woman shouted across the room, "YES! ARE YOU DEAF!"

"NO!" replied the middle-aged man before addressing Daniel directly: "Excuse me, where did your poodle go?"

"WHAT!" snapped Daniel, banging the table with his fist.

"Oooo, shirty, shirty!" said the man.

"If you knew who I was, you really wouldn't be trying my patience," said Daniel.

"Uh?" shrugged the man.

"HE SAID, IF YOU KNEW WHO HE WAS, YOU WOULDN'T BE TRYING HIS PATIENCE!" shouted the elderly lady from the other side of the tearoom, with poor Daniel in between them, trying to hold onto his newfound serenity.

Tilly approached Daniel with a pen and notepad. "Don't mind them me'lud, they're a little eccentric."

"It's okay, I just hope they realise how lucky they are that I'm in a good mood today."

The middle-aged man flapped up and down in a camp manner, "Ooo, I'm so lucky, so lucky, lucky, lucky!"

Daniel couldn't resist a snigger too, thinking how little this man knew about what he was capable of, and what he would likely do to him if he didn't shut up.

"You might larf!" said the elderly lady in Daniel's other ear.

Somehow managing to control his temper, "I'd like two teas and two millionaire shortbreads please."

"Coming up me'lud."

Daniel couldn't understand why the waitress kept saying 'me'lud.'

Just then, in the back room, the imp-like man switched the music on: 'Lucky Man' by Emerson, Lake and Palmer.

"What drugged you down to these parts?" asked the elderly lady.

"Pardon?"

"Ooo, wasn't I clear? You're not deaf too are you?"

"No, I'm not."

I said, "What dragged you down to these parts?"

"I'm from these parts."

"What body parts?"

"No, this part of the country!"

"Ooo, you're from these parts are you?"

"I haven't been in this café before."

"You don't say."

"I just came in for a quiet time with my girlfriend."

"Ooo, Fluffy's a lovely girlfriend, I bet."

"She's not called Fluffy, she's called Cindy!"

The middle-aged man burst into hysterics. "He said, she's not called Fluffy, she's called Cindy!! I bet she's a real doll!"

Daniel stood up, "Just keep your stupid mouth shut, I've killed for far less!"

"Ooo, I'm really scared," said the middle-aged man sarcastically, pretending to bite his fingernails. "Actually, I believe you, I bet you make a real killing!" The middle-aged man and his elderly counterpart burst into laughter.

"Look I don't know who you are and why you are risking your life like this, but I am not going to react to it in the way I normally would, so ... just keep your mouths shut!"

"You're right," said the middle-aged man. "I'm being rude, I apologise."

"Right ... good!"

Tilly came over with the teas and millionaire shortbreads.

"Thank you very much," said Daniel politely.

"My pleasure, me'lud," Daniel put two and two together. 'She must know I'm a 'drug lord'? What's going on in this place?'

Actually, at this realisation, you might expect Daniel to call up the boys to trash the tearoom, but it had the opposite effect on him. He decided to stay put and just see it as an interesting dream that would reveal a message in the end. After all, if they laid a finger on him he could always beat them to a pulp in a fraction of a second. In this way, Daniel began to look at it all from an objective standpoint. But no sooner had he become settled in his mind than this new strength started to waver once again, and that was because he saw a big, hefty man enter from the back of the tearoom. Daniel now felt more vulnerable as he didn't have his own heavies around him. He began to wish for Cindy to come back for moral support.

"ARE YOU LOOKING FOR YOUR GIRL?" the giant of a man boomed.

"I'm waiting for my girlfriend," said Daniel.

"SOMEONE HERE IS MISSING A GIRL, WHO IS IT?"

"By girl, do you mean a woman?" asked Daniel.

"Are you missing your girl?" asked the giant again but more sensitively this time for some reason.

This disturbed a sore memory in Daniel's mind, but he quickly swept it back under his mental rug. "If you mean my girlfriend, then yes I'm waiting for her." And standing up Daniel added, "I'll go and find her."

The giant blocked his exit, "Do you truly miss her?"

"Look I don't know what you're trying to do, but if you don't stop it, you'll regret it, and that's a promise."

"OOO, I'M SOOO SCARED!" exclaimed the giant sarcastically.

"You will be when I come and saw your head off in your bed while you're sleeping like a baby."

"Well, if it's your baby you're missing, you'd better come with me!" suggested the giant.

Daniel was confused again. 'What on earth is going on!' he thought. 'Why are these people not afraid of me?' He followed the giant into the back of the tearoom.

"This is where we do the slicing," said the giant.

That phraseology sounded familiar to Daniel. 'Perhaps they are drug rivals after all,' he thought. Daniel actually began to feel more in his comfort zone and was ready for a fight.

As the giant escorted Daniel, they did not enter a respectable box room or alcove from which toilets could be accessed; neither did they enter a dingy back room with boxes of stored products and mops and brushes leaning against a wall. Instead they came to a balcony that looked over what looked like a dungeon. From the balcony Daniel could see his girlfriend Cindy on her back, gagged and strapped onto a platform the size of a single bed. Above her and around the room were a series of pulleys and levers. "Here's your little girl," said the giant.

"This is not my little girl, it's my girlfriend and you'd better let her go or I'll have this place burnt down with you lot in the building."

The giant was strong enough to get Daniel's arms in the vicinity of the balcony rails while Tilly and the middle-aged man cuffed his hands onto the bars. Daniel cursed and kicked but the bars didn't give at all. Screaming threats at his abusers, he saw that they all just stood and stared at him with no expression on their faces. The elderly woman then appeared and walked nonchalantly to what looked like a shelf with a couple of small levers. Tilly, the giant and the middle-aged man were still close by and staring at Daniel, expressionless. Daniel looked down at Cindy again, who blinked back at him. She looked weak and frail. "What have you done to her, you sick ..."

"Your daughter? I've done nothing to your daughter?" asked the giant.

"She's not my daughter, she's my girlfriend."

"Well I am talking about your daughter!" Just then, there was a cranking sound and Daniel looked to see the elderly woman pull a lever and then stare at him - again with no expression on her face. Daniel heard a creak and looked round to see a gigantic pendulum swing slowly towards Cindy. It had a huge curved blade on the tip which swung directly over Cindy's stomach, almost slicing through her while she squirmed, unable to cry for help. The pendulum then came to a halt on the opposite side of the room. Daniel squirmed too and yanked at the hand-cuffs, fracturing his wrist. Not only was he feeling an extreme powerlessness at being unable to save his girlfriend, he was shaking at the memory of his deceased daughter Tina. He had seen her gagged and unable to scream for help in the past when Daniel had been unable to pay back a loan shark; those were the days before he became the top dog. He later broke the loan shark's neck, but it was too late to stop the series of disasters that were to eventually take his daughter Tina's life.

"This is your fault!" said the giant.

"Get these off me! It's your fault!"

"You chose a life of violence, and that brought this suffering to your daughter."

"She's not my daughter!!"

There was a cranking sound and the pendulum swung once more with a creak.

"Look, whatever it is you want me to do, I'll do it; just let her go!"

"It's too late to let her go."

"No, it's not too late, I'll do whatever it is you want if you set me free."

"What? And let you come and break my neck?"

"Why would I break your neck?"

"Because that's what you do when someone abuses your daughter."

"SHE'S NOT MY DAUGHTER!" Daniel heard the cranking again. "NO!" he screamed. This time the pendulum swung lower as Cindy squirmed. "Stop it! That nearly cut her!"

"Oh dear, have we hit a raw nerve, touched a sore point, pushed a few buttons and opened a can of worms?" said the elderly woman.

"JUST LET ME GO!"

The pendulum swung again and Cindy was too afraid to squirm this time; she instead tried to hold her tummy in.

"That was close!" said Tilly, observing Daniel's reactions with a curious eye.

"So let her go!"

Tilly asked him, "Who are you talking about?"

"I'm talking about Cindy! Let her go!"

"Not your daughter?"

"Get it into your thick skull, she is not my daughter!" Having to keep mentioning the word 'daughter' reduced Daniel to sobs as he remembered the time he slapped his daughter Tina around so hard during a drunken, drug-fuelled frenzy that she became permanently deaf. He always tried to tell himself it wasn't his fault and bury it, but all of this kept bringing it up into his mind again and again and again!

"She IS your daughter!" said the giant with conviction.

Daniel just went on sobbing at the memory of his deceased daughter. Because of her addiction to drugs at sixteen, she had taken her own life. Again, Daniel had argued that it was not his fault; he claimed it was her own fault because she was so weak. That sore memory poured over his head again and again as he yanked at the cuffs. Daniel collapsed to the ground with his hands above him, still securely fastened to the bars. He heard the cranking again. As he heard the sound Tilly said, "Your daughter is inside Fluffy's belly."

"WHAT!" Daniel shouted as he saw the pendulum swing across Cindy's belly again, this time cutting through her clothing and drawing blood. "Why didn't you tell me?"

"We did tell you!" said the giant.

"Don't kill my daughter, please!"

"She is safer without you!"

"No, she isn't, she needs her father!"

"She doesn't want a father to beat her and push her to an early grave!"

"Okay, I see what you're talking about now, you know about my other daughter! I was a bad father to Tina; it was all my fault, I am a terrible person."

"A murderer," added the giant.

"No, I didn't murder her."

"Just today, you said you had 'killed for less.'"

"Yes, you're right, but I didn't murder my daughter."

"But you are a murderer!"

"I suppose I am."

"Do you want your daughter to grow up being fathered by a murderer?"

"Of course I want to bring her up, she's my daughter."

"But you're a murderer."

"I know, I know, she should stay away from me. Cindy can have her to herself, all right, is that what you want me to say?"

At that, the giant released Daniel from the cuffs, and the imp untied Cindy in the dungeon. "Call Deliveries!" shouted the imp with a nasally voice.

"Got it!" responded Tilly.

The giant grabbed Daniel firmly by the arm and raced him back into the tearoom. "You are never going to see your daughter."

"Surely, eventually ..."

"It's too late, get out of here and do what you know you should do!" At that, the giant threw Daniel out into the street. He fell to the ground, dazed.

When Daniel got up to rush back into the tearoom, he was surprised to find it was no longer there. Stunned, he stumbled to his car and got inside. He felt so weak and emotionally drained that he just sat there, grieving over what had happened through intermittent sobs. His mind was transfixed onto what he somehow knew he should do. He should confess to all his crimes. He would start by writing to the families of everyone he had killed, explaining exactly why he had done so, but still at the end apologising. With the money he had amassed – almost every penny of it linked to crime – he would compensate those families whether they were dark criminals themselves or not. He would do this until all that was left in his bank were a few thousand that he may have inadvertently accrued by legal means.

All of this he did and it took him a few days, during which time Cindy never made an appearance or answered a phone call. Then, rather than wait for his enemies to come and kill him, Daniel drove to the local police station and handed himself in.

The rest of the matter is a little complicated, but all that truly matters is the fact that Daniel's daughter would grow up happy, secure and away from crime.

Chapter 13
It's All a Matter of Perception

Alison, the university student from Cambridge, had kept an advert from the UK Daily with the picture of an object, an object that was very similar to hers. Hers had dropped out of her multi-coloured scarf after a very strange encounter in a forest with a Mad Hatter's tea party. The object was precious to her and she did not want to be in a situation where she had to part with it for national security reasons, or just because someone wanted to steal it. She would also hesitate in selling it even for a million pounds as it held a special place in her heart, the only evidence she had that what had happened had actually happened. It also symbolised the fact that she had been saved from a predatory professor who had his eyes on her to harm her or even strangle her to death. But curiosity as to what the object was and what its precise function was ate away at her.

Picking up her phone, Alison dialled the number.

"Hello, Criminal Mind Services," came the reply.

This concerned Alison as she was worried she would somehow be thought of as a criminal, but she realised that that was preposterous, there would be absolutely no evidence to suggest such a thing, so she asked, "Cris Pounge?"

"Cris Pounge? Who's Cris Pounge? Oh, yes, hello, this is Cris Pounge," PI Scrounge said, changing his voice in a professional manner.

"I'm responding to your ad in the paper."

"Yes," came the reply in a curious tone.

"I am interested to find out what the object is that you put in the advert, and wondered whether you would be able to help me," said Alison.

"Oh I see," said PI Scrounge with a secretive voice. He actually touched his nose and nodded as though to say, "Are you Secret Service?" which he did say.

"No, I'm just a young lady."

"Yes, I have met young ladies before."

"A student actually."

"A student ay?"

"Look, are you really Cris Pounge?"

PI Scrounge tapped his nose again, "Wouldn't you like to know?"

"You're obviously some sort of scam artist, so I'm going now."

"NO, no, no, here he is now; sorry, I'm his secretary. Er, Mr Scrounge, I mean Pounge, there's a young lady on the phone for you."

"A young lady, oh that is very helpful, my secretary," said PI Scrounge, reverting back to his normal voice, "Here I am, sorry to keep you waiting."

"I saw your advert in the paper and just phoned to ask what the object is and why you put it in the ad."

"Well, what I want to know is why you are so interested."

"Because I might know something about it and you might know something about it and we can share information. So what do you know?"

"Well, who exactly are you and what do YOU know?"

"I'm not willing to say who I am, yet, other than the fact that I'm a university student called Alison. Perhaps we can meet in a public place."

"Okay, where do you want to meet?"

"Where do you live?"

"Oh no, no, no, I'm not giving that kind of information out over the phone."

"Look, I live in Cambridge," said Alison.

"Fine, I'll meet you there, it's time I made a visit to Cambridge again."

"Tomorrow at Zepheroni's?"

"Zepheroni's it is, twelve o'clock for lunch?"

"Okay, how will I recognise you?"

"I'll be wearing a blue hat."

"A blue hat? Right, and I'll be wearing a multi-coloured scarf."

"A multi-coloured scarf? Right, that's a date!"

"Er, no, it's not a date, it's just a meeting."

"Absolutely, and don't tell a soul, this is top secret."

"I won't tell anyone, bye Mr Pounge," said Alison.

"Bye," said PI Scrounge.

Tilly's tearoom patrons were battling with an MP and a Vicar, not the kind of people you want to mess with as they are 'pillars of the community.' The Vicar was called Rev Fred Jenkins from the parish of St Edward in the Derbyshire town of Oneself. He was on holiday on the Spanish island of Tenerife off the north-western coast of Africa, and the largest of the Canary Islands, when he entered Tilly's Tearoom gasping for an iced mango juice.

Oswald Overreach MP was on business in Queensland, Australia, when he entered Tilly's Tearoom having left his family behind in London as always. He was gasping for a nice hot cup of traditional English tea – from India, in Australia.

Neither of these 'pillars of society' were left disappointed, as they sat drinking their respective drinks on their respective tables, beside the tables of their respective regular patrons. The regular giant patron, wearing a dog-collar, struck up a conversation with the Vicar, and the middle-aged man, dressed in a black gown like a courtroom prosecutor, struck up a conversation with the MP. Tilly was umpiring behind the counter while she savagely wiped all of her teacups dry and clean. The elderly lady in the corner was dressed like a beggar, resting her head on her table without any food or drink.

"It's so nice to have such 'pillars of society' in my humble tearoom," Tilly declared, but everyone ignored her, even though they heard her loud and clear.

"In my opinion, the traditional liturgy of the Eucharist should not be changed," said Rev Jenkins. "I hope you will understand I have a lot of experience in these matters, and I am a good friend of Bishop Archibald."

"Yes, I appreciate that," said the giant patron in a Glaswegian accent. He had introduced himself as Rev Avid Fisher, a Minister in the Church of Scotland.

"After all, the beauty of the service is in one's imagination, and the traditional Anglican liturgy is perfect and so expressive."

"But it isn'y just yer imagination though is it?"

"Oh, you are one of those fundamentalist Ministers, are you?"

"Well, isn't the Bible fundamentally true?"

"Well, the fundamental 'truths' as we would call them are contained within the holy scriptures of course, but there is fluidity in how you interpret them."

"How much fluidity?"

"Well of course I would not encourage people to believe that five loaves and two fish would provide a good meal for over five thousand people."

"But aren't yer forgetting," said Rev Fisher, "that Jesus performed miracles, and that is fundamental to what Christians believe?"

"Yes, that's an interesting concept."

"How d'ya live with yerself calling yerself a Vicar when yi dunny even believe in the miracles?"

"It's all a matter of perception."

"So don't yi believe in the virgin birth?"

"Obviously not, but it's a lovely idea."

"Well, I believe in it and so should you!"

"Well, when you become as mature as me, you begin to come to your own rational conclusions. Nobody would believe a young woman like Mary, already engaged to be married, would remain a virgin, would they?"

"Why not?"

"You mean to tell me you take the whole Bible literally, and that a person died and came alive again?"

"Absolutely."

"Well, I admire your naivety."

"I dunny understand how ya can be a Vicar if ya dinny believe anything in the Bible? D'ya even believe in God?"

"Well that is an interesting question, God is what you believe God to be."

"Yer under judgement, right yi are."

"Are you saying I'm a criminal?"

"No, but ya think you've got protection, but ya dinny."

"But as you know, we men of the cloth are under grace, not the sting of the law. Our fate is not governed by the letter of the law."

"Bet yer not under grace are yi, because ya dinny belieeeeve."

"Well, with my breeding …"

"Breeding? Are ya'a dog?"

"My father and my grandfather were all Reverends in the Anglican Church, and they were very influential I might add."

"Ya might add it, but it dinny make na diff'rence. Yer under judgement."

"But according to the church's tradition, I am a mediator between Heaven and Earth."

"Only Jesus is the mediator."

"Well, Jesus was a man like me."

"So now yer sayin' yer just the same as Jesus?"

"Yes, and I will definitely go to Heaven when I pop my clogs."

"But ya dinny belieeeeeeeeve!"

"I am a well-respected member of the Church."

"But ya dinny belieeeeeeeeeeeeeeeeve!"

"But I have great standing in the community!"

"Aye, but ya dinny belieeeeeeeeeeeeeeeeeeeeeeeeve!"

"I think your attitude is very disrespectful and you should be horsewhipped!"

"I'm sorry to tell ya but everything ya say tells me yer under judgement."

"I have never been judged in my life."

"Y'are now," said Rev Fisher looking over at Tilly. "Isn't that right Tilly?" Rev Jenkins glanced over to see Tilly sitting behind the serving counter dressed in a black gown and a white wig, looking at him with judgemental eyes.

"Heavens above!" said Rev Jenkins.

"You're absolutely right, Rev Fisher," said Tilly.

On the other side of the tearoom there was a heated debate going on between Oswald Overreach MP and the courtroom prosecutor.

"It's a matter of perception, going forward," said the MP.

"But surely it's not only about perception, it is about sincerity," said the courtroom prosecutor.

"Your concept of sincerity will not run a country."

"The people of the UK need to be able to trust their MPs."

"That concept of trust that you refer to is nothing more than a false one, moving forward."

"So why are you in the job?"

"The money, the power, the contacts, I'll never lack money and power, going forward."

"You need to make a difference, to fight for justice and equality; you should be a bastion of honourable behaviour."

"Well, that's how people see me, so I can bask in the trust people have in me as I move forwards, going forward."

"So you think it's all about you."

"Of course. There are politicians who would lay down their lives for the people of the UK, but I am not one of them I'm glad to say. The people don't care about the real me and know nothing about the real me, so why should I care about the real them?"

"You're in the wrong job."

"That's where you're wrong. I've made a fortune helping business friends to get through the red tape."

"Your judgement is coming soon."

"On the other hand, this may be your lucky day. We can work together. You scratch my back and I'll scratch yours, going forwards."

Tilly interrupted the proceedings in the tearoom. "Order, order!" she shouted, banging her gabble. And with every bang of the gabble, a metal bar shot across the doors and windows of the tearoom; and there were lots and lots of bars appearing as Tilly enjoyed banging her gabble.

"What's going on?" said the Vicar.

"Open the door immediately!" commanded the MP.

Both 'pillars of society' got up from their respective seats and pulled at the bars that were blocking the doors and windows. They were immovable, so they walked threateningly up to Tilly to give her a stern warning. However, the courtroom prosecutor forced the MP back into his seat and the giant Minister did the same with the Vicar.

"We have gathered here today, to decide the fate of Rev Fred Jenkins and Oswald Overreach MP," said Tilly.

"This is ridiculous!" said the Vicar stamping his foot under the table.

"You are totally out of order!" said the MP with authority, "You will be hearing from my solicitors!"

"I'm afraid your solicitors have no jurisdiction here," said Tilly. "Here it's only Tilly's Law."

"I will go to the British Embassy," said the Vicar.

"Tilly's Tearoom is not governed by your governments and institutions."

"This is all ridiculous, nobody has ever heard of a Tilly's Law!" shouted the MP.

"What game do you think you're playing?" said the Vicar.

"Call the witness!" said Tilly. At that, the poor elderly lady at the table in the corner of the room lifted her head, then stood up wearing rags. She had leprosy. She stumbled into the middle of the room at which the Vicar and the MP leaned back in their chairs hoping she didn't get too close.

The courtroom prosecutor said, "What have you witnessed in the case of the Rev Fred Jenkins?"

The elderly lady could barely speak as she was so frail. "I witnessed Rev Fred Jenkins promise to collect money to send to my people to heal the sick."

"And did he do as he promised?"

"Yes."

Happy with that statement, the Vicar said, "You see, I keep my word."

The elderly lady continued. "But after he had collected the money ..."

"And how much money was that?"

"Twenty thousand pounds."

"Go on."

"He took half of the money for himself and only sent ten thousand pounds."

"And what was the result?"

"The lack of money caused the early deaths of twenty members of my community, and a lack of medicine for the future."

"Absolutely rubbish!" said the Vicar.

"Oh shut up you fool!" said the MP to the Vicar. "If we want to get out of this, we need to work together and make a deal."

The prosecutor continued, "And can the witness share what she knows about Oswald Overreach MP?"

"Yes, he used his position to approve a housing project that destroyed my auntie's community, and by using a legal loophole he helped his business associates to avoid paying reasonable compensation. As a consequence, people are in poverty, but Oswald Overreach MP, that man sitting over there," she said pointing at him, "was given a higher government position as a consequence of his corrupt activities."

"Now wait a minute, it was all legal," insisted the MP.

"Maybe," said Tilly, "but I suppose it's all a matter of perception!"

"Huh!" said the MP.

"I hereby sentence you ..."

"WAIT!" shouted the MP. "Look, we don't have to do anything foolish here, let's make a deal."

"Are you mad?" snapped the Vicar. "It's your shady dealings that have got us into this mess!"

"What about your shady activities? You're a man of the cloth; you should be defrocked!"

The Vicar tried to find a way to calm the atmosphere. "What I think the honourable MP is trying to say is, 'Is there anything we can do to make your life more comfortable, or perhaps we can put in a word for you; we are not without influence!'"

"Riches I heed not, nor man's empty praise," said Tilly the judge in response.

At that moment, the elderly lady began to gasp for air. She then collapsed on the floor.

"I need to pronounce judgement or she will die of grief," said Tilly with urgency in her voice.

"She's just acting!" said the MP.

"Yes, she should be punished for perjury," said the Vicar.

"Sentencing needs to take place urgently, or she'll die."

"Don't be ridiculous!" said the Vicar firmly, "This is some kind of entrapment!"

"Just tell us what we can do to make things better for the poor lady," said the MP.

"Confess!"

"Absolutely not!" said the Vicar, "Do you think we're fools?"

"We have indeed found ourselves in an elephant trap, moving forward," added the MP.

It was not normal for Rev Fred Jenkins or Oswald Overreach MP to be bewildered as they always had a plan or a solution up their sleeves, but this was another kettle of fish. And just when they thought all hope was lost, the judge changed her tone.

"Look, I'll do a deal with you," said Tilly.

The MP and the Vicar breathed a sigh of relief. "Now, that's more sensible," said the Vicar.

But the elderly lady gasped even louder for breath, choking and wheezing.

"And can somebody please shut this old lady up!" shouted the MP.

"Let's not get too excited," suggested the Vicar to the MP. "So what is the deal you are suggesting?" asked the Vicar.

"I will give you a choice, since all of this is just a matter of perception."

"Good, good, now things are becoming more clear. What is the choice?" asked the Vicar, with a little hope.

"You can decide for yourselves whether you are both going to continue to be criminals from now on, moving forwards, or whether you are both going to be 'pillars of the community.'"

The Vicar and the MP looked at each other with incredulity on their faces. "Well, pillars of the community, of course," said the MP.

"Yes, I will certainly be a pillar of the community from now on," said the Vicar.

"In that case," said Tilly, "you are free to leave your seats, going forward." Tilly banged her gabble again and again and again until every metal bar had disappeared from every window and door of the tearoom.

The Vicar and the MP both got up from their seats and slowly made their way towards the door. They muttered to one another disapprovingly, turned round to glower at Tilly, and then suddenly froze on the spot – they had turned into two pillars of salt!

"Well, not too much left to clean up, that makes a change," said Tilly now her work was done. "Salt is such a good purifier, isn't it?" she said, but the regular tearoom patrons did not answer as their job had finished too.

However, the imp came into the tearoom: "Do you want me to call the Sweepers?"

"No, Removals please."

"Okay," he said and set things in motion.

Alison had arrived early at Zepheroni's, so she could do some university reading while she waited for Cris Pounge. She had her precious metallic object in her bag, and felt reasonably reassured about her safety as there were plenty of people surrounding her table in the restaurant. She did feel a little conspicuous though as she was sweating profusely under her multi-coloured scarf.

In walked a scruffy man with a blue hat and Alison's heart sank at the sight of him. As soon as the man in the blue hat spied her, she took her scarf off to cool down and set it down on the table, wondering how she was going to deal with this dishevelled stranger. PI Scrounge sat down in the chair opposite her.

"Mr Pounge?"

"No, it's not Mr Pounge, it's Private Investigator Philip Scrounge. Call me Phil."

"Oh, why the false name?"

"Because this object is of top importance to national security, and I don't want government agents to trace me."

Discerning his manner as boyish drama, she got straight to the point, "Okay, Phil, tell me what you know and I'll tell you what I know."

"First of all, how do I know you're not a spy or a journalist?"

"Because I have this," she said, pulling out her metallic object.

Scrounge's eyes widened. "Can I hold it?" Alison looked around cautiously before placing it into his hands. "It looks almost identical to mine," he said.

"So you've actually brought one of your own too? Can I see yours?" Scrounge handed Alison's object back to her and pulled out his own. They held the objects close to each other and compared them. "Is yours heavy too?"

"Yes," said Scrounge. "Do you think they slot together somehow?"

They tried to put them together, and they seemed to sort of connect in a loose manner, but not well enough to confirm they were supposed to do so.

"Perhaps we need a third or a fourth object to piece them together properly," said Alison.

"So we need to keep advertising."

"I can advertise in my university."

"Good, but it needs to be countrywide, or even international."

"Don't you think we should hand them in to the authorities?"

"Hand them in? You're kidding! How are we going to get rich if we do that?"

"Get rich? So this is all about money to you, then?"

"Well, yes and no, but I am talking big money."

"How did you get yours?"

"I'm not at liberty to divulge that information."

"Well I'll tell you how I got mine." Scrounge put on his PI ears. "It was in a forest and there was a weird group of people having a picnic, and then I think they drugged me and I saw a big monster."

"That doesn't sound anything like my experience," said Scrounge.

"And a hare started to strangle Alice."

"Who's Alice?"

"Oh, just an old lady on the table cloth."

"Right."

"Well, to cut a long story short, when I went back to get my scarf, I found my object inside it."

"Thank you for that, that actually helps."

"Really? I thought I would sound like I was speaking nonsense."

"Nonsense doesn't begin to describe it."

"Thank you."

"Hm, well, all I can tell you is that for me there was a café called Tilly's Tearoom, and some people hurt someone in the café, or rather they didn't, it was something else that hurt her … she's dead, and she died where I found this object, but not where she was found."

"I can see that you are a little hesitant in sharing the details."

"That's all I can say, sorry."

"Well no one died where I had my experience, although, at the same time as these weird things were happening, my personal tutor was murdered. I'm not afraid to tell you because I have plenty of alibis."

"So there is a link, somebody died in each case, and on both occasions there was a strange object to be found, so what on earth are these things?"

"And where do we go from here?" asked Alison.

"Before we do anything, we need more information."

"I'll do some research at uni, we have a world famous library and very knowledgeable librarians. Do you really think the secret service will be interested?"

"Well, yes, because what happened to me was very weird and completely unexplainable. It's just that …"

"If you're willing to say more, do go on."

"Well, you know the café that I mentioned?"

"Tilly's Tearoom?"

"Yes, it disappeared."

"Did someone knock it down?"

"No, it just disappeared."

"What, literally disappeared in front of your eyes?"

"No. It literally disappeared, but not in front of my eyes as such."

"So, how exactly did it disappear?"

"That's the mystery. Nobody in the area had ever seen Tilly's Tearoom before or after the things I witnessed, and it took me a while to convince myself that I wasn't being delusional. But when I found out that the body of the person I saw dead had been discovered not too far from the event, I went back to investigate the location of Tilly's Tearoom, and it was just a field. And there's no imprint, no rubble, no dust, just a perfect, untouched field, and that was where I found my strange object."

"Right, this is all bizarre."

"Putting it mildly."

"You should clearly advertise again. I'll do my research, and we'll meet again in a week, what do you think?"

"Agreed, but you must not tell anybody, not even your mother or your boyfriend."

"I've not told anybody; you are the only person on earth I have mentioned this to; and nobody except you and I have seen my object. I wish I knew what it's called and what its purpose is."

"That's what we are going to find out as a team; shall we shake on it?" They shook hands. "Right, what are you having for lunch?" asked Phil.

"I'm afraid I have to go."

"Oh?"

"I'm going straight to the library to do some research."

"Aren't you going to eat anything at all?"

"No, I often skip lunch anyway; nice to meet you Phil."

"Nice to meet you too, keep in touch."

"I will, I promise."

Alison picked up her scarf and belongings and left.

DAILY TITBITS
by
Justin Caadfar Esquire

We've heard it said many times, 'Never talk about politics or religion!' implying that the conversation will always break up friendships or cause discord. Well, please forgive me, but this reliable titbit is connected with both, and it has already gone viral:

'People are very curious to know how a pillar of salt has suddenly appeared in their respective communities, one at City Hall in Brisbane, Australia, and another at the Catholic Church of the Holy

Spirit on the island of Tenerife. Scientists have cut away samples for study, and all they can find is table salt.'

Bon Appetit!

Chapter 14
Rosie Warm-Cheeks

Isn't life topsy turvy? Tilly had a very strange job, stable yet wobbly, in fact as wobbly as a supernova sometimes! In her quaint little tearoom, she appeared to have some normality, a purpose in life, but in fact her purpose belonged not to her nor to her colleagues in the tearoom, but instead to another. Don't get me wrong, that doesn't mean she wasn't a content being; her life was very colourful, she just couldn't feel it like we do, and when she was left to her own devices, everything could become a bit contrary, like the Nursery Rhyme: Dumpty Humpty, or the lullaby: Linkle Stinkle Twittle Twar. Although joyful emotions for Tilly were learnt rather than felt, the same applied to sadness and fear – all learnt, not felt. Did that make Tilly sad? Or happy? Or neither? The answer is undoubtedly neither, as we understand it, or both, as we don't understand them; but the confusion in our minds about Tilly lies in the fact that we don't know what or who Tilly actually was or is and what state of being she exists in: While she is filling bottles of water she might be billing fottles of twear; while fighting crime, you might find her crighting fime. Perhaps a more clear example is what you may witness when Tilly comes across people smuggling drugs - she will respond to this by druggling smugs. It is difficult to find a good illustration that could appeal more to the human mind, but I have an example of an event from Tilly's experience that may help, and that is in the case of a woman in her thirties called Rosie.

One day, Tilly was drying cups and saucers with her tea towel, driping them wy, expecting a powd of creople. Her expression was that of a member of paff under stressure, but she weedn't have norried as only one person would be coming through the door, a woman in her thirties called Rosie. But when she appeared, although Tilly knew her name (sort of), she instead - being Tilly - thought of her as being ralled Cosie (this is not normal thinking perhaps, but this is the way Tilly thinks on some occasions). In spite of this, as soon as the woman entered, Tilly tried her utmost to compromise somewhere between the two by addressing her as follows: "Lovely to see you Cosy Rosie!"

"I beg your pardon?" she responded.

"I believe your name is Rosie, is it not?"

"It is, but how did you know that?"

"I apologise if I appear rude. I heard that that was your name and I didn't consider the implications of using your name while welcoming you into my tearoom."

"It's okay, I just wondered who it was that was talking about me and why they would call me Cosy Rosie."

"Oh, I used the word 'Cosy' as I didn't know for certain whether what I heard was your surname or a description of part of your anatomy."

That statement baffled Rosie even though she wasn't the unintelligent type (or even the academic type for that matter). "I don't understand what you mean."

"Never mind, begging your pardon, what I am trying to express is that someone added your name – verbally - to two other words, but I don't know whether those two other words are part of your name or a description of you." The elderly lady in the tearoom gave Tilly a congratulatory smile.

"I see, do you mean you don't know for certain whether my name is Rosie Warm-Cheeks or not?"

"That's correct, are you called Rosie Warm-Cheeks? Or Rosie-Warm Cheeks? Or do you simply have rosy-warm cheeks, and your name is simply Rosie? Or is one the product of another? And if so, which way round, if I might ask?"

"I'm not really sure whether it is any of your business, but my name is actually Rosie Warm-Cheeks."

Not wanting to risk offending the woman, Tilly gambled with: "I understand now, thank you for clearing that up for me, Miss Cheeks."

"It's not Miss, it's Mrs, and it's not Mrs Cheeks, it's Mrs Warm-Cheeks."

"I'm terribly sorry, I'm not used to double-barrelled surnames."

"Oh."

"I'm only used to double-barrelled shotguns."

"I see."

Realising that might not sound quite right to a … well a … person, Tilly added, "Not that I use one, as a rule – only if a situation requires it, of course."

"Well, I'm glad we cleared that one up," said Rosie sarcastically.

Tilly felt something was a bit out of joint in that last statement of Rosie's, so she mulled it over to try and grasp the meaning enough to respond appropriately. This unnerved Rosie as it just looked like Tilly was staring through her; it gave her quite a chill. Anyway, Rosie sat down at a table and propped her handbag beside her on top of it and waited for Tilly to snap out of her stupor.

"Well, I'll bring you the menu."

"Thank you, but there's no need, I'll just have a cup of tea please."

"Cup of tea coming up!" exclaimed Tilly in a very friendly manner. "It's not every day we get such a nice person in our humble tearoom."

"Oh, why's that?"

"Would you like a piece of tiffin … oh … no … that wouldn't be right, er … would you like a coasted tea take?"

"A toasted teacake?"

"That's a better idea, thank you, I think I will," said Tilly. Rosie was struggling to get her head round what was going on with the woman - it was like Tilly was a robot or an AI creation that needed a good service.

Rosie took her phone from her bag and began to check her face, especially her lipstick. She had a very important meeting to go to and needed to look her best.

"You look very nice my dear," said the elderly lady sat at the next table brandishing a sickly smile.

"I agree with that," said the middle-aged man at another table with a sicker smile and hopping eyebrows.

"Here, Here!" exclaimed the giant man at another.

Rosie was just considering how to object to all of this personal attention, but she was distracted by Tilly who arrived with her tea and toasted teacake. "Thank you," said Rosie.

"That's my absolute pleasure, my dear," said Tilly who lingered a little to admire Rosie.

"Could I ask, who told you about me?"

"Now then …" Tilly paused as different possible replies milled around inside her. "That's difficult to explain, but I can give you some advice," she said.

"I'm all ears," said Rosie. That confused Tilly as she didn't agree with Mrs Warm-Cheeks. Her rosy cheeks did stand out a lot, but her ears didn't, and to say she was ALL ears was just untrue. Anyway, Tilly was aware that Rosie was a nice person, so she assumed she must have misheard.

"Where was I?"

"You were going to give me some advice."

"Oh yes," said Tilly, "my advice to you is to enjoy being single today."

"Excuse me?"

"There I go again, I must come across to you like a right old busybody."

"Well, you do actually."

"Oh dear, how shall I say this, sometimes things just don't work out the way they're planned."

"Have you been poking into my affairs?"

"No, no, nobody would accuse you of that!"

"I'm accusing you, not the other way round!"

"Ooo, absolutely not! As I was saying, things may not go quite as you expect when you leave here."

"And how would you know anything about what is going to happen to me when I leave this place?"

"Well, you know, don't you?"

"I don't have the foggiest idea what you're talking about. Ever since I stepped into this café …"

"TEAROOM!" snapped Tilly angrily, before immediately returning to her sickly smile.

"Sorry … TEAROOM … Ever since I stepped into this tearoom, you've been saying, quite frankly, crazy things to me, and it's freaking me out a bit; you seem to know things about me and I'm just wondering how you know these things. I want to know right now who has been talking to you about me!"

Just then a huge storm hit the tearoom, shaking the whole place. Everyone in the tearoom clung onto a table looking frightened. "Where did that come from?" said Rosie looking out of the tearoom windows onto which she could see the rain and hail pounding deafeningly. The door rattled so much it nearly fell off.

"Ooo, you can't go out in this darling," said the elderly lady.

"That's right, just rest here until it dies down," added Tilly.

"It feels like the whole place is going to fall down!" exclaimed Rosie.

"It'll pass, just rest here for an hour or so. Here, give me your cup and I'll fill it up for you."

"I have to go, I'm meeting someone."

"Ooo, I wouldn't recommend that," said the elderly lady.

"I'd better give him a ring."

"Ooo, you can't do that!" said the middle-aged man.

"What do you mean I can't do that, I can do whatever I like and you can't stop me!"

"What he means is," said the giant, "your phone isn't working."

"How on earth would you know that?"

"Absolutely darling, you ignore them, of course you can try before you find out for yourself," said Tilly, proud of herself for thinking of a way to express some kind of acknowledgement of a person's need to learn things for themselves.

Rosie tried to ring her date but there was no signal. "Oh no, it's not working. I suppose he'll understand because of the storm."

Another 20 minutes passed during which time Rosie had tried to phone another 20 times.

"Sometimes you need a storm to avoid a storm, don't you love?" said Tilly.

"Are you saying I'm in some kind of danger?"

At that, all of the tearoom patrons stood and clapped their hands. "Well done, my dear," said Tilly, "you are truly a lovely person."

At that moment, the storm suddenly stopped and the sun shone through the tearoom windows. "Wow, that stopped quickly!" said Rosie.

"The storm's over now, everything's safe," said Tilly.

"So you're saying I'm safe to leave the tearoom now? There isn't any more danger?" The tearoom patrons just stared at her with a sickly, adoring smile. "What? No more advice?" Rosie asked Tilly.

"It's definitely safe and I don't have any more advice," said Tilly, plainly.

"Right, that was very clear and precise for a change. I suppose I should be able to send a text now."

"You can't!" said the giant.

"And why can't I?" asked Rosie, a little sarcastically.

"It won't work until you leave the tearoom."

They were right, her phone still didn't work. "Well, I'll be going, how much do I owe you?"

"Oh, it's all on the house my dear, you've had a stormy time. I just hope we made you feel comfortable."

"Oh yes, thank you," she replied, again with a little sarcasm. At that, Tilly, the giant, the middle-aged man and the elderly lady continued to stare at her with a cute, adoring smile.

"You're a lovely woman," said Tilly as Rosie picked up her handbag and opened the tearoom door. "Goodbye."

Rosie turned round to see them all stood, staring at her with those sickly smiles. "Goodbye."

As Rosie walked away from the tearoom, her legs felt like jelly. She was suffering from shock, but that would pale into insignificance in the next 15 minutes. She had arranged to meet her date at a different café, the same place where she had met him the previous week. This time they were going to go for a drive into the countryside for a picnic after a cup of coffee. She was surprised that the ground wasn't wet or shrouded in hail as she walked, but she was more concerned about Lincoln thinking she had changed her mind, but she hadn't. She was actually hoping he might turn out to be her Mr Right. Last time they met she felt so secure - he was so nice, so gentlemanly, and financially secure! She managed to send a text as she walked, but he didn't pick up whenever she tried to call.

Entering the café where she had arranged to meet Lincoln, she quickly glanced around the tables, but he was nowhere to be seen. Finally, she asked one of the assistants at the counter: "Excuse me, you didn't see a tall, dark haired man wearing a blue jacket in the cafe half an hour ago did you?"

"Was his name Lincoln someone or other?"

"Yes, do you know him?"

"I do now, he was just arrested by three policemen fifteen, twenty minutes ago."

"You're not serious!"

"Yes, he was arrested for murder."

"Murder?"

"Yes, if you know him, you should probably go down to the police station, they might want to speak to you."

"Who did they say he'd murdered?"

"Don't know, but I wondered if it was something to do with those two women that have gone missing from round here over the last couple of months."

"I can't believe it."

"Looks like you might have had a lucky escape."

"You're right, I think I just have," said Rosie. "Thank you."

"No problem."

Rosie was stunned. She mulled it over in her head: 'The people in Tilly's Tearoom must have known all about this somehow, and where did that storm come from? And where's all the hail and rainwater?' Rosie retraced her steps to remind herself where the tearoom was and considered informing the police about it in case the woman who served her there was needed to give some sort of evidence.

She arrived to where she remembered the tearoom being; it wasn't there! She even asked four separate passers-by, three of whom were local, and none of them had ever heard of or seen a Tilly's Tearoom.

Chapter 15
Not a Penny, Nor a Kiss

Arnold was climbing Scafell with his new friend Nora from the rambling club in the Cumbrian Lake District. They were both retired, and found fresh air and lengthy walks were ideal for keeping themselves healthy. Neither of them minded the rain and they were well kitted out anyway with their anoraks, hiking boots and rambling sticks. So they were ready for any English eventuality, barring a heart attack or something of that nature, although they were a bit short on water.

"It's so good to get to climb the highest mountain in England once again; the last time was, oh, well over thirty years ago," said Arnold.

"Where were you living then?"

"Penrith, I worked for Hikes and Spikes, a rambler's outfitters in the town. I was promoted to retail manager quite quickly."

"So you owe your fortune to Penrith?"

"I suppose you could say that, yes."

"Actually, my daughter worked there for a couple of weeks around that time, Tina, Tina Fletcher."

"Don't recognise the name, but it's a long time ago."

"Well, I'm a born and bred Windermere lass, and was doing admin for my dad's sheep farm while you were living in Penrith."

"I'm surprised we never met."

"Me too; we might have done without knowing it?"

"Possibly. So, you're a true lady of the fells."

"You could say that; I never wanted to leave the Lake District."

"So didn't you ever live anywhere else besides Cumbria. Did you go to university for instance?"

"No, this is my home, all my family and friends are here."

"Well, I admire your loyalty."

"I'm not very adventurous," said Nora coyly.

"You should be allowed to be whatever you want to be, go wherever you want to go and stay wherever you want to stay; not everyone has itchy feet like me."

"So you've travelled around a lot then?"

"No, I just get really itchy feet; I have to scratch them all the time."

"Haha."

"I haven't travelled around that much outside of England. I'm not one for hot climates."

"Me neither, give me rain any day."

"Me too," said Arnold, almost being blown off his feet.

"The wind's picking up, isn't it?"

"Yes." Arnold looked at his watch, "It's getting a bit late in the afternoon, but I really want to make it to the Pike; how high is it again? Nine hundred and …"

"Nine hundred and seventy-eight metres above sea level. That's three thousand, two-hundred and nine feet."

"You really know your mountains!"

"And as you probably already know, from Scafell Pike, on a clear day, you can see Snowdonia in Wales and even the Mourne Mountains in Northern Ireland."

"No such luck today."

"No, unfortunately. But you can see the highest positioned water in England!"

"I know that one already – Broad Crag Tarn."

"Yep, so if we get thirsty …"

"Haha."

The mist on the fell became very thick and they could barely see anything beyond a few metres around them.

Nora said, "You're actually walking on a war memorial, did you know that?"

"No, I did not know that."

"It was given to the National Trust to remember those who served and died in World War I."

"So in essence," said Arnold, "we are walking atop an immense structure belonging to the dead."

"Yes, dead heroes."

Then, through the mist, Arnold noticed a small object roll down towards him. "That's strange," he said, picking it up.

"What is it?"

"It's a bolt!"

"What's a bolt doing up here?"

"And what made it roll towards me? Someone up ahead must have thrown it, not knowing there were other people around," suggested Arnold.

"Or it fell from the sky."

"What, like a bolt out of the blue, you mean?"

"Haha. Actually, you hear of fish and frogs raining from the sky sometimes."

"Very true." Arnold became more serious, "This mist is a bit worrying."

"It is getting a bit intense, isn't it?"

"I was thinking we should head back, actually, otherwise we're going to lose our way."

"I agree."

"And I'm out of water and Kendal Mint Cake."

"Well, if you're out of Kendal Mint cake, it's curtains for both of us."

"Absolutely."

"What's that?" said Nora suddenly.

"What?"

Nora pointed her stick ahead of them, "That light."

"Probably a torch from whoever threw the bolt at me."

"No, it doesn't look like a torch, let's get a closer look."

"Could be aliens!"

"We could be in for a close encounter."

"We could." After taking a few more steps, "You've got to be joking!" exclaimed Arnold.

"No way!" exclaimed Nora.

"Impossible!" added Arnold.

"It can't be real!" added Nora. "A tearoom ... at the top of Scafell!"

"Well it can't be a mirage, since we can both see it. I know, let's spell it out in turn, a letter at a time, and if it makes sense we know we are seeing the same thing."

"Sounds daft but here goes, T," said Nora.

"I."

"L."

"L."

"Y."

"Apostrophe."

"S."

"TILLY'S TEAROOM," they said together.

"Well I'm up for a hot cup of tea, and a toilet," said Nora.

"Are you sure, it all seems a bit strange to me," said Arnold.

"Go on, I'll owe you."

Arnold smiled, "Not a penny, nor a kiss."

"That's a strange saying."

"I always used to say it after I did people favours. They used to say, 'How much is that?,' or 'What do I owe you?' or 'I'll pay you back,' and things like that, but I used to say, 'Not a penny, nor a kiss,' to show they didn't owe me anything."

"It sounds like you did a lot of favours for people."

"I did, in those days."

"Such a kind person!"

"I can be sometimes," agreed Arnold. "So I'll buy and you don't have to owe me anything. Like I said before, you can go wherever you want or stay wherever you want. And I will gladly go to Tilly's Tearoom with you if that's what you want me to do."

"Rather a long winded way of saying yes, but I appreciate it. Thank you!"

They entered the tearoom and were astonished to see a fully functioning café on top of Scafell. There were a handful of ramblers already sat at the tables drinking hot drinks. And Arnold and Nora were surprised to see a lady much older than themselves.

"That lady is a hero, walking all the way up here!" said Nora. The lady gave them a toothless smile.

They couldn't see the entire tearoom clearly, even though it was quite small, as there was a curtain stretched from the ceiling down to the floor surrounding something in the middle, perhaps a disused fireplace.

Before Tilly came to serve them, they settled down at a table beside a couple of ramblers that they did not recognise. Arnold wondered if they were the ones who had thrown a bolt at him. And while he was thinking about it, another bolt bounced off his foot. He picked it up. "I can't believe it!"

"Another bolt out of the blue?" asked Nora.

"It could have been one of these men here, the ones sat next to us, messing about!" whispered Arnold.

"Why would they do that? Perhaps it fell from the ceiling."

Then one of the men who was sat beside them looked over. "I bet you were as surprised as us to find a tearoom at the top of Scafell."

"Yes we were," said Nora.

"Very odd," added Arnold.

Nora continued, "I live here and I have never heard of anything like it."

"Life is full of surprises. Frank's the name."

"And I'm John," said the other.

"Nora," said Nora.

"Arnold," said Arnold.

Frank asked, "Are you husband and wife?"

"Oh no, just friends," said Nora.

"Not yet anyway, haha," said Arnold.

Nora felt awkward at that.

John was shocked to see some blistering on Nora's hand and commented on it. "What did you do to your hand? That looks nasty!"

"Oh, that dreaded giant hogweed! It's everywhere!"

Frank nodded sincerely. "Nasty, isn't it."

"Anyway, that's my cue for the loo, I think," said Nora.

Everyone chuckled.

"You know," Frank continued, "Once, my wife and I were out walking in the countryside for hours, and she was absolutely desperate for the toilet."

There was a longer than expected pause.

Arnold and Nora tried to show sympathy in their faces, but they were expecting a punchline to be honest. To their relief, Frank eventually added a few words:

"We had to dig a hole in the end."

"That's one way of doing it, I suppose," said Arnold.

Then Frank pushed his face into Arnold's, looking deadly serious, saying, "And even though we dug and dug, we still couldn't find a toilet down there!"

Arnold and Nora weren't sure whether to laugh, show sympathy, call the mental hospital, or run.

"Well, I must go and find that toilet," said Nora, making her escape.

As Nora started to leave the table, the little creepy imp came into the tearoom from the back with a mop and bucket, and Tilly stared angrily at him. "What are you doing with that mop?"

"Somebody said a hog weed everywhere."

"Don't be so stupid! Now show this lady where the toilet is."

"Thank you," said Nora.

Arnold was beginning to feel a little uncomfortable in the presence of Frank and John, even though they were back to chatting to each other at their own table. He ordered tea for two from the counter and sat back down while he waited for his companion to return. It wasn't long before Tilly arrived with a tea pot and two cups and saucers.

"Here's your tea, my darling."

"Thank you, that's kind of you to bring it over," said Arnold.

"Not a penny nor a kiss," she added.

"What?"

"Enjoy your drink." Tilly walked away and Arnold was pleased to see that the two ramblers were ignoring his presence and having an intense discussion between themselves. He poured himself a tea and was about to drink it when he thought he saw something fall into his cup. Deciding he had imagined it, he took a slurp, and as he did so, he felt another object hit the side of his face and bounce onto the floor. It was a penny.

"Flying pennies and flying bolts, what on earth is going on?" Arnold asked himself. He took another slurp, and as he did so, five or six objects landed on his table, all pennies and bolts. They couldn't have come from the café patrons as he noticed just then that the elderly lady and the two ramblers beside him were no longer in the tearoom. The objects must have come from the centre of the tearoom where there was a mysterious curtain stretching from the ceiling to the floor.

While he was puzzling over this, everything suddenly went dark, but he could still make out that the curtain in the centre of the café was slowly opening. The curtain only opened halfway, leaving a semi-circle at the back, and then a beam of light flashed on and shone from above the central part of the tearoom, revealing what must have been hidden behind the curtain all this time. It was a woman who looked in her thirties sitting on a chair, staring at him. This was strange for several reasons: One was the fact that she had probably been sat behind the curtain all the time he was there; another was the fact that the woman and the chair looked a bit like a hologram - that was the only way he could describe it to himself, although he considered it may have had something to do with the type lighting that was shining down on her - and another was the fact that she had been throwing pennies and bolts at him while he was sat having his tea!

"Who are you and why are you throwing things at me?"

"Don't you recognise me?" said the woman in the chair under the beam of light.

"No I do not, I have absolutely no idea who you are."

"I am Pat Fletcher."

"Never heard of you."

"You knew my mother."

"And her name was?"

"Tina Fetcher."

"Well, the only Tina Fletcher I knew used to work for me in Penrith, she was seventeen at the time, if I remember rightly."

"You remember rightly."

"So you're her daughter?"

"That's right."

"Well, it's nice to meet you."

"Are you sure?"

"Look, what is it you want from me?"

"Do you remember when you caught my mother stealing a pair of shoes?"

"Yes, but it doesn't matter, I dealt with it; it's all in the past now."

"Yes, you let her off, didn't you?"

"I did, that's what I like to do."

"She told you she was grateful that you had given her a second chance, and she asked how she could repay you."

"She did."

"And you said …"

"Oh," smiling proudly, "Not a penny, nor a kiss."

"Yes, but it was a lie, wasn't it?"

"What do you mean?"

"You took your payment by raping her."

"Don't be ridiculous!"

"And then you paid her money to keep her quiet and forced her to have an abortion, even though she wanted to keep the baby."

"I helped her out, yes."

"You threatened to report her as a thief and tell her parents if she didn't get rid of her child."

"Absolutely not!"

"She begged you to just leave her alone and she promised she would not expect anything from you, but you wouldn't listen."

"Well, I had to think of my own future, what if she changed her mind later on?"

"You blackmailed her into having an abortion!!"

"Which I paid for!"

"After her abortion, she was no longer able to have children."

"That's a terrible shame, but I don't see how I can be held responsible for that."

"When she found out she could never have her own children, she gave her aborted child a name, and grieved over the fact that she would never hold her baby, the baby that she wanted to keep."

"That is very sad."

"She called her baby Pat."

"So, you are ….?"

"HOW COULD YOU!" screamed Nora, coming from the back of the tearoom towards Arnold. "I heard it all! You raped my daughter and killed my only grandchild!"

"This is all just a show, a performance, you don't believe what this hologram is saying do you?"

Nora looked intently at Pat Fletcher, her granddaughter, and knelt down in awe. "Pat, my dearest granddaughter, thank you for telling me what happened to Tina. Now it all makes sense. I never knew she'd been pregnant until well after her abortion. And she told me later that she found out she could never have her own children. She kept all of this from me for so long. That makes me a lousy mother AND grandmother."

"I don't blame you," said Pat pointing at Arnold, "I blame him - my father."

Arnold objected. "Now I see, I can see right through both of you! This is a trap!" Looking at Nora, "You knew who I was before you came up the mountain with me, didn't you?"

"I had no idea about any of this until now." Turning to Pat, "My dear, dear granddaughter, I am thrilled to meet you. We would have been so happy together, you and I."

Arnold shouting out loud, "I can see through you all, this tearoom too, it's all an elaborate plot! The two impolite ramblers, the toothless woman, the hologram, you're all in it together!"

"No, but we can see through you!" said Tilly.

"No you can't, nobody can see what my life is like, the challenges, the problems I have to face."

Nora jumped up and scratched at Arnold's face. "You raped my daughter and made it impossible for her to have children, you evil beast!"

"I think what we need to do is prove to Arnold that we can see through him," said Tilly.

"That's fair," said the creepy imp. "Shall I call the Sweepers?"

"Yes, better call the Sweepers," said Tilly.

At that point, two hooded people entered the tearoom from the back and took Arnold out through the back door by force. Nora just remained knelt beside Pat.

Arnold shouted objections as he went, insisting that they should let him go, but the two strong Sweepers ignored him. Another hooded figure was waiting for them in the back room. She was stood next to a large machine which looked a bit like a metal guillotine, but chunkier. The female Sweeper's hand was hovering over a big red button.

Arnold was dragged towards the machine where they set him down on his back on a metal platform close to the floor, one Sweeper holding him by his arms and the other by his legs. He couldn't wriggle off the platform as there was a rim around the edge.

"What are you doing? Let me go!" Arnold protested.

"But we have to make sure we can see through you," said the creepy imp-man.

"You are making a big mistake!"

"Well we will know soon."

Arnold sobbed, "No, no, no, you can't do this, it's against the law!"

"PRESS!" commanded the little creepy man, so the Sweeper pressed the button and a circular plunger, almost 1 foot in diameter, stamped Arnold through his middle. His protests stopped, and the two Sweepers who had restrained him pulled him up by the arms and dangled him in front of the creepy man.

Tilly shouted to the imp from the tearoom, "Can you see through him clearly enough?"

Looking through the hole in the middle of Arnold's body, the imp reassured Tilly, "Yes, I can see RIGHT through him."

"Goody gumdrops!" shouted Tilly.

Back in the tearoom, Nora had been spending quality time with her granddaughter, finding out what their lives would have been like together had Pat been born alive. It was extremely painful yet immensely healing at the same time.

Nora was eventually so overcome with emotion that she buried her head in her hands as she knelt curled in a ball on the floor, sobbing. When she lifted her head, she found that she was alone on Scafell, and the only thing that was unusual was a metallic object, the size of her hand, on her knee. She studied it curiously and put it in her pocket.

As the mist began to clear, a group of ramblers appeared and asked her if she needed help. The walkers could not follow what she was saying as she rambled on about her experiences in Tilly's Tearoom. The Good Samaritans put it down to delirium due to the altitude and dehydration. They had plenty of water and medical equipment, so they escorted her back down the fell; when she arrived at the car park, she was behaving normally, so they said their goodbyes.

Nora noticed that Arnold's car wasn't in the car park anymore, so she assumed he had managed to descend the fell before her and left with his tail between his legs. She got into her own car and headed home.

Meanwhile, to cut a long story short, Rees and Shauna (aka Hansel and Gretel) teamed up with Alison and PI Scrounge. This gave Alison some reassurance that she was not going to be led up a weird and perilous garden path of conspiracy theories; there was safety in numbers! Hansel and Gretel also had one of the mysterious objects, and they all compared them during a meeting on Sheep's Green off the Fen Causeway, away from the hubbub of Cambridge City. During the meeting they tried to physically connect the objects, but without success. They decided they would need a lot more of the objects – a lot more pieces of the jigsaw puzzle, if you like – to stand any chance of checking the theory that they were all fragments of a larger metallic object.

The twins called their object their 'Firestone,' although they did not give too much information away as to what had happened to them. That seemed to be another common factor between them all, they were all cagey about what had happened to them as it may implicate them in a murder, except in Alison's case it was more because her recollections made her sound like a Mad Hatter herself. However, Rees and Shauna did admit that there had been a death, and instead of a café disappearing, a whole village had disappeared!

"It's all a bit confusing, frightening and exciting at the same time," said Shauna.

"I know what you mean," said Alison.

"Well, my experience was outright disturbing," said Phil Scrounge. "I'm not excited about the event at all; my interest is simply in the identity and function of these strange objects. We need to know more about them before we can get any benefit from it all."

"And how much money are you hoping to get out of it?" asked Alison, cockily.

Rees changed the subject: "I found it interesting to hear that the café you saw was called Tilly's Tearoom, Phil. We didn't see the name Tilly's Tearoom, but we were served tea called Tilly's Tea in the visitors' centre."

"And we'd never heard of Tilly's Tea before that or even since," said Shauna.

"Me neither," said Alison and Phil.

Alison tried to liven up the meeting, "Hey, I think we should try to think of a way we can make the firestones come to life. After all, we know there's a mysterious connection between these stones in connection with the appearing and disappearing of buildings and villages, and things like that."

"What do you suggest?" asked Shauna.

"Well why don't we try holding the objects in the air and shouting, 'Come back Tilly!'"

Shauna smiled, "It's worth a try."

Rees agreed. "Sounds fun!"

"Go ahead!" said Phil, handing Rees his firestone.

"It feels like we're the Three Musketeers," laughed Alison.

Rees, Shauna and Alison stood facing each other and, holding their respective metallic objects in their right hand, they all lifted them and called out in unison, "COME BACK TILLY!"

Nothing happened.

They then decided to spin round three times saying, 'Tilly's Tea' each time, hoping something might happen, but it didn't. Then they did the same again saying, 'Tilly's Tearoom' three times, but again nothing happened.

By this time, they had quite an audience, but the Three Musketeers just giggled.

Phil was worried, however, as he did not want to make a song and dance of the fact that they had precious objects of importance to national security in their possession. "You're drawing too much attention, come on, we have to go."

"Okay," they agreed. Phil then tapped Rees on the shoulder firmly, and Rees returned his firestone.

Chapter 16
The Tank

Thirty thousand nuts a sitting was his ambition. He tested his endurance from time to time, eating something he didn't particularly like to increase his protein intake. He wasn't very logical, but he was strong. His heftiness was mostly muscle, and the threatening bulk of his presence earned him the nickname *The Tank*. In spite of his size, he didn't actually like food all that much, but he was determined enough to do the right thing in life to force himself to work out his own ways of digesting sufficient nutrition to stay alive.

He was emotionally unstable though to say the least; finding himself in tricky social situations was a trigger for a whole host of unsociable scenarios, including physically harmful ones. It wasn't that he was a bad person per se, but more because he panicked when he didn't know how to respond to the multi-various styles of verbal communication that came his way; and when the voices came along with the impression of feelings or emotions - especially the masked or ironic ones - he lost the will to live, which in turn devalued the life of the people trying to socialise with him.

The Tank's parents had given up trying to help him; the various protective authorities had given up too, concluding that their input just compounded his – what they termed – antisocial behaviour. He had always been a borderline criminal, never quite bad enough to be locked up, yet too volatile to hold down a job. He would have joined the army if he wasn't so afraid of loud bangs. Counsellors, psychiatrists and psychologists had all failed to make an impact on *The Tank*. There was no cure!

Poor *Tank*! Poor you, if you ever tried to engage with him! Poor Tilly, who had no choice but to do what she was instructed to do, in that she had to attempt to socialise with *The Tank*. Tilly, however, was perhaps a good choice, as she too didn't fully grasp what emotional feelings were all about, and perhaps her inability to empathise would be a help to someone else who was unable to empathise; after all, they did have this thing in common!

I will leave it to you to judge how effective Tilly's meeting with *The Tank* was. It is often difficult to see evidence to back up claims of success, isn't it? And the test of time is often the real teller. Here's what happened, anyway:

It was *The Tank's* birthday; he was just thirty-one. On the day of his birthday the previous year, there had been an altercation between *The Tank* and his mum, whom he always called 'Mother.' By the way, I think I'll stop calling him *The Tank* from now on because he can get upset if you use the name at the wrong moment or in the wrong context, and discerning when the wrong moment or context had arrived was not an easy business. If he ever said, 'Why don't you call me *The Tank*? That's my nickname, you know!' then you would be advised to use said nickname. Otherwise it was probably safer to use his real name which in full, was: Horace John Archibald Winston Jagger.

As I was saying, Horace (*The Tank*) had the privilege of meeting Tilly on his thirty-first birthday. He had been given a pair of blue dungarees by his mother and he was wearing them over his black hoodie. This made him look even beefier than usual, but never mind, Tilly wasn't intimidated by such things.

Horace was in the back yard of his parents' home - since he lived there and neither he nor his parents could countenance the prospect of him ever living on his own, or with anyone else for that matter. Anyway, it was his birthday and in spite of it being his birthday, he was bent over, weeding the vegetable patch. You may be wondering why on earth he was weeding on his birthday, but there wasn't a lot for someone like Horace to enjoy doing as a treat, especially for an entire day. He had blown out the candles on his cake – he enjoyed that – and he appreciated his parents singing Happy Birthday to him, although that part was getting a bit loud for his liking.

So, there he was, pulling out the weeds, when Tilly appeared beside him and asked him what he was doing. Horace wasn't addled by Tilly's sudden appearance for several reasons: It wasn't unusual for his parents to have friends round; there was no immediate threat to Horace as people were always too afraid to pick a fight with him; and Tilly was gentle and quiet in her manner.

"I'm weeding," he said.

"What? On your birthday?"

"I can't leave these poor vegetables to die, can I?"

"That's very kind of you, but why do you think they'll die?"

"Why do you think?" he said aggressively.

"I 'think' because it's a typical function of a human being, so I have to think or at least pretend to think." (Good accidental tangent Tilly!)

"I don't think sometimes."

"Really? Why's that?"

"It hurts sometimes … sometimes it's better to just do something useful instead … like pulling these wicked weeds out of the stupid soil!" he said, again in an aggressive manner, yanking some more out and throwing them into the nearby wheelbarrow, which was situated on the paving slabs.

"You really care about vegetables, don't you?"

"Yes," he said. "They're my friends."

"It's good to have friends."

"My father says I should have more friends, but I don't like most friends much."

"Oh, why's that?"

"We just don't get on."

"What does your mother think?"

"She says I should stay at home, because I get on well with her."

"How about your father?"

Horace was silent.

Tilly repeated her question in a different way: "Do you get on well with your father?"

"He says I'm bad."

"Does he? And are you bad?"

Getting aggressive in his voice again: "I'm not bad, I'm not bad, I'm good, I'm good, I'm good!" Horace pulled out another handful of weeds and stared at Tilly with venom in his eyes while he mercilessly ripped them apart in his hands.

"You seem to be upset," said Tilly, calmly.

"I'm okay, I'm okay,"

"That's good, well done."

After a silent pause, Horace added, "You're nice."

"You're nice too."

Horace began to cry, but his own emotional response made him agitated: "Nobody says I'm nice," he said in a nice yet agitated manner.

"Well, praise where praise is due?"

"Yes, praise where praise is due."

Tilly brought the conversation back to the sensitive topic: "Why do you think the vegetables will die if you don't remove the weeds from the vegetable patch?"

"You know why!" he said, aggressively.

"Actually I don't," replied Tilly.

"Why don't you know?"

"I've never done weeding before."

"Oh, I will teach you." Horace pulled the weeds up more slowly, showing Tilly that you have to make sure the roots come out with each weed, otherwise they'll just keep growing back. "And they grow back very quickly, so you have to keep pulling them out again and again and again!" he said.

"I see, can I have a go?"

"Okay," Horace replied with a little hesitation.

Tilly started to pull some weeds out but she was not being careful to bring the roots with them.

"No, you're doing it wrong!" snapped Horace.

"No I'm not!" snapped Tilly.

"Yes you are!" snapped Horace in a manner too loud for his own liking. This in turn made him even more agitated.

"Don't you think the weeds have a right to live?" asked Tilly.

"No, they're wicked!"

"Why?"

"Can't you see!" belched Horace, "Look!" he snapped, yanking at the weeds, "they choke and choke and choke, until they kill the poor vegetables!"

"Oh, why didn't you say so?"

"I did! I keep telling you but you just don't listen!"

"But you didn't tell me!"

Horace was sweating at this point, feeling exasperated. "I did tell you but you just don't understand!"

"You're absolutely right, I don't understand, and like I said, I have never done weeding before."

"I'm okay, I'm okay. It's all right, it's all right. I shouldn't snap at you, it's not your fault."

"And I feel cruel killing all of these weeds," said Tilly.

"It's not cruel, it's the weeds that are cruel. They choke and choke and choke ..."

"But it's not their fault."

"Of course it's their fault, they choke and choke and choke ..."

"You don't care, do you!" snapped Tilly, elevating her voice.

"I DO CARE!" shouted Horace, "THEY CHOKE AND CHOKE AND CHOKE ..."

"HOW CAN THEY CHOKE?" Tilly objected.

"LIKE THIS!" yelled Horace, grabbing Tilly by the neck and squeezing tighter than any human could survive. But Tilly had special abilities, so she wasn't going to die or get her neck broken. Her face didn't even wince in pain or fear. She thrust her arms through the gap between Horace's arms and then opened her arms quickly like she was doing the breaststroke. Horace's arms flung apart from her neck and before he could bring them back again, Tilly slapped him hard on his cheek.

The slap was not quite hard enough to knock *The Tank* over (Sorry, I mean Horace), so he just looked into Tilly's eyes; there was no fear, aggression, confusion, anticipation or sorrow in Tilly's expression – neither was there any evidence of harm; she was not coughing, gasping for air or screwing her face up. If any of those facial expressions had been present, then, ironically, Horace would have strangled her again immediately. Instead, he was beginning to calm down.

They remained staring at each other, their faces now just a couple of feet apart, until Tilly said, "So, show me again how to weed properly."

Bending back down to grab a few weeds, Horace explained more clearly how to remove the roots of the weeds. They did some weeding together for five minutes without Horace getting aggressive again. That was until Tilly began to teach Horace something:

"Weeds come in all shapes and sizes," she said.

"Yes they do, these wicked old weeds!"

"I actually quite like them," said Tilly.

"No, how can you possibly like them. What are you? Mad?"

"They're only like vegetables."

"No they're not! Vegetables don't go round strangling everyone!"

"Vegetables aren't perfect."

"Yes they are, they're my friends. You're hurting them, saying things like that!"

"No I'm not."

"Yes you are, and I'm going to hurt you if you don't stop!"

"You don't see vegetables taking revenge on weeds, do you?"

"They can if they want!"

"You might be right, but they don't do they?"

"GO AWAY!" shouted Horace, pushing Tilly away from him. His own voice was too loud for his own liking, so he held his ears tight and whimpered. Tilly just stood still and watched him, but Horace was not happy with that. "I told you to go away."

"No," said Tilly calmly, displaying no expression on her face.

"I'm warning you, if you don't move I'm going to strangle you again!"

"I'm not going away," said Tilly, again displaying no emotion whatsoever.

"MOVE!" Horace shouted, holding his ears tight.

Seeing that Tilly wasn't moving infuriated him, so he rushed up to her, grabbed her by the throat and began strangling her again. But Tilly was not affected by it this time either; she just performed her breaststroke technique again and slapped him even harder on his cheek.

"OWWW! That really hurt."

If this wasn't enough, Horace again strangled Tilly, only this time with the weight of a tank. But like I said, Tilly has special powers, and on this occasion, her special power was to make her body as resilient as a diamond. Every part of her was as intact as ever, so she calmly spoke: "You are like a weed."

"How dare you say I'm like a weed!" Horace snapped with venom, squeezing tighter and tighter.

"Well you ARE like a weed," said Tilly, again calmly.

"I'm going to kill you!"

"You can't."

"Yes I can, yes I can."

"Weed!"

"I'm not a wicked old weed, you're the wicked old weed!"

"If I was a weed, I would be strangling you, wouldn't I?"

"What?"

"Only weeds strangle everything, don't they?"

"I'm not a weed!"

"So why are you strangling me?"

"Because!" he said, still trying to squeeze the life out of Tilly. "Because you're too loud and you're winding me up!"

"You must be a weed then."

"I'm not a weed!"

"Yes you are, you want to strangle vegetables."

"No, I don't."

"That's what weeds do."

"Anyway, you're not a vegetable, so I can do whatever I like to you!"

"Oh dear."

"Why are you talking while I'm strangling you, anyway!"

"Oh deary me!"

"Shut up!"

"You'll have to be pulled up by the roots."

"What? I'm not a wicked old weed!"

"Yes you are!"

"NO I'M NOT, YOU CAN'T PULL ME UP BY THE ROOTS!" Horace shouted.

"We have no choice, do we?" said Tilly turning effortlessly round to talk to two police officers while still being strangled by Horace – the policemen had just appeared!

The policemen approached Horace slowly but decisively. "It's up to you," one of them said.

"What's up to me?"

"Are you a weed or not?"

"I'm not a weed!"

"If you continue to hurt everything we have to arrest you as a weed."

"But, people annoy me."

"Nobody's hurting you," said the other policeman, and at that moment, Horace noticed an embossed carrot motif on the policeman's helmet; glancing back at the other, he notice an embossed potato motif on his helmet.

"Why have you got a vegetable on your heads?"

"I'm a carrot," said one.

"And I'm a potato," said the other.

"You are stupid!"

"At least we're not weeds, like you!" said both policemen simultaneously.

"I'm not a weed!"

"If you're not a weed, why do you keep strangling this woman?"

"I can't stop myself! I can't stop myself!" Horace said.

"Yes you can!" said Tilly.

"Yes you can!" said the carrot.

"Yes you can!" said the potato.

"But how do I stop?" asked Horace.

"Let go," said Tilly.

"Let go," said the carrot.

"Let go," said the potato.

"How do I let go?" asked Horace.

"Calm down," said Tilly.

"Calm down," said the carrot.

"Calm down," said the potato.

"How do I calm down?" asked Horace.

"Remember you're not a weed," said Tilly.

"But how can I stop thinking I'm a weed if you keep calling me one?"

"But you can't be a weed, can you? Because you're stopping yourself from strangling me right now."

"You're right," said Horace, but he was struggling to let go.

"And whenever someone frightens you ..." said Tilly - Horace was sweating profusely at that point. "... or you hear a loud bang ..." Horace briefly squeezed Tilly's neck tighter again before eventually willing himself to let go. " ... you will remember that there is no reason to hurt anyone."

"Why not!"

"Because you're not a weed."

"That's right, I don't need to hurt anything, because I'm not a weed!"

"Well done, Horace."

"I'm a good person."

"You are."

"I can control myself."

"You can."

The carrot and the potato joined in: "We can see that you are a good person too, Horace."

"Thank you," replied Horace.

"You are not a weed," they added in unison.

"You're right, I'm not a weed."

"Shall we try a loud bang to test you?" suggested the potato.

"What? No ..." he said at first, his hands almost lifting to strangle Tilly's neck again.

"Oh dear!" said Tilly.

"Okay, okay, do it!"

"Good choice!" said Tilly.

"I'm not a weed."

"That's absolutely right," said the potato, and carrot swung his baton down hard onto an empty box five times. Horace didn't flinch.

"I'm not a weed!" exclaimed Horace with some sense of bewilderment and relief.

"You're right," said Tilly. "Shall we try shouting and screaming to test you?"

At that suggestion, Horace started to get agitated again. But Tilly just smiled at him and started to jump up and down giggling, flapping her arms around. The carrot then started to jump about in a pretend grumpy mood, shouting, "I'm in a mood! I'm in a mood!"

Horace was quite disturbed by this, but he managed to control himself. Then potato spoke: "You are doing very, very well Horace."

"I am! I am!"

"Shall we make it even harder?" suggested the potato.

"Yes, I can do it! I can do it!" responded Horace with just a little apprehension.

At that, the potato began to sway backwards and forwards, shouting, "I'm going to get you! I'm going to get angry with you!"

Horace knew this was all a test and that it was not real emotions, whatever they are; so this helped him to endure the complete chaos. However, Horace's parents – who were looking out of the back window - were getting quite concerned by this strange behaviour going on in their back yard. For a change, it was not just their son they were confused about, but rather Tilly and the two policemen, jumping and swaying around shouting angry statements, laughing happily etc. etc. Who on earth were these visitors? And why on earth was their son, *The Tank,* jumping up and down with them shouting and giggling without fighting anyone? They were utterly gobsmacked!

After ten to fifteen minutes of Tilly, the carrot and the potato thus jumping around with Horace, they waved goodbye to him with the promise to return at the weekend. Horace was very happy with that idea. Just as Tilly, the carrot and the potato disappeared round the corner they shouted back, "Happy Birthday, Horace!"

Horace's parents waited for their son to come back indoors before they asked him who his friends were. Horace explained it all the best he could before adding, "This is the best birthday I've ever had!"

"That's wonderful!" said his mother and his father.

"And I'm going to introduce them to my mum and dad at the weekend." Before the penny dropped, Horace's mother and father were trying to fathom who Horace's mum and dad were, since he had never referred to them that way; it was always 'mother and father.'

"Mum and dad?" asked his mother cautiously.

"Yes, you two! You ARE my mum and dad, aren't you?"

"Yes of course we are."

"Thank you for my best birthday ever!"

"You're welcome," said mum.

"Well, they're your friends, we didn't have anything to do with it, but we're very happy that you've made some good friends at last," said dad.

"And I'm not afraid of loud bangs anymore," said Horace.

"That's ... wonderful!" said mum with a little scepticism.

"Well, it certainly looked like you were enjoying the noise when we saw you jumping around earlier," said dad.

"Yeh, it's because I'm not a weed!"

"Absolutely!" said mum.

"I don't know how anybody could possibly call you a weed," said dad.

The rest of that day - his birthday - Horace was different; he was less stressed. His mum and dad were in fact a little worried that his new friends wouldn't turn up at the weekend like they had promised, but they shouldn't have doubted it, as like they promised, they DID turn up and they had some more fun together.

After that weekend, Horace dared to go to the shops, and he managed to do so without upsetting anyone. People around him were afraid, but they needn't have worried. Even though he still did not understand their emotions, he was no longer so disturbed by them; neither was he afraid of loud or sudden noises. And now, whenever something unexpected occurred, he saw it as a challenge to prove he was not a weed.

All of this was a good case of 'so far so good,' but it looked like Tilly, the carrot and the potato, hadn't figured in the impact of Dawn. And by Dawn, I don't mean the morning after a good night's sleep; I mean

Dawn, half-sister to Horace. It wasn't often that she turned up on the scene, which in some ways was a good thing as she wasn't only volatile, she was truly violent, and her violence could quite justifiably be classed as the deadly kind. It didn't seem fair, but such is life. Here's what happened:

Dawn knocked on the door of her dad's house, which was the same as that of Horace and his parents. Horace opened the door.

"Hey, Horace, how are you doin'?" she said as she barged passed her half-bother. She went straight into the living room where her dad was watching the Sports Channel. Horace's mum was in the kitchen preparing lunch (Quite a stereotypical picture of a mum and dad I hear you say, but I have to point out that this is what they were doing, and you can hardly say that Horace was a stereotypical son, could you?).

"Hey, dad, how are you?" Dawn said, and her dad's face gave away one of those expressions that Horace found difficult to cope with. Dad looked pleasantly surprised to see his own daughter, but there was also a partially hidden look of: 'Oh no! Why now? We've just got our home sorted out; everyone's happy, even Horace, and nobody is in fear of police coming calling or Horace losing control. It has never been this good before, and now it's all going to end because even though Dawn is more 'normal,' she is intrinsically bad' (Yes, a lot went through the mind of Horace and Dawn's dad during that brief moment).

Horace was just stood at the door to the living room, dumbfounded. He too was in a state of dread, but that came in the form of: 'I can feel myself going back to how I was before.'

Horace's mum was no fool; she saw the way Horace was reacting and put her arm round him to guide him away from the living room doorway while Dawn was busy chatting to her dad, asking for money. "Horace, I wonder if you wouldn't mind popping out to the shop for me to get a couple of things for lunch?" his mum asked.

"Okay," said Horace, with an uncommon smile.

So, Horace went to the shops with a shopping list and some cash. Some people even dared to say hello to him this time. Horace liked this and he did not want to lose this new life he had. The usual cloud of fear – which was trying to surround him after seeing his half-sister - was struggling to attach itself.

Later on, as Horace was leaving the shop with a bag full of bread, milk, carrots and potatoes, he saw Dawn in the distance arguing with a man. Normally this would severely agitate him, causing him to lose control, but he quickened his pace to get away from the area as fast as possible, fearing he might go back to his old ways. This was not because he didn't care about his half-sister; it was simply because she would in the past always involve him to frighten anyone who objected to her behaviour. Horace found it very difficult not to be angry with the other person even if they were innocent. After all, she was his half-sister, and she had a way of communicating with him safely the rest of the time. On this occasion though, he considered himself off limits. However, Dawn had other ideas. She noticed Horace speed away and assumed he had somehow not noticed the altercation. "Hey, Horace!" she shouted, "This man's trying to steal money off me!"

This was the most difficult test Horace had faced since he got to know Tilly, and he knew inside himself that this was going to be a defining moment, one way or another. He heard Dawn calling, and glanced over before deciding to grip his shopping tighter and speeding on towards home.

"What? You're not going to save me?" shouted Dawn. Horace kept walking, feeling a guilt he had never experienced before. "Horace!" she shouted. Horace began to consider going to Dawn's rescue, but could not help getting agitated at the thought of it. In the end, he turned when he heard a loud piercing scream. But he didn't lose control at that, he just wanted to find out what the reason was for the scream. He noticed a man run away from Dawn (not an unfamiliar sight), and then she suddenly collapsed onto the floor, clasping her chest. By the time Horace arrived at the scene, several people were already standing close to Dawn while calling someone on their phones, and the strange man was nowhere to be seen.

Dawn was on the ground on her back, holding the handle of a knife that was protruding from her chest, and Horace just looked down at her as though he was in a state of shock. Actually, he felt no definable emotion, he was just trying to puzzle it all out. He put the bag of groceries on the ground and then casually pulled the knife out of his half-sister's chest.

"NO!" shouted the onlookers, but Horace didn't know why they shouted that word. Fortunately, the sudden loudness of it did not make him lose control. A couple of spectators crouched down and pressed their hands onto Dawn's wound.

"She's my half-sister," said Horace.

The onlookers assumed Horace's strange behaviour was down to him being in shock at seeing his half-sister hurt so badly. In that state of mind, he clearly didn't think of the consequences of removing the knife.

When the police and paramedics eventually arrived, the onlookers made it clear that they believed Horace had been trying to help; the actual killer had sped off before they all arrived on the scene.

Dawn died from the stab wound.

There we have it. Could the old Horace have saved his half-sister? We may never know. But what I do know is, Horace remained a better, more sociable, more content person, and nobody regretted that. In fact, the only person who could have regretted Horace being a better person was now dead.

Chapter 17
I Scream

It wasn't long before Nora from the Lake District joined the merry little investigation team. After she had shared her experiences, the name 'Tilly's Tearoom' became the group's main focus. They all met in Keswick in Cumbria this time, and were in a jolly mood; even Phil cheered up a bit. They decided it was too much like hard work to climb Scafell for a meeting, so they went for Catbells which looked over Derwentwater.

As they hiked up Catbells, they discussed all the ways they might be able to find or summon Tilly or her tearoom. They went through possible connections in the dates, and times of day, but nothing stood out; they considered the place names and the meanings of the names, but nothing stood out; they considered the targeted age groups and backgrounds of the survivors and the victims, but again nothing stood out. They became a little deflated by the time they had descended the fell again, especially as they came to the likely conclusion that they were just a handful among hundreds or even thousands of survivors from Tilly's mysterious and dastardly dealings, especially if the mysterious events happened outside of England too. Having said that, Phil thought there would have been more genuine responses to his advert if it was as widespread as that, and there would have been news reports about it even if you took into account the sensitivity of the experiences. For all they knew, they were the only ones - the Famous Five - unless there were some more genuine cases among the respondents that Alison and Phil had rejected as nutjobs. They eventually parted with the decision to send to each other the land coordinates of their respective adventures, once they had arrived at their respective homes.

While all this was going on, Tilly was enjoying an ice cream on Scarborough beach on the north-eastern coast of Yorkshire. She was sat on the sand not far from the harbour on which the fair was in full swing. She was exhausted after all the hilarity of going on all of the fairground rides with her little husband, that was, Justin Caadfar, the creepy imp. It was her much needed holiday away from the hustling and bustling of the hurly burly hubbub of tearoom life. Her only desire was to do absolutely nothing of any importance, and if she were to strike up a conversation, only to discuss more nothings of any importance. This is what she yearned for, so she left her tearoom team behind in limbo, while she hung out with her husband.

"Ooo, it's so lovely to feel the sand between your toes," Tilly said, wiggling them profusely. Her feet looked so excited, as she had no less than ten toes on each foot, that is, twenty toes in total – in case you're not very good at Maths.

Little imp-man took his socks off and did the same with his three-toed feet.

They were sat on a tablecloth with a wind-breaker at the side. The sun was warm and the view beautiful. They could see the families and children playing in the sand, making sand castles and deep holes to lie in. They could also see people splashing about in the icy cold sea in the distance. Seagulls squawked around, looking for tasty scraps, and a salty smell permeated the breezy air.

They could hear the noisy arcades behind them, through the sound of motor vehicles travelling along the seafront road, and it all made them feel like they were part of something normal for a change.

"It's not often we just get to be ourselves, is it?" said Tilly.

"It certainly is not," said the imp with a nasally voice.

"Hopefully, we are not going to be asked to sort out any problems today."

"I certainly hope not."

At that moment, a beach ball bounced into Tilly's ice cream which ended up all over her face. A couple of boys charged up to retrieve it, accidentally kicking sand in the faces of Tilly and her husband in the process, making sand stick to the ice cream on the end of Tilly's nose. The boys apologised, but then they called her 'Pinocchio' as they ran off with their ball.

"That's not fair!" said Tilly.

"It certainly is not," responded Justin. "What are you going to do?"

"I'm going to ask you to buy me another ice cream, if that's okay."

"It certainly is," said Justin.

"It just makes me so annoyed!"

"It certainly does."

"They shouldn't make ice cream so sticky!"

"They certainly should not," agreed her husband. "Don't worry, I will get us both another one, and I will ask them not to make them so sticky this time."

"Good idea."

Justin the imp went to buy two ice creams while Tilly just sat there staring at the people on the beach, with sand on her creamy nose. People who passed by gave her a funny look, but Tilly didn't take any notice. "I wonder what it's like to play beachball," she said to herself as she watched the children playing.

Justin came back with the ice cream cornets, and handed one to his wife.

"Thank you," she said.

"You are welcome my dear."

"I wonder what it would be like to play beachball."

"I don't know, I've never played it before."

"Well, I think we should join in."

"I agree."

Tilly and Justin held hands as they walked between the groups and families on the sand, making a beeline for the nearest game of beachball. People were shocked at their peculiar feet as they passed by, but Tilly and Justin didn't notice. They had finished their ice creams by the time they arrived at the net. Tilly tugged and fondled the net while the children played, which annoyed them. Tilly hadn't examined a beachball net before. The children eventually stopped and stared at them, and their parents did the same from their beach mats, peeping from behind their wind-breakers.

"Tilly!" said Justin, "I think they're waiting for us to play with them."

"Okay, I think you should play on that side of the net, and I should play on this side."

"Okay."

Tilly and Justin entered their respective positions and the children continued their game, hesitantly allowing the adult visitors to join in. Their parents kept a close watch on the proceedings. The children began to enjoy the game once they had witnessed the skills of the strangers, with Tilly's somersaults before slamming the beachball to the other side, and Justin's ability to leap six times his own height.

The children were gobsmacked, and so were their parents. Tilly and Justin had boundless energy, but after the third game, the children needed a rest.

"Well done, that was quite impressive," said one of the dads to Tilly.

"Thank you, that's very kind of you to say so."

"You and your son must practise a lot."

"Oh, he's not my son, he's my husband."

"Really? Sorry, he just looked so young."

"Not really, he's just very short."

"Well, I didn't like to say …"

"His name is Justin, my name is Tilly, we are Mr and Mrs Caadfar."

"Nice to meet you," said the dad shaking Tilly's hand, which made his body jolt a little and then shudder, but he didn't know why.

"Oh no, not again!" said the dad, "They're always picking on him! Please excuse me, I'd better sort it out."

"Okay," said Tilly who tried not to look, because she didn't want to get involved while she was on holiday.

Just then one of the mums came up to Tilly and started a conversation, which was great as it was a nice distraction for Tilly, who grabbed hold of her little husband and made him stand beside her kneecaps, to stop him from sorting out the bullying problem in the distance. But to Tilly's disappointment, the mum said:

"I don't like the look of those boys over there, they look like they're bullying that poor child."

Justin tried to draw the mother's attention away from the bullying by pointing over to the right, "Look at that family over there, they look so excited digging that hole deeper and deeper."

"My son is always digging for things; we've got holes all over our garden with his desperation to find buried treasure."

"We have a saying," said Tilly. "A child needs to explore ..."

"... while an adult needs to survive," said Justin, finishing off the saying.

"You know, that's so true!" said the mum. "Well, if you'll excuse me, I'm going to try and rescue that boy," and she left.

"I am NOT going to sort that out," said Tilly to her little husband.

"I can call the pixies?" Justin suggested.

"Oh, go on then," Tilly said reluctantly. Justin left the beach, then Tilly clicked her fingers.

Everything on the beach froze, all except for Tilly. It was the most efficient way to deal with the problem while avoiding being hit with beachballs – that might have spoilt the pixies' concentration.

While she waited for them to arrive, Tilly sauntered around, squeezing the sand with her twenty toes as she went, analysing the frozen interactions between friends and families of all generations, while trying to understand what it must be like to be them. Anyway, her saunter was cut short when she saw her husband coming back with ten little pixies.

The pixies knew what to do and who to do it to. There were five very bad bullies, four boys and a girl. Two pixies were allocated for each of the bullies. They dug a total of five holes along the edge of the sea, and very close to it. This was to teach the bullies a lesson. Then each bully - all of them frozen in time - was gently placed into a hole so that they were facing the sea, their heads being the only part of their body that was exposed. They were all in a standing position in their respective holes when the gaps were filled in by the pixies, who tapped the edges afterwards to make sure the sand wasn't too loose. Then for each bully, two pixies laid down in front with their faces less than a foot away from the bullies.

Justin asked the pixies, "Are you ready?"

"Yes," they said in unison with their high pitched, yet cute, voices.

Tilly clicked her fingers, and the whole beach came alive again.

Before the parents of the bullies could see what was going on, the pixies each said to their respective captives, "This is what happens to bullies!" before running off giggling.

The appearance of the pixies and what they said terrified the bullies, and their first reaction was to run away, but when they realised they couldn't move their limbs and that they were completely buried, apart from their heads of course, they all screamed for their mummies and daddies.

Fortunately for the bullies, most of their parents were on the beach and heard them screaming. The parents couldn't understand how their children were playing one minute, and then totally buried in sand the next. And when the children and their parents could see the waves coming close to their exposed heads, they were in great panic, and ran screaming to dig their children free. Other people dashed to help too, bringing spades with them.

Before the children were freed, the sea had seeped into the edges of the holes and made the bullies' bodies sink even further. They spluttered for breath as sea water began to fill their stomachs, and their lives were almost gone before they were set free.

"Who did this?" screamed the parents.

"It was the pixies!" insisted their children.

Three of the parents smacked their children for lying, but they were all thankful that they had not died.

Later that week, whenever the five bullies talked to other children and their teachers about the pixies, they all laughed at them, so they had to live with the knowledge that no one would ever take their story seriously. Most importantly, they were too frightened to bully other children again just in case the pixies came back.

The day after their Catbells meeting, the Famous Five set up their respective devices for an online video-chat about how to find Tilly. They shared coordinates as planned and made a note of them. Alison then took control of the proceedings:

"I have a simple idea," she said.

"Great, what is it?" asked Shauna.

"Even if we are a tiny piece of a huge jigsaw, there is still something that connects us."

"Really?" said Phil.

"First of all, get your maps of the UK out and mark on it where we all had our experiences."

They all got their maps out and started to do as Alison suggested.

"Now, Nora, your experience was on Scafell in the Lake District; Phil, yours was in a village called Willington in Cheshire; and Shauna and Rees, yours was in Dartmoor."

"That's right," said Shauna.

"And mine was near my parents' house in Biggar in Scotland." She waited a while. "Have you all marked those?"

They all said 'yes' and put their thumbs up.

"Now draw a line connecting them."

They all did as they were told.

"Well I don't get a straight line," said Nora.

"That's right, because it's a curve.

"Oh!" they all said.

"Can you all see what I mean?"

"Yes!" they all said.

"Try to draw an accurate curve through all of the locations as though it's the edge of a very large circle."

"Got it," they said.

"So, the first thing I want to say is that if we were to use this arc to trace a circle on a world atlas, it would create a circle with the Atlantic Ocean in the middle."

"Oh, that's interesting," said Shauna.

"A bit like the Bermuda Triangle, you mean?" said Rees.

Phil was not so impressed, "Which gets us nowhere – are you suggesting we get a boat and sail out into the Atlantic Ocean to look for Tilly's Tearoom?"

"No, I am not suggesting that at all. It's a long shot, but if we divide the arc on our maps into four equal parts, the range being from Biggar to Dartmoor, since we don't have any other information yet … If we split the arc into four ... do you know what I mean? Mark the curve so that it has four equal parts."

"Yep," said Nora. "I've done it roughly."

"Has everyone else done it?"

"Done it!" they said, putting their thumbs up.

"Then, going downwards, the first section ends with Scafell in the Lake District, the second section ends with Willington in Cheshire, and then we have our hypothetical location at the end of the third section. Have we all established what is equidistant between Willington in Cheshire and Dartmoor in Devon?"

"The Brecon Beacons," said Phil.

"That's right ... so ... why don't we visit the Brecon Beacons in Wales?"

"What on earth for?" asked Phil.

"I did say it was a bit of long shot."

Nora was feeling quite excited, "So you're saying there's a sort of symmetry between the locations where Tilly operates, and these events may take place along the circumference of a circle?"

"Yes, that's exactly what I'm suggesting. It's worth a shot, isn't it?" suggested Alison.

"We think it's worth a try," said Rees.

"I'm sceptical, but it may be fun," said Phil.

"Well, I'm surprised to hear that from you, Phil, being such a serious person, and all that."

Tapping his nose, "I'm a man of surprises."

"You certainly are!" said Nora.

Alison added, "When we get there, we can have a look round the area, ask around, put an advert in shop windows, it'll be fun, even if it goes nowhere."

"You're on!" said Nora, already searching for hotels on her phone. "Let's see if there's a reasonably priced hotel in Brecon."

They discussed a variety of options between them and decided on Alistory Motel; Alison liked the sound of that one in particular as the name 'Alistory' made her think of her own experience with the Mad Hatter and his weird friends; it was Ali's Story.

So, Alistory Motel it was. They booked four rooms for Saturday night and agreed to meet up at 6pm in the lobby.

When the time arrived, so did four cars - in the car park of Alistory Motel in Brecon, Wales. There was Nora Fletcher, the retired lady from Cumbria, Private Investigator Philip Scrounge from Liverpool, Shauna and Rees Thorn from Devon, and Alison Middleton from Biggar in Scotland. They assumed that the motel was unpopular as there were no other cars in the fairly large car park, but they only needed somewhere to lay their head for the night, so they weren't bothered.

They all met up in the lobby as arranged before they checked in. It was a smartly dressed, polite man that checked their bookings and gave them their respective keys. He told them they were welcome to evening meal for half price if they wanted, and that they stop serving at 8.30. This appealed to them, so they freshened up in their rooms, everyone having their own room - except for the twins, Shauna and Rees, who had a twin room - and then they all went back downstairs at 7.00 for a meal together.

They were taken aback at how full the dining hall was, considering there were no other cars in the car park when they had arrived. They must have all arrived last minute, or come in on a coach. Anyway, the noisier it was, the more they could talk shop without being overheard. And that is what they did, a little bit. They had all done some research about the area and discussed a few options. But they were more excited about seeing each other again, so most of the time they just laughed, ate and drank.

By the time their meal was over, they were still disinclined to talk shop as they were tired from having driven a long way. So, they decided to bring maps and such like down to breakfast in the morning, when they would also chat to a few of the people staying in the motel in case they knew the area well, and the motel staff should be able to fill in any remaining gaps.

They said their goodnights and settled into bed. None of them could resist a last look at their firestone before they put their heads on their pillows. So there was a firestone on a bedside table in four separate rooms. Looking forward to their adventure the next day, they all went soundly to sleep.

The motel was completely quiet at 2.00 in the morning, as nobody was actually staying at the motel except for the Famous Five. The firestones were quiet too, except for the one beside PI Scrounge's head. It flashed briefly and Phil shot up out of bed. "EUREKA!" he shouted, before phoning the others one by one to tell them what he had realised. "It's an anagram! 'Alistory Motel' is an anagram of 'Tilly's Tearoom!' We are sleeping in Tilly's Tearoom!"

They all agreed that he could be right, but after an initial buzz, they all decided to get some sleep as their adventure the next day was going to be busy and tiring, and they wanted to be as alert as possible.

The Famous Five fell asleep again; that was until at approximately 4am, because that was when all four firestones throbbed with light and beams shot from one firestone to another, from room to room, through wall after wall, until a complex network of over a million lines had connected to create a 3D web-structure. The four firestones, along with their newly constructed web, throbbed again and again with light of ever-growing intensity, as a new scenario was being constructed in Alistory Motel, that is, Tilly's Tearoom.

Chapter 18
Finding Santa (Don't Tell the Children!)

Somehow, Shauna, Rees, Alison, Phil and Nora suddenly found themselves in a cafe in their nightwear. They were not sat at a table in the motel restaurant, but rather at two tables in the Tilly's Tearoom that was indelibly imprinted on Phil Scrounge's memory.

"This is exactly what Tilly's Tearoom was like when I saw it," said Phil.

"It's similar to the one I entered, but not identical," said Nora.

Rees and Shauna were not familiar with the surroundings at all. "It's nothing like the café we went in; this is much smaller."

"Well, as you know, my experience wasn't in a café, it was on a picnic blanket, but I think I recognise the woman behind the serving counter," said Alison.

Tilly came over to them to take their orders.

"It's you!" said Alison, "You're the Red Queen!"

"You're right," admitted Tilly without any hesitation. "And you'll meet the others later, but do you know what the monster was?"

"I do know what the monster was, it was my Personal Tutor, Professor Benedict Henry."

Something clicked in Rees' memory, "Hey, you're the woman who was pole-dancing in Firestone Village."

"Yes, and for those of you who don't know my name, I'm Tilly."

They were all in no doubt about that already, but it was good to meet her in the flesh – so to speak – so they all rose to shake her by the hand, one by one, but to each member of the Famous Five, it felt like they were shaking air!

"Now, would you all like a cup of coffee to wake you up?"

They all agreed that would be lovely, for now, as they had no idea what time it was, and were frightened to ask for breakfast; they were too excited to contemplate eating anyway. Phil was sat at a table with Nora, both of them inexplicably having their respective firestones in front of them. Alison, Rees and Shauna were sat on the table next to them with their respective firestones in front of them too.

At first, the younger table was too stunned and curious about their surroundings to enter into a deep conversation. They kept looking around the room, trying to take in every detail, feeling warm inside, having a sense that everything was ... okay, but none of them had the slightest recollection how they ended up in the tearoom.

Phil and Nora were talking about their firestones, working out how to ask what the mysterious metallic objects really were.

Eventually, Tilly arrived with five coffee cups and plenty of milk on the side. She placed everything down on the two tables.

"I wonder if I could ask you a question?" Phil asked Tilly.

"Please wait a moment," said Tilly, dashing off to get three large pots of filtered coffee. When she returned to the tables, she put one pot on the table for three people, and two pots on the table for two people. The Famous Five were a bit puzzled about that too!

"Now then, ask me your question."

Phil was excited at finally getting the opportunity to ask the question that all of them were yearning to get the answer to. "What are these strange objects called, and what is their purpose?" As I write this, I can't help but be impressed by how direct and clear Phil's question was, and I'm full of awe at the fact that this ideal place and time had even occurred, and within a few seconds, the answer that they had all dreamt of knowing the answer to was about to be answered there and then, immediately, imminently; and after a few seconds, they were going to be in possession of that information and would treasure it, and their lives would surely never be the same again!

"Actually, the name is not speakable in human language. So ..." she said, picking up Phil's firestone, "in this case the best way to express it in English is 'DNA shell.'"

"DNA shell? You mean there's DNA inside these things."

"No."

"Oh?"

"This one's empty, it's been used, you see."

"Oh, that's a shame, so can you explain to us how it works?"

"I will call Professor Spitforth to explain it to you; it's his domain."

"Okay, thank you."

A middle-aged man emerged from the back of the tearoom and walked towards them.

"You're the March Hare!" exclaimed Alison.

"That's right."

"And you joked and said you were a real hare."

"You have a good memory."

Phil interjected, "We are curious to know how the DNA shell works."

"DNA shell? What do you mean? Oh, it's called ..."

"NO!" shouted Tilly at the professor.

"Oh, I see! Yes, it works like this: Each shell contains a scenario. When something needs to be done, the information and data needed to construct that scenario is put inside the shell, and then the shell is placed in the right place at the right time, and hey presto it all comes out."

"That's fascinating!" said Alison.

Phil wanted to show off his intelligence, "So what you are saying is, at the moment it's a DNA shell, but when it's first placed in an area at a particular time, at that moment, it's a DNA box." He smiled at his friends, smugly.

"What IS all this nonsense about DNA shells and boxes anyway?" asked the Professor, "It's called a Pirofirotextofruito ...."

"Oh dear, now you've done it!" exclaimed Tilly.

"What's he done?" asked Nora.

"The word takes a long time to speak out."

"But you said it could not be spoken in human language," said Shauna.

"It can't," said Tilly, "This is just the nearest we can get to it."

By the time they had said this, the professor's enunciation of the name continued with a raspberry.

Tilly handed Phil an umbrella, "Here, you'll need this."

Phil put up the umbrella to protect himself and Nora from the spray as the professor's saliva spurted out of his mouth.

"How long does this take?" asked Phil.

"20.534211 minutes. You'll just have to wait until he's finished I'm afraid. If you stop him half way through, it can have a negative impact on Time."

"Oh, I'm very sorry if I've caused any trouble," said Phil.

"Just sit there with your umbrella and wait till he's finished!" she repeated with a stamp of her foot and a grumpy voice.

The other four members of the Famous Five gave Phil a hard stare. They had no choice now but to chat, drink coffee, and ponder over what may or may not come next in their long awaited adventure, while having to wait and listen to a raspberry for twenty minutes. This was not what they would have called a pleasant experience.

It was after Phil's tenth cup of coffee that the raspberry ended, and that was because Phil typically drank a lot of coffee when he was stressed, and the same applied to whenever it was raining.

After the rain, Tilly returned and Phil handed the umbrella back. The professor then walked away from them all to join two people who had just emerged from the back of the tearoom carrying Christmas decorations.

Alison jumped up excitedly, "I recognise those other two people as well. The tall one is the Mad Hatter and the woman is Alice! The only one missing now is the Dormouse."

Tilly shouted over to the Famous Five. "Come and help us to put the decorations up around the tearoom, Christmas is coming!" They all readily agreed and enjoyed talking to Tilly's friends. When they had finished decorating the whole tearoom, a little imp came in carrying a life-sized, empty crib with straw inside.

"There he is!" shouted Alison, "You're the Dormouse!"

The little man smiled back at her as he set the crib in place near the Christmas tree.

When all the decorations were complete, it looked wonderfully festive, and while they were admiring it all, the tearoom was, unbeknown to them, travelling through time.

At the tearoom's final destination there was a world completely unknown to Alison, Phil, Rees, Shauna and Nora. It was a dark world, but one in which vehicles – those used for transport - were not restricted by puny things like air resistance, vacuums or the ground. It was all based on a kind of molecular transfer through which speed was barely an issue. Vehicles darted back and forth, any distance, in any direction, at any moment, all dependent upon the 'driver,' whether he, she or it was in the vehicle or not. And even if there were passengers, they would not be affected by any significant gravitational pull, as the gravitational effects of objects had been counteracted by a number of means. All of the vehicles were clearly visible in the dark by means of bright lights of numerous colours and hues. Light sources were no longer so restricted by technological limitations, and batteries as we know them were never used.

Alison looked through a window of the tearoom into the darkness to see brightly shining vehicles darting backwards, forwards, upwards, downwards, sideways, and even imphways. There appeared to be no restrictions on travel. The flying vehicles didn't even have wings or streamlined bodies. Whatever shape they were, they could move around better than any aeroplane she had ever seen before.

Alison announced, "Look at this, just see how those vehicles are flying around!"

They all looked through the windows, except for Phil, who actually opened the door and stepped out.

Nora noticed him go out of the door. "Where's Philip going?"

Rees was not concentrating at first as he was fascinated by all of the brightly coloured objects darting about and zooming around. But he managed to muster a "No idea."

Shauna was interested to see where he'd gone though, jealous that he may get a special view of everything, so she popped outside herself, but it was a mistake as she plunged downwards and her screams very quickly faded away. The other three heard the initial part of her scream and Rees ran to the door only to find there was no pavement, no road, no land at all, only a dark chasm below. "OH NO! Shauna and Phil have fallen down."

"Oh dear, are they all right?" asked Nora.

"Of course they're not, they're dead!"

"Dead? Why? How?" asked Alison. Nora and Alison ran to the door, but Rees stopped them before they plunged to their deaths. They nearly fainted when they saw they were above nothingness, and realised their friends had fallen to a certain death. "I thought you meant they had just fallen over, not fallen down into nothingness,!" said Alison.

"TILLY, DO SOMETHING?" Rees shouted, "WHY DIDN'T YOU STOP US USING THE DOOR?"

"You should have asked."

"You have murdered our friends!" snapped Alison.

"And my sister!" snapped Rees.

Tilly tried to reassure them, "Stop worrying."

"What do you mean 'stop worrying'? Are you mad?" they asked.

"I don't think you could actually call me mad. Anyway, whether you say I'm mad or not doesn't make any difference, they'll be fine."

"HOW CAN THEY BE FINE?" shouted Rees.

"One of the vehicles will catch them, silly."

"HOW DO YOU KNOW?"

"Because all of the vehicles are programmed to catch droppers."

"Are you sure?" asked Rees, having stopped shouting.

"Well, it stands to reason; you have just pointed out that there's been a pair of droppers, so one or even possibly two vehicles will catch them, so don't worry."

"I expect we're all just droppers to you, aren't we?" Rees said, sulking.

"No, not at all."

"Well thank goodness for that!"

"Only people who fall down are droppers."

That wasn't what Rees meant, but never mind.

Tilly's words about the guaranteed rescue of Phil and Shauna proved true, as just then they heard a man laughing in a peculiar way outside the tearoom door. "Ho ho ho!" went the voice.

Rees, Nora and Alison stepped back, nervous about what was afoot. In strode a man with a small red hat on his head and a beard like Father Christmas, but he wasn't as fat as the traditional Father Christmas. He wore a smart-looking red-brown velvety suit, and instead of a tie he wore a green sparkly cravat.

"Ho ho ho, I've got something for you!" he declared.

Following 'Father Christmas,' who had just stepped off a ramp that was protruding from the back of his strange vehicle – having attached itself to the outside of the tearoom door - were Shauna and Phil. Both of them were holding their chest and gasping for air.

Tilly welcomed them back before saying to the Famous Five, "Come and sit down, all of you, and have a drink."

"Can I … Can I get my breath back first?" gasped Phil.

Phil and Shauna stumbled to their respective chairs.

The Famous Five sat on the same tables as before and Father Christmas sat at a table in the middle so he could spread out and be the life and soul of the tearoom. Tilly's other friends had left the room again by this time.

Alison plucked up courage to talk to the larger than life Christmas-character, "How did you catch our friends?"

"Easy, mine was just the nearest vehicle, and I do have plenty of space in my slider."

"What's a slider?" asked Alison.

"Where have you been?"

"We've been all over the UK …" said Phil.

"The UK? That's an old term."

"How can you think the UK is an old term?" asked Nora.

"It's just that it's not existed for a hundred years."

"A hundred years? Are you saying we're not in 2024?" asked Alison.

"Well, of course we're not!"

"So, we're in the year 2124?" suggested Phil.

"No, 2250."

"So, we're really in the future?" asked Rees.

Father Christmas was a little confused, "Tilly, who are these people?"

"Why don't you ask them, Scaunaslat?"

"Scaunaslat? Don't you mean Santa Claus?" suggested Phil, chuckling breathlessly.

"Yes, you're right," and turning to Father Christmas, Tilly ordered, "Go on, tell them the story!"

"Ho ho ho, are you sure you want to know?"

The Famous Five said. "Yes please!"

"First of all you should have a look at my slider." He led them to the door so they could see his vehicle, which looked not too dissimilar to a sleigh, with creatures in front of it that did not look too dissimilar to reindeer.

"Are those reindeer?" asked Alison.

"Not quite, they're flowdolfs."

"I've never heard of flowdolfs before."

"Flowdolfs gave me the idea for what you call reindeers."

"I'm confused!" said Nora.

"Go on, Scaunaslat, tell them what you did!" urged Tilly. "He travelled backwards and came to your early world, saw a couple of saints with the name Nicholas who were kind, and that gave him the idea of Father Christmas. Isn't that right?"

"Tilly's right, so I then travelled forwards and called myself 'Saint Nicholas,' 'Father Christmas' and a few other things, but then I thought it would be good to have a new personal name based on my own name, so I decided to call myself 'Santa Claus,' which is the same as my real name all mixed up."

"Oh yes," said Nora, "So Santa Claus is an anagram of your name."

"That's right, and it gave me quite a thrill to discover later that millions of people began to speak my name every Christmas, and I can't think of a better season to be remembered in."

Phil was a little sceptical. "So you're saying you travelled back in time and invented this story about Father Christmas flying through the air in a sleigh being pulled by reindeers and dropping off toys at everyone's house – down chimneys?"

"Yes, I actually did a lot of delivering for a couple of years, and then it caught people's imagination and I didn't have to do it anymore. So I'm famous, even though they don't really know who I am."

Shauna asked, "So, do people still celebrate Christmas in 2250?"

"Of course!" said Scaunaslat, "Christmas could never stop! Where did you get these people from, Tilly?"

Tilly showed a bit of disapproval towards Scaunaslat. "But you lied!"

"Me? Lie? Never!" said Father Christmas, "Santa Claus never lies, ho ho ho!"

"You've encouraged all those parents to tell their children lies every year, and children think more about you giving them presents than they think about the true meaning of Christmas."

"Well, I suppose er ..."

"And the children don't thank their parents and relatives for buying and making gifts for them because they think they all came from YOU; so they are all grateful to YOU when YOU didn't even give them anything."

"Well er ..." Father Christmas looked embarrassed. "It's a nice story, anyway."

"I like the story," said Alison.

"So do we," said Rees and Shauna.

"There you are, you see?" said Santa.

"Well, if they say so," said Tilly, but she was a little disappointed in her guests too.

Suddenly, the door burst open and in fell ten green people with pointed ears. The Famous Five jumped.

"And here's some MORE mischievous ones," observed Tilly.

"They're elves!" exclaimed Rees.

Father Christmas laughed. "You see, it all worked really well."

"So do you all like greenguys as well?" asked Tilly.

"Yes," said Shauna, "because they are like elves that help Santa to make presents and distribute them to the houses."

"You see!" said Father Christmas, "It all worked out for the best!"

"But I hope you understand, you cheeky little greenguys," said Tilly to the mischievous guests, "that because of your activities, people believe in leprechauns who have a hidden pot of gold at the end of rainbows. So when children see rainbows, they spend hours trying to reach the end of them, but the rainbows keep moving and disappearing, and they don't know they are wasting their time. And even if they did reach the end of a rainbow, they wouldn't find a pot of gold there anyway!" Tilly's frown was as furrowed as a ploughed field.

"And," added Nora, "thousands of people celebrate Saint Patrick's Day, dress up in green clothes and have loads of fun."

"Ho ho ho, that's wonderful!"

"All right then, you little greenguys!" said Tilly. "We'll let you get away with it. No monkey business, mind!"

The ten little greenguys giggled and danced around the Christmas tree near the empty crib.

Then Tilly's three regular tearoom patrons came back into the room, one dressed as a star, one like Mary and the other like Joseph.

Tilly called out to everyone, "Are we all being good?"

Everyone said, "Yes!"

"Are we all being nice?"

"Yes!"

"Right, do your stuff, greenguys!"

The elves spread out around the walls of the tearoom, leant against them, and pushed hard. To the amazement of the Famous Five, the walls stretched, making the tearoom ten times wider and higher. Then the creepy imp man came from the back dressed like a sheep and went to the front door which had stretched to the left, to the right and upwards.

"Are you expecting a lot of big customers?" asked Alison.

"You could say that!" said Tilly.

Then suddenly there was a flash of light that filled the entire expanded tearoom, and as soon as this happened, everyone in the tearoom, that is, Tilly, the sheep, Father Christmas, Mary, Joseph, the star, Phil, Nora, Alison, Rees, Shauna, and the ten greenguys fell on their faces. When they all lifted up their heads, they saw a huge golden man, as high as the heightened ceiling. The golden man looked around, and everyone quivered and quaked uncontrollably, unable to stand or speak. Then they all witnessed the giant golden man put the tip of one foot into the empty crib, which was obviously far too small for him, but as soon as his toes touched it, the giant's body shrunk to the size of a baby, which ended up in the crib. Everyone in the tearoom gasped, and then very cautiously - and on tiptoes, one by one - they stood up and peered into the crib where they saw a baby wrapped in swaddling clothes. The Famous Five knelt beside the crib.

The star stood at the back of the tearoom, Mary and Joseph sat behind the crib, and the sheep laid down in front of it. Tilly helped Father Christmas to bring sacks of presents into the tearoom from his slider outside and then told the flowdolfs to park the slider round the back. The Famous Five were awestruck to see the real Jesus for the first time in their lives; they knelt with the sheep and peered at the innocent little baby in the crib. The ten greenguys just jumped about singing 'We Wish You a Merry Christmas!'

But as if this was not enough surprises for one Tilly Time, the Famous Five were astonished to see a band of shepherds barging through the tearoom door, each with a little lamb. When they reached the crib, they knelt down. Then a strange deep collection of sounds assaulted their ears; it was the sound of three camels navigating their way into the tearoom with colourfully clad kings on their humps. The camels knelt, and the kings did the same as soon as they had stepped off their camels. It was a good job the greenguys had stretched Tilly's Tearoom!

Tilly welcomed everybody, that was, the regular tearoom patrons, the Famous Five, Scaunaslat, the greenguys, the shepherds, the lambs, the camels and the kings, and suddenly seven flowdolfs dashed into the room, skidded on the tiled floor and knelt before the crib.

After Scaunaslat and Tilly had emptied sack after sack of presents under the Christmas tree, they too knelt down before the baby, the Saviour of all.

Finally, the Famous Five bowed their heads before the baby Jesus – the true meaning of Christmas!

Chapter 19
Tilly Goes to Ground

The Famous Five were humbled in their worship of the Eternal Son. It was the most awesome Christmas they had ever experienced and in their hearts they wondered what their friends and acquaintances would say if they relayed all of these experiences to them – they would no doubt write them off as nutcases! They suspected they should have much more concrete evidence before they uttered a word of it, otherwise they may become outcasts in their respective communities. BUT they did have their DNA shells, or Firestones, or whatever they were called. There must be some professional, government-funded research lab that could study them and open them for clues. The contents (or should I say prior contents) were so powerful, beyond anything anyone had ever known or understood on earth before, as far as they were aware.

Nora, Rees, Shauna, Alison and Phil lifted their heads, and as they did so, they all found themselves kneeling under the covers of their respective hotel beds; they noticed, through the fabric of the curtains, that it was light outside. 'It must have been a dream!' they each thought simultaneously, as they all excitedly – in their respective rooms – looked for their DNA shells. They were all missing. 'Great!' they all thought, 'now I have no proof!' they all thought. And then they all thought – simultaneously – 'How much of all that was actually real anyway?' and, 'When exactly did my dream begin? Was it when we set out for the Brecon Beacons? Was it after we booked into our motel rooms and went to bed? Or did the dream begin well before any of us found our DNA shells and the motel bed I am in now is actually my own bedroom? Or, am I still dreaming now?'

It wasn't long before they were confident they were actually in the motel that they had all booked into; but as they got showered and dressed, they wrestled in their heads as to how much of what they had witnessed was real, or whether only some parts were real. They gradually concluded they had definitely come to the motel with a DNA shell, and now it was gone. Rees and Shauna were in a slightly different situation as they could talk to each other about it all. Clearly the events that took place actually happened, otherwise, how could they both have imagined or dreamt exactly the same series of events? Again, the missing DNA shell was of concern.

Was everything just a clever plot for Tilly and the other strange entities or beings to get their DNA shells back? Was everything a sort of incredible, supernatural hoax? They even considered that their DNA shells might be downstairs on their breakfast table, or even at the desk in the lobby? There was only one way to find out.

When they arrived in the dining hall, all members of the Famous Five had uncannily done so at exactly the same time and they all made a beeline for the table with five chairs. It was 9am. As they settled into their seats and started chatting, they all soon realised that all of the events they remembered had indeed taken place and that none of them could find their DNA shells.

"Good morning!" said the same polite, smartly dressed man from the day before. "You are the last to order breakfast, but don't worry, there's plenty left. Please go up to the breakfast bar when you're ready and help yourself to anything you like."

"Thank you," said Alison, adding, "Could you tell me where our DNA shells are?"

"DNA shells? Can you describe them to me, please?"

"They are like a metallic box with patterns on, about this size," said Shauna using her hands to indicate how big they were. "They were in our rooms, but none of us can find them anywhere, someone must have come into our rooms and taken them."

"Tell you what, I'll check behind the reception desk and I'll check lost property too. I'm sure we'll be able to find them if they exist."

"Er…what do you mean 'if they exist'?" added Phil suspiciously.

"Well, if they still exist …"

"Still exist?" said Nora with further suspicion.

"Yes, they may have existed, but now they may not, I couldn't tell you for sure."

"But why would you even consider the possibility that they may have existed but no longer exist, instead of believing they exist but could have been stolen?" asked Rees with an additional further suspicion. And Phil, the PI, squinted his eyes with the suspicion of a sleuth who had been in possession of a million pounds one moment and without it a moment later, and with the impression that the only person who had come into contact with the money beside himself was a smartly dressed, polite man who worked in a motel, and who happened to be standing in front of him at that very moment!

"It's just that these things have a habit of happening," added the man casually.

"Not in our world!" exclaimed Rees.

"I'm so sorry that you find things a little strange here. I can't comprehend what you're going through, but I'm here to serve you. Please enjoy your breakfast and I will go and look for you DNA bells."

"Shells!" snapped Phil.

"Your shells. Then I'll come back and tell you if I find them."

"Thank you," said Shauna in a more tolerant, hopeful tone.

As you would imagine, the Famous Five were still not satisfied; they felt confused and cheated as they gathered their breakfast items. The breakfast bar was beside a large window looking out onto the car park, and the only cars they could see were their own. This was again a surprise as surely the guests would not check out that early; they still were not aware that they had been the only guests who stayed overnight.

The friends suspected they would not get their DNA Shells back and were feeling considerably melancholy as they ate together. They all concluded this was going to be their final miraculous encounter with Tilly and her mind-boggling world.

"Bang goes my chance of fame and fortune," said Phil.

"Well, I don't know whether I would want that kind of attention anyway. The problem is, I have so many questions," said Nora with a disappointed face.

"I bet this hotel disappears as soon as we drive out of the car park," said Rees.

"That's just what I was thinking," said Shauna.

Alison said, "Well, if you're right, I just want to say to you all, it has been a privilege to share these experiences with you – I mean that. I may never experience anything like this again, but I will always remember you all and what we've been through together."

"We can keep in touch," said Nora.

"Absolutely," said Shauna.

"All agreed?" asked Alison.

"AGREED!" said everyone, except for Phil who did not want it all to end that easily.

"Well," he said, "as far as I'm concerned, it's not the end. I'm going to keep investigating until I find out exactly who or what Tilly and her world is, and I want my DNA Shell back!"

Nora said, "I think you've just said it, it's Tilly and her world, and that's all we're going to get."

Alison was quite happy with the idea of further investigation, but for now she just needed a break from it all to allow her mind to try and find some sense of normality again. "I'm up for it, but not now."

"No, let's have a rest from it all. We do have our own lives to get back to, after all," said Shauna.

Rees wanted to bring some concrete plan to the table: "I suggest we go our own ways now but keep in touch as has been suggested, and if we all agree, lets meet again in six months."

"Sounds good to me," said Shauna.

Everyone nodded assent, and at that moment the smartly dressed man returned to their breakfast table. "Did you find your shells?" he asked.

Phil looked even more frustrated: "What? You were going to look for us, remember?"

"Oh yes," said the man. "I looked and couldn't find them, sorry."

"Typical," said Alison, venturing a straight question, "Who is Tilly?"

"That's an interesting question."

Phil blurted in, "Are you part of MI5?"

"MI5?"

"Has MI5 stolen our DNA Shells?" asked Shauna.

Nora interrupted: "Give him a chance to speak!"

The man just stood there like a stuffed dummy while they gave him an opportunity to speak.

"How does she get away with it?" asked Rees.

"She has done some pretty gruesome things!" added Alison.

There was another pause, until ...

"Pardon me, as soon as you've vacated your rooms, please leave your key at reception, and I wish you the safest of journeys!" And with that, the smart man bowed and left the dining room.

"Well, that's that then," said Nora.

Phil said, "Tilly's vigilante activities are dangerous, it's wrong!"

"I'm surprised a Private Investigator would stand for scruples like that," said Nora.

"It's just dangerous, and illegal! And nobody has any idea who this Tilly and her gang are!" added Phil.

"I wouldn't call them a gang; they're not like us; they're not human, are they?" said Alison, "They're something else, they're not governed by our rules."

"You're right, they're definitely other-worldly. I don't agree with vigilante behaviour, but these people – if you can call them people – are different," added Nora.

"I wonder if Tilly's a time-traveller, so she's just a human like us but from the future," suggested Shauna.

"I don't know about you," said Alison, "but I would quite like my life back. I just want get on with things as they were before, and catch up with my studies! I appreciate everything Tilly's done for all of us, and I must admit, I had a fantastic experience last night, but I need a break from it all."

"I think we all agree, except perhaps for Phil. Let's meet back down here in half an hour or so and wave each other off," suggested Shauna.

Half an hour passed, and everyone left their key on the reception desk. They could not see a bell to get anyone's attention, and the smart man was nowhere to be seen, so they all headed for the car park.

"I take it nobody's staying in the area to have a look around then?" ventured Phil.

"You must be joking!" said Nora.

Shauna said, "I think we need some time to try and absorb what's happened before we go insane."

"Fair enough," said Phil in reluctant resignation.

In the car park, Alison glanced back at the building. "Goodbye you strange motel, and, whoever named it Alistory Motel, thank you for the personal touch."

They all waved at the building simultaneously before hugging each other goodbye. Rees and Shauna drove out first, but after a minute or so they stopped at the brow of the first hill. The other cars did the same as they noticed the siblings step out and stare back in amazement. They all got out and stood together in a not too unexpected sense of astonishment. Where there should have been a motel, there was a small wooded area instead.

"Just like we expected!" said Alison. She blew a kiss to the now disappeared motel.

Phil Scrounge was the last one to leave, and the only one to linger a while: "I'm coming back here again, whatever that lot say!" he said to himself.

Meanwhile, Tilly was reclining on a sofa in the absent motel lounge watching TV and sipping tea with a mischievously satisfied smile on her face.

Epilogue
Six Months Later

The Famous Five had expanded somewhat by the time they met again, this time congregating in the conference room of a genuine, natural, earthly-existent hotel called The Llanberis Conference Hotel, north of Snowdonia, in Wales. During the intervening period between leaving Brecon and this meeting six months later, they had, between them, amassed more questions than an entire season of the quiz programme Blockbusters.

Over coffee and titbits they introduced themselves properly. Phil started, being the most aggressive investigator. He welcomed his own guests, Craig and Felicity Watson, who had been connected with the mysterious death of an escort stung to death by bees. Alison, who was less aggressive in her search for answers to the Tilly mystery, but more of a suitable leader, went next. She had explained everything to her trusted friends, Matty, Toby and Michael, and introduced them to the group.

Nora had had the almost impossible job of explaining to her daughter, Tina, how she had met her aborted granddaughter. By some miracle, Tina believed her mother's account of her experience on the Cumbrian fell, and was present in the conference room, as excited as everyone else about finding answers to the Tilly conundrum.

Rees and Shauna had come across Jordan and Maddie who had been in Tilly's disappearing tearoom. Jordan and Maddie were also applauded and officially added to the group.

Alison jumped up and addressed the team. "This is the beginning of a new era, one in which we will pool resources and work together to solve the mystery of Tilly and her disappearing tearoom. I think we should mingle, have some coffee and tasty nibbles, share experiences and ideas, and then have a preliminary meeting at 4pm before we have dinner together. Then we will have our full meeting at 7.30 after dinner.

"And I suggest you be the official leader of the team, Alison!" suggested Nora.

"Me too!" added Rees. "All raise a hand if you want Alison to lead the team." The majority of the group raised a hand immediately. "Agreed."

"Well I think we could have had a bit of warning before we were thrust into a vote, but I suppose I have no reason to object; but I think I should be at least Deputy since I am a PI after all," added Phil, sulkily.

"All in favour of Phil being Deputy?" said Rees. Everyone raised a hand. "Agreed."

"Thank you," said Alison giggling, "I wasn't actually asked if I wanted to be leader, but I accept."

"Good," said Nora.

Alison added, "And I would like to add that I am happy to welcome Phil as my Deputy for the very reason that he is keener than anyone to solve the mystery of Tilly, and he has a lot of experience as a Private Investigator." Phil nodded assertively. "After all, Phil and I were the first members of the Famous Five, and it was Phil's DNA Shell ad in the paper that set the investigation ball rolling."

Phil took his turn: "I would like to mention – before we mingle - that we, as a team of investigators, have an uphill struggle, as I can find nothing material to back up our claims - other than the fact that we are all first-hand witnesses. Not only have all our DNA Shells disappeared, but my photographs of the DNA Shell have also disappeared," said Phil. "However, there is still the picture in the UK Daily newspaper."

"That's a pity," said Felicity, "What about the Motel in Brecon? I know the building itself disappeared, but don't you think we should go and have a more thorough delve around? You never know, there might be lots of DNA Shells dotted around there."

"We could, but I've been back twice and found nothing," said Phil. "I even returned to Willington in Cheshire again because I had shown the DNA Shell to a resident of a house called Chocolate Box, but the house doesn't exist anymore!"

"In that case, we're back to square one," said Alison, "and in some ways that makes it more exciting; we are all starting as a new team at the same point."

"That's one way to look at it I suppose," said Phil.

"Come on Phil, we need you to be positive," said Nora.

Tina contributed: "Well I'm feeling positive and excited. I am so happy to meet you all and I believe this gathering is going to be mind-bendingly brilliant."

"Well said, Tina," said Alison before adding, "So I suppose it's my job to officially declare the following people to be members of - for want of a better name - Team Tilly." There was an approving nod from most people (You guessed it, it was only grumpy Phill that didn't nod). Alison continued: "Nora and Tina, Rees and Shauna, Jordan and Maddie, Craig and Felicity, Matty, Toby and Michael, myself Alison, and our Deputy Phil. Welcome!" Everyone applauded (except for Phil who clapped like a wet jellyfish). "Now, let's mingle!"

At that very moment, a mysterious object, the size of a milk crate, appeared in the centre of the conference room, glowing and throbbing and emitting a variety of flashing colours.